To Bob & ...
with best ...

The King's Codebreaker

Andrew Douglas

Andrew Douglas

The King's Codebreaker

Edited by Tom Swanston

Matador
5 Weir Road
Kibworth Beauchamp
Leicester LE8 0lQ, UK
Tel: (+44) 116 279 2299
Email: books@troubador.co.uk
Web: www.troubador.co.uk/matador

ISBN 978-1848764 019

A Cataloguing-in-Publication (CIP) catalogue record for this book is available from the British Library.

Typeset in 11pt Bembo by Troubador Publishing Ltd, Leicester, UK
Printed in Great Britain by the MPG Books Group, Bodmin and King's Lynn

Matador is an imprint of Troubador Publishing Ltd

For Susan

Chapter 1

Thomas Hill was not much of a drinking man – half a bottle of claret or a couple of pots of ale might last him an hour or more – but two or three times a week, having closed his bookshop, he liked to walk down to The Romsey Arms. The inn was only two hundred and ten paces from the shop and if there was news of the war that was where he would hear it. He knew it was two hundred and ten paces because he had counted them. It was the mathematician's curse – forever counting things.

The war. The wretched war. Bloody and brutal, and so far pointless. As far as Thomas could tell from the newsbooks that found their way to Romsey, neither side had shown much evidence of a coherent strategy, or even of real determination to win a decisive military victory. While talks dragged on between the King and Parliament, William Waller and Ralph Hopton danced minuets around each other in the West Country, the Earl of Essex had settled comfortably into Windsor, and John Pym, reportedly dying from a cancer in his stomach, was busy building defences around London. Prince Rupert was thundering about the country at the head of his cavalry, attacking Lichfield, Brentford, and anywhere else that took his fancy, and now there were rumours that his brother Maurice had joined him for an attack on Bristol. Thomas knew better than to believe all the reports and, in any case, they were often contradictory. Sir Jacob Astley had been reported killed at Gloucester two days before arriving in excellent health at Oxford. And there were strange stories of ghostly battles at Edgehill and witchcraft in East Anglia. In time of war, Thomas had decided, rational men very easily became irrational.

One thing, however, was now clear. The talking had achieved nothing and there would be more bloodshed before England knew peace again. With the King gathering support in Oxford, and London in the hands of Parliament, something violent and bloody was inevitable and probably soon. Either the King would advance on London, or Essex and Cromwell would try to surround Oxford. More bodies disembowelled by the sword and the pike, more eyes sliced from their sockets, more limbs left for the crows, more widows and orphans left destitute. Even in this little town, there were ten women widowed by the war, including his sister Margaret, and twice that number of fatherless children, his nieces among them. There were a one-legged tailor, a blind innkeeper, and a farmer with half a face. The other half had been taken by a man with an axe. The farmer had lived, but when he returned his wife had taken one look at him and fled. The wags in the town said that even the man's sheep looked away when they saw him. Yet Romsey itself had seen no fighting – imagine Stratton or Hopton Heath, where there had been battles. Was there an able-bodied man left standing there? God forbid that the war should really come to Romsey.

It was early August and the evening was warm, so Thomas wore no coat, just his white ruffled shirt with a high collar and a clean pair of linen breeches tied at the knee, a few shillings in his pocket. He seldom wore a wig despite his lack of hair. Wigs were hot and bothersome. He reckoned he could tell how busy the Romsey Arms was by the time he reached the baker's shop on the junction of Love Lane and Market Street. If he could hear voices, it was busy; if he could see drinkers overflowing outside the inn, it was very busy; but if he could see or hear nothing, he might have only himself for company. That would be disappointing. He much preferred gossip and banter and he liked being the source of news. A writer and bookseller was expected to know everything before anyone else.

As he approached the bakery he knew it would be gossip and banter. And on turning into Market Place, he guessed it might be rather more. At least a dozen men were outside the inn and by the sound of them, had been there quite some time. Their coats were a hotchpotch of colours but they all wore broad-brimmed, feathered hats, and tall leather riding boots. Each man had a bandolier over one shoulder, a sword at his waist and a tankard in his hand. They were Royalist dragoons. Boisterous, loud, celebrating dragoons. Thomas quickened his pace. This would be news. Terms for peace agreed perhaps, and an end to the war at last. He all but ran the last few yards.

'Well now, gentlemen,' called out a tall blue-coated dragoon above the hubbub, when he saw Thomas, who had noted the black and white feathers and red band round the man's hat, which had immediately marked him as their leader, 'and who have we here? Doesn't look like the enemy, more's the pity. Not much taller than my wife, a bit on the skinny side, and short of hair. Clean shaven, clean shirt, clean boots. But you can never tell. Be on your guard, men. Who are you, sir, and have you the money to quench our thirst? If not, be on your way. We're hot and dry.'

He might have spoken in jest or he might not. Thomas decided to risk it. 'My name is Thomas Hill, sir. I have a bookshop in this town. Alas, I don't have enough in my pocket to buy ale for all of you unless you will settle for but a sip each. Perhaps if you pool your resources, however, you might have enough to buy me a glass of claret. The landlord here keeps a good cellar.'

The tall dragoon stared hard at Thomas, then laughed loudly. 'Good man, Master Hill. A glass of claret it shall be. A bookshop, eh? And what improving work would you recommend for a humble soldier of the King?'

'A difficult question, sir, as I know nothing of your tastes and I would not want to cause offence.' replied Thomas, looking his man up and down, 'I read that in London all manner of books are joining the King's Book of Sports on the fire and it's much the same in Oxford. So nothing religious or political. Let me think. Not classical, I fancy, nor poetic. Henry the Fifth, perhaps, or Julius Caesar – warriors both. Or philosophy. Or something more practical – a worthy volume on horsemanship or husbandry?' He paused as if in thought. 'No. Philosophy it is. De Montaigne, my favourite philosopher of all.'

'Who? Doesn't sound English.'

'He was French, sir. Just as this claret is.' said Thomas, taking a glass from an outstretched hand, and raising it to the dragoon. 'Your excellent health.'

'And yours, Master Hill. We'll talk of philosophers later. Let me first introduce myself. I am Robert Brooke, captain of this troop of drunken scoundrels, whom I'm instructed to take to join Lord Goring. It seems his lordship is in need of our assistance, though by all accounts he needs little assistance in the matter of refreshment.'

George Goring had changed his allegiance from Parliament to the Crown the previous year, and Thomas knew of his reputation as a drunkard. He offered a small bow. 'Captain Brooke. An honour. And what news do you bring? An end to the war or is that too much to hope for?'

'Indeed it is. There can be no end in sight while Fairfax and Cromwell are at large, nor any of their henchmen, and that's an end to it.'

'Alas,' replied Thomas, 'it seems so, though I wish it could be done peacefully. We hear there's been fighting in the north and the west. Adwalton Moor and Landsdown, was it not?'

'It was. And splendid victories both. At Adwalton, the magnificent Earl of Newcastle sent Fairfax and his son running like hounds on the scent, and at Landsdown our Cornish pikemen gave Waller's rabble bloody noses. The war goes well.'

'Happily, we have seen little of it in Romsey, though we thirst for news.'

'Then I shall have the honour of giving you some.'

'And what news is that, captain?'

'We come from Bristol, which, praise God, is now in Royalist hands. Three days ago the Princes Rupert and Maurice took the city. It was a glorious triumph, and I'm proud to say that my men and I were part of it.'

'Bristol. Noted for its ale, I believe. You didn't go thirsty then?'

Brooke let out a raucous bellow. 'We certainly did not, my friend. Nor hungry once we'd cleared the shitten scum out of their shops and houses and filled our stores with meat and bread.'

So much for an end to the war. Thomas said nothing. He could guess what was coming. Plunder, destruction, rape, murder. The usual story. Another dragoon piped up. This one was short, with a face ravaged by drink, a big belly, and the voice of a fishwife. 'Those arse-licking, traitorous, bastards got what they deserved. When Prince Rupert asked them politely to open the gates, they refused, the donkey-headed dung eaters. We had to breech the walls and storm the city. Good men died.'

'So they did.' agreed Brooke, 'We had to make an example of the place. They should have opened the gates. It was a bloody business getting in. Women and children were killed. I hate the sound of screaming women. It puts my teeth on edge. But it was their own fault. Later we hanged a few for good measure.'

'They'll open the gates to the King next time.' said a dragoon, raising his tankard, 'The city's ours now, and everything in it.' Thomas had heard enough. Another city destroyed, men hanged, women raped and murdered, children butchered. And these so-called soldiers boasting about it. 'Well, bookseller,' went on the fat dragoon, 'and what have you to say to that? A great victory, eh?'

Thomas really did not want to say anything. He turned to go. Before he had taken a step, however, he found himself flat on his back in the dust, struggling to breathe. The dragoon had punched him hard on his breastbone, knocking him backwards, and was now astride him, his backside planted on Thomas's chest. Thomas was quick on his feet and much stronger than he looked, but it all been so fast that he barely knew what had happened. He gasped for air and opened his eyes. A bulbous, red-veined nose, two watery eyes, and a stinking, black-toothed mouth, were inches from his face. He shut his eyes again and held his breath. The stench of the man was revolting, never mind his weight on Thomas's stomach. And he could feel something sharp pricking the skin under his left ear. The fat dragoon had pulled a knife from his belt. Blood trickled down Thomas's neck. The man hissed at him. 'So, Hill. You choose to ignore my question. Perhaps you didn't want to hear about our great victory. Perhaps you're a piss-drinking roundhead after all. Is that it? A piss-drinking roundhead is it, Hill?'

Thomas felt the point of the knife digging into his neck. He turned his head to the other side and vomited. It ran down his chin into the dust. He retched and coughed, his eyes clamped shut. Then, suddenly, the weight on his chest was lifted and he was being helped to his feet. He heard the voice of the captain. 'God's wounds, man, we're soldiers of the King, not highwaymen. You've had too much ale again. Master Hill meant no offence, and even if he did, there's no reason to kill him. Go and find a bucket of water and stick your ugly head in it until you're sober. Or as sober as you ever are.' The dragoon, stunned by a heavy blow to his head with the hilt of the captain's sword, struggled unsteadily to his feet, and, cheered on by his colleagues, stumbled off in the direction of the duck pond. 'My apologies, Master Hill. The man's a drunken oaf. Are you recovered?'

From the winding, Thomas was recovered. From the shock, he was not. 'Thank you, yes, captain.' he replied quietly, wiping away blood and vomit with a white hankerchief, 'I meant no offence but I don't care for violence of any sort.'

'A soldier must do his duty and obey orders. War is violent.'

'Then let us pray that this war ends soon. Enough English blood has been spilled on the land.'

'I too pray that it ends soon, and with victory for our King. Now will you take another glass of claret with me while that fat fool has his head in a bucket?'

'Thank you, captain, but I shall be on my way.'

'But what about your French philosopher? Mountain, was it? You were going to share his wisdom with me.'

'Montaigne, captain, Michel de Montaigne. He lived in the last century and said many wise things. Here's one with which to bid you farewell. "To learn that we have said or done a foolish thing is nothing; we must learn a more ample and important lesson: that we are all blockheads." God be with you, captain.' Thomas bowed, and set off back up Market Street towards Love Lane. Watching him go, the captain took off his hat and scratched his head. 'If any of you understood that, be sure to enlighten me. Now go and see if that fat-bellied idiot is alive. We must be on our way.'

Still a little dazed, Thomas walked slowly. When he reached the bakery on the corner, he stopped to breathe in the aroma of tomorrow's loaves. His sensitive nose twitched in pleasure. The dragoon had smelled like a midden. Revolting. It was a blessed relief to get the stench out of his nostrils. He breathed deeply and looked around. From this point in the village he had a good view of the countryside. To the west he could see the great oaks of the New Forest, and to the south fields of wheat and barley yellowing in the summer sun, copses of oak and elm, and the Test winding down towards Southampton. Every time he stood here, he knew why he had come back. God forbid that it should be ravaged as so much of England had been ravaged.

Margaret was sitting outside the shop on her wicker chair, enjoying the last of the evening sunshine. When she saw Thomas coming up the street she put down her book and watched him. He's a good man, she thought, a good brother and a good uncle. The girls adore him. 'There you are, brother,' she greeted him, 'and walking steadily, I'm pleased to see.' She had never seen him less than sober, but teasing ran in the family.

'Certainly, my dear, though I was sorely tempted. A troop of dragoons on their way through were washing the dust out of their throats. I'm surprised you didn't hear them from here.'

'Royalists, Thomas?'

'Yes, Royalists. I'll tell you their news later. Are the girls in bed?'

'I've just put them down. They'll be asleep.'

Pity, thought Thomas. He liked telling them a story before they fell asleep. It was usually something from the Bible or the classics. Hercules was popular, so was David, though five-year old Polly was already expressing doubts about a giant as big as Goliath being felled by a little pebble. 'There's chicken from yesterday, if you're hungry,' said Margaret, 'and plenty of cheese.' So far, the privations suffered by so many towns and villages had not come to Romsey and no-one was starving. 'You can tell me what the dragoons had to say while you're eating.'

In between mouthfuls, Thomas told her the news of Bristol. He left out the worst bits and Margaret knew that he had. She too had heard it all before and she too was sickened by it. 'God forbid that Polly and Lucy should grow up in such a country. They've lost their father and, if it goes on much longer, they'll lose their childhood. Polly asked me today what happened to the farmer's face. We saw him in the market. What am I to tell her? That he tripped over a plough or that it was hacked off by a man with an axe? One's a lie, the other would give her nightmares. She's only five, for the love of God.'

Thomas sighed. 'I have no answers, my dear. A war that was supposed to be about the principles of government is nothing of the kind. Men change sides as it suits them and mercenaries fight for whoever offers them most. It's a war driven by fear. Fear of a King with a catholic Queen, fear of puritanism, fear of the Irish, fear of losing. Perhaps all wars are the same. We all fear something.'

Margaret smiled. 'Philosophical, as ever, Thomas. Does your great Montaigne have anything helpful to say on the matter?'

'Probably. I offered the captain of dragoons a little something to send him on his way.'

'Good God, Thomas. Something from Montaigne? You're lucky he didn't run you through on the spot.'

'Am I?' he asked thoughtfully, but told her nothing of his brush with the fat one.

When Margaret was five, Thomas's mother had died giving birth to him. Their father, a Romsey school teacher, had brought them both up to love learning for its own sake, and, from an early age, to think for themselves. 'It is the duty of a father to teach his children how to think, not what to think.' the old man had been fond of saying, 'If only more fathers understood that, there would be fewer wars and less poverty.' Thus encouraged, Thomas had learnt to read and write by the age of five, and to read Latin and French by eight. Much as he loved words, however, he loved numbers better. Numbers fascinated him, especially the ways in which a simple symbol could reveal the truth about something. Pythagoras and Euclid had led him to Plato and Aristotle. While Margaret had stayed at home to run the household, at fifteen Thomas had gone to Oxford. A scholar of Pembroke College, he had studied mathematics and natural philosophy, had excelled at tennis on the court at Merton, had been much in demand as a dance partner for his boyish good looks, nimbleness of foot, and grace of movement, had first bedded a girl, and had learnt to make up for his lack of height and weight with speed of hand and quickness of eye. More than one fellow student had come to regret a drunken insult or unwise challenge to Thomas Hill.

Yet for all this, Thomas had always found it difficult to conform. He avoided societies and associations, attended chapel only because he had to, moved in small circles, and preferred the company of teachers to that of students. After three years, he had intended to stay in Oxford to continue his studies, but when his father had become ill, had returned to Romsey to help care for him. After the old man had died ten years ago, Thomas had stayed in the town, bought the house and shop in Love Lane, and settled down to the quiet life of writer, bookseller, and occasional publisher of pamphlets on matters philosophical and mathematical. And when Margaret had married Andrew Taylor, he had been content with his books and his writing for company. But the war had changed that. Andrew had left Margaret and their two daughters to join the King's army and had been killed in a skirmish near Marlborough. Margaret had sold their house in Winchester and returned with the girls to Romsey. Now they all lived together.

It was only a small shop, made smaller by shelves and tables overflowing with books and pamphlets, Thomas's writing table and chair, and two more chairs for the use of customers and visitors. The latter being more common than the former, the shop barely provided them with a living, but Thomas's inheritance and Margaret's money from the sale of her house kept them comfortable. While in Oxford and London both sides burnt books they found offensive – how an inanimate object could give offence was a mystery to Thomas – he lived his life happily surrounded by them, appreciated the scholarship of even writers like the self-regarding John Milton, with whose opinions he largely disagreed, and waited for peace to return. He knew it might be a long wait.

Ten days after his brush with the fat dragoon, Thomas and Margaret made their regular trip to the market with the girls. For three centuries market day had been by far the most important day in Romsey. Farmers sold eggs, poultry, meat, vegetables, and fruit, clothiers and haberdashers set up stalls to show off their finery, and everyone from the mayor and aldermen down came to meet friends and exchange news. The town population of little more than a thousand seemed to double on market days. Polly and Lucy wore their best bonnets, Margaret her shawl and her long string of pearls; she insisted on them when out with Thomas. 'You're a respected man in this town, Thomas.' she had said more than once, 'You're educated, you write important pamphlets, and you're looked up to by everyone. It wouldn't do to let you down.'

'Thank you, sister.' he replied, thinking privately that Margaret exaggerated a little for the girls' benefit.

Since the visit by the dragoons, the town had been quiet and little news had arrived with the merchants who came from all over the county to buy the wool finished and dyed in the town. Hoping that market day would prove more informative, they shut the bookshop and walked hand-in-hand down Love Lane and Market Street to the square between The Romsey Arms and the old Abbey.

While Margaret took the girls to buy flour and eggs, Thomas wandered through the market. Stopping briefly to talk with the Court Recorder and a town burgess, he made his way through the crowd to the inn, where thirsty farmers and merchants were kept happy by six women paid two shillings each to make sure every mug was kept topped up from the big jugs they carried in and out. Chosen by the innkeeper for their speed with the jug, the size of their bosom, and their ability to keep his customers coming back for more, not one of them would go home that evening without having made at least one visit to the little copse behind the inn. The innkeeper allowed them to keep whatever rewards they received for these absences, as long as they were no more than ten minutes each. He reckoned ten minutes was good for business. 'Morning, Master 'ill. Pot of ale, or a little walk by the river first?' One of the girls had seen him coming. She knew what his answer would be.

'Neither, thank you, Sarah. Next time, perhaps. Have you heard any news today?'

'Not much. Unless you count Rose. 'er belly's full again, silly bitch.'

'Does she know whose it is?'

'Ha. Course not. Stupid cow.'

'Ah well. Perhaps he'll grow up to be a bishop.'

'Bishop, my arse.' roared Sarah, chest heaving and ale slopping out of her jug, 'Thief more like, same as 'er eldest. 'anged he was, and only ten. Good riddance, I say.'

'Let's hope not. No other news? Then I must go and find the girls.' Having filled one basket with eggs and another with a small sack of flour, the girls were found admiring ribbons at a haberdasher's stall. 'Ribbons, ladies? I thought we needed eggs.'

'We've bought the eggs, uncle Thomas,' said Polly sternly, 'and the flour. And now we need ribbons. Pink ones.'

'Good morning, Master Hill', said the haberdasher, tipping his hat, 'pink certainly suits both the young ladies.'

'Oh, very well. Pink ones it is. Shall I help you choose?' But before Polly could decline her uncle's offer, a thundering of hooves brought the market to an abrupt standstill. Twenty horsemen wearing the round helmets and leather jerkins of parliamentary cavalry galloped into the square. Their mounts, teeth bared and flanks glistening, were reined sharply to a halt outside the Romsey Arms. Every head in the market place turned towards them and every eye searched for a hint of menace in their demeanour. These were the first soldiers of Parliament the town had seen. Margaret instinctively gathered the girls to her, and Thomas put himself between them and the troopers.

All but one dismounted and faced the crowd, reins in one hand, the other on the hilts of their swords. The man who must have been captain of the troop alone remained mounted. He addressed the crowd, his voice carrying easily around the square. 'Here this, people of Romsey. We are soldiers of Parliament, on our way to Southampton. We need food and drink, and our horses need rest. If you co-operate, there will be no trouble. This evening we shall depart. Until then we will take our ease here.'

Thomas turned to Margaret and whispered, 'Take the girls home. Keep an eye on the street. If you see soldiers coming, hide in the usual place. Here's the key. I'll be back soon.' Leading the girls by their hands, Margaret slipped unnoticed out of the square and up the street towards the bookshop. When they had left, Thomas sat on the Abbey steps and waited. He did not trust these soldiers. Having refreshed themselves in the Romsey Arms, they would start foraging for food and plundering whatever else caught their eye. That was what soldiers did.

He was right not to trust them. Before long, two troopers, each holding a bottle of claret by the neck, stumbled out of the inn. They were followed by two more, these two holding Sarah and Rose by the hair. The men were laughing and the women cursing. Rose struggled to free herself and yelled at the man holding her to leave her and her baby alone and go and stick his prick in a sheep. He slapped her hard, shook her like a rat, and told her he had humped prettier ewes than her. Sarah was trying to reach her man's eyes with her fingers. 'Put that scabby thing in me, and you'll never see it again,' she screeched. So, thought Thomas, this is how God-fearing soldiers of Parliament behave with drink inside them. This was to be no shilling tumble by the river. Sarah and Rose, hard-bitten whores though they were, were frightened. Thomas looked around. The twenty or so watching were unarmed, unconcerned, and unwilling to interfere. There was nothing he could do. He should go home.

Not all the troopers had gone into the inn. Some had taken the horses off to find stabling; others, the most avaricious, had set about hammering on doors and demanding to be let in, threatening to burn down any that were not swiftly opened. On Love Lane, Thomas could see a two-handled cart standing outside a large house owned by a wealthy wool merchant. Inside, he heard voices raised and a woman wailing. When he reached the cart, he looked in and saw that it was loaded with cloth, plate, bottles, and an enormous pair of silver candlesticks. Two troopers came out of the house, carrying a heavy gilt mirror. They dropped the mirror clumsily into the cart, shattering its glass. One of them pointed at Thomas. 'You there, who are you and what are you looking at?' It was a rough London voice, coarse and ugly, more at home in Spitalfields than Romsey.

'My name is Hill. I'm looking at nothing and I'm going home.'

The trooper eyed him suspiciously. 'And where is that?'

'A little further up the lane.'

'Well, Hill, you look a generous fellow. I think we'll come with you.' said the other one.

Thomas shrugged. 'As you wish, but I'm only a bookseller. You'll find little of value unless you're fond of books.'

'We'll see about that, master bookseller. Lead on, and you may show us your wares.' Thomas had no choice. Walking as slowly as he dared, he led the two men with the cart towards the bookshop. He could only hope that Margaret was watching out, as he had told her to. He spoke loudly. 'It's only a small shop. I have little money there.' Perhaps Margaret would hear him in time to hide with the girls. From these two thieves, she would certainly be in danger.

When they reached the shop, the door was locked. Thomas put his hand in his pocket for the key, and swore silently. He had given it to Margaret. Without a key, the soldiers would know that the door had been locked from the inside, and that there must be someone there. He almost panicked. 'Fire and damnation. My key's gone. It's been stolen, or I dropped it in the market.'

'No matter, bookseller. I have a key.' replied Spitalfields, and with two hefty kicks, broke the lock. The door swung open. 'There. Now let's see what you have for us.'

As Thomas had warned them, in the shop he had little but books and pamphlets. The narrow door in the rear wall was closed. Thank God, Margaret must have seen or heard them, and taken the girls to the hiding place. All was quiet. The troopers looked around. 'Where's your money, bookseller?' demanded Spitalfields.

'I have very little, as I told you.' Thomas went to his writing table, took a small bag of coins from a drawer, and tossed them to the trooper. The trooper opened the bag, looked inside, and scoffed.

'Is this all? I don't believe you, you lying turd-sucker. Where's the rest?'

'That's all there is.' The trooper took two steps forward and aimed a blow at the side of Thomas's head. Thomas ducked it, only to catch another one from the other side. He stumbled and fell.

'Then we'll look for ourselves, shit-eater.' While Thomas sat on the floor, the two men attacked the shop. The drawers of the desk were pulled out and the contents – more paper, quills, and ink – strewn about the shop, books were dragged off the shelves, and the front window smashed with a chair. Thomas said nothing. Wanton destruction he could cope with. God forbid there would be anything worse.

When the whole floor was covered with damaged books, paper, and ink, and the desk and chair reduced to firewood, the two troopers stopped for breath. 'So. No money in here.' said one, pointing at the narrow door. 'Where does that lead?'

'To my rooms. A kitchen and bedrooms, nothing more.'

'Come on, Jethro. We'll take a look.' The door was unlocked. They went through, and up the short staircase immediately behind it. Thomas sat on the floor and held his breath. If the girls were going to be found, it would be now. He listened as the men climbed the stairs and into the bedrooms above, their boots clattering on the floorboards. He heard beds being tipped over and a mirror being smashed. He shut his eyes and waited.

Eventually, the men stomped back down the stairs and into the shop. They carried a few plates and a silver cup. 'Is this all you've got, bookseller?'

'I fear so.'

A sword was unsheathed and pointed at his throat. 'No hiding places, bookseller? You look prosperous enough.'

'No. All my money is in the books. Or it was.'

'And whose are the women's clothes? Women's and children's.'

'My sister and her daughters are away in Winchester.'

'A pity. Though if she looks like you, we'd have to put a sack over her, eh Jethro?' Luckily, she doesn't, thought Thomas, but said nothing. 'Come on, we've wasted enough time in this shit-hole.'

Thomas got up and watched them swagger back down the lane. They had taken a little money, some plates and a silver cup. They had wrecked his bookshop and destroyed many of his books. They had smashed furniture. But they had not harmed Margaret or the girls. When he was sure it was safe to do so, Thomas went back into the shop and through the narrow door at the back. He stopped at the bottom of the staircase, knocked three times on the first stair, and said 'Montaigne' loudly. Then he stood back as the first three stairs detached themselves and put out a hand to help Polly and Lucy crawl out from the tiny space behind. They had both wet themselves and were sobbing miserably. They were terrified. Thomas hugged them. 'All's well, now. The soldiers have gone. We're quite safe.' Margaret emerged behind them, stretching her back and legs. Her face was ashen.

'Did they hit you, Thomas?' she asked, peering at him, 'Your face is bruised.'

Thomas put his hand to his cheek. 'It wasn't much. The books suffered more.'

In the shop, they looked aghast at the devastation. Polly held on to her mother and Lucy started wailing. Margaret picked up some pages from a small volume from which the cover had been ripped. 'I fear that the Prince of Denmark has suffered somewhat,' she observed, looking at a page, and picking up another, 'and so has Romeo. How wanton and stupid and cruel. What did they think they would gain by this?'

‘God alone knows. I told them I had no money except for the purse, and they took your silver cup.’

‘And broke the door and the window, I see. Well, Thomas, we must mend both at once and start to clear up this mess. Go upstairs, girls, please, change yourselves, and do what you can to sort out our clothes. I’ll be up soon.’ The girls, drying their eyes, did as they were told. ‘They’re shocked, Thomas, as well they might be. Polly asked if they were the men who killed her father.’

‘What did you tell her?’

‘I said they weren’t. She might have screamed otherwise.’

‘Thank God they stayed quiet while those animals were here.’

‘Thank God, indeed. Royalist drunkards one day, Parliamentary thieves another. What next, do you think? A Spanish Armada?’

Thomas laughed. Humour in times of trouble. Montaigne would surely have approved. ‘Probably. Now we’d better set to. I’ll mend the door and board up the window. You salvage whatever books you can. I may be able to put some together again as long as they’re complete.’

‘Very well. Then I’ll go up to the girls. We’ll have to explain this somehow, at least to Polly.’

It took all afternoon to clear up the shop and the bedrooms. Ruined books went on the kitchen fire with the desk and chair, and Thomas had a pile to rebind. Upstairs, the beds were righted and clothes sorted out. The door and window were secured. By evening, they were exhausted. Margaret put the girls to bed and sat with Thomas in the kitchen. In his hand, he clutched a copy of Montaigne’s Essais. Miraculously, it had escaped unharmed.

He opened a bottle of his very best hock. 'Just the time for it.' said Margaret, taking a sip. They sat quietly and shared the wine.

It was almost dark when they heard a knock on the door. Margaret started. 'Please God, not again. I couldn't bear it.' she whispered.

'Hush now, Margaret. It was a gentle knock. Probably just a neighbour. Nothing to fear. I'll go and see who it is.' More nervous than he pretended, Thomas went cautiously to the door. 'Who is it?' he called.

'A friend. I seek Master Thomas Hill.'

'I am Thomas Hill.'

'Kindly open the door, sir, and you will see that I mean you no harm.'

'My home and shop were destroyed this very day by soldiers of Parliament. How do I know I can trust you?'

'Abraham Fletcher.'

Thomas wondered if he had heard correctly. Abraham Fletcher? His old tutor at Oxford? Surely not. 'What of Abraham Fletcher?'

'He sends greetings.'

Thomas hesitated, then made a decision, knowing that he might regret it. He unlocked the patched up door and opened it. Outside stood a man in the grey hooded habit of a monk. When he pushed back his hood, Thomas saw a cheerful, bald, blue-eyed face, with a long nose and a strong jaw. It was not a face he knew. 'Thomas Hill?' inquired the monk. Thomas nodded. 'I am Simon de Pointz. I carry a message from the King.'

Chapter 2

The monk dropped his bag on the kitchen floor and stood with his back to the stone oven. Thomas and Margaret waited for him to speak. Even with a slight stoop to his shoulders, he was a head taller than either of them. Entwining his fingers, he stretched his arms, and sighed with relief. 'God knows but that bag was heavy. It's far enough from Oxford without having to carry a load.' Neither Thomas nor Margaret spoke. 'Well,' he went on, 'you must have an explanation. May I sit?' Without waiting for an answer, he hoisted his habit above his ankles and sat. 'First of all, Abraham Fletcher sends you his greetings. He's well, and hopes you are the same.'

'Thank you,' replied Thomas stiffly, 'and what does Abraham have to do with your being here?'

'It was Abraham who suggested you to the King.'

'And why would he do that?'

'That is a question which I can answer only in part.'

Thomas spoke sharply. 'In that case, Father de Pointz, I may be able only to listen in part.'

The monk laughed. 'Abraham said you might be difficult. I'll explain as best I can. The King, as you doubtless know, is in Oxford. Queen Henrietta Maria joined His Majesty there a month ago. Her Majesty recommended me to carry this message.'

'Why you?'

'The Queen is a devout lady. I've been with her for three years and travelled with her from Holland.' He grinned broadly. 'Now that was a voyage. Nine days at sea, the weather so bad that the ladies had to be strapped to their beds. Eventually we turned around and went back. We waited ten more days before trying again. By the grace of God it was calmer the second time. We stayed a while in York, before meeting the King at Edgehill and travelling with him to Oxford. I am a devoted servant of Her Majesty and, happily, she trusts me.'

'And what is the message you carry?'

'The King is aware that at Oxford you distinguished yourself as a mathematician and became expert in the matter of ciphers.' Thomas nodded. It was true that he had won prizes for mathematics and had much enjoyed studying the science of codes and ciphers. So much so that he and Abraham had amused themselves by sending each other coded and encrypted messages – scurrilous poems, invitations to dinner, barbed criticisms of colleagues – and challenging the other to decipher them. As a new code or cipher had to be devised for each message, they had both become adept at inventing and breaking all manner of alphabetic ciphers, and numeric and homophonic codes. 'For reasons that I cannot disclose,' continued de Pointz, 'His Majesty has need of your skills and has instructed me to escort you to Oxford.'

The looks that Thomas and Margaret exchanged were part astonishment, part alarm. Margaret recovered first. 'Reasons that you cannot disclose? My brother abhors violence, as I do. Why should he leave his sister and nieces unprotected to help prosecute a war which should never have started, and in which innocent women and children are dying every day? This is not a war against a cruel invader. It's a war between Englishmen on English soil. How can it possibly be condoned?'

'Are there not important principles at stake?'

'What principles can justify innocent blood being spilled?'

'Principles of justice and liberty?'

'You speak as if such principles were espoused by one side alone. They are not. The King would rule without reference to his subjects, Parliament would restrict our civil and religious freedoms.' replied Margaret with unaccustomed force.

'And what principle are the King's mercenaries fighting for? The right to kill for money, I suppose?' demanded Thomas, 'And what of the turncoats? A sudden epiphany? I doubt it. This war, like all wars, is about self-interest. Claims of justice and liberty are no more than fancy covers on a miserable book.'

The priest held up his hands. 'Master Hill, I cannot persuade you against your will.' He smiled. 'Nor can I take you to Oxford by force. I can tell you that Erasmus Pole, the King's cryptographer, has died, and that Abraham Fletcher has particularly recommended you to replace him. That is all I can tell you. The King has sent for you, and you must decide whether to obey his summons. If I return without you, he will be disappointed, but I don't think he will send Prince Rupert with a troop of cavalry to do what I had failed to do. Either way, I must leave tomorrow. Not even time to call on the Benedictine nuns in your lovely Abbey.'

'So, Father de Pointz, you arrive unannounced at our door, you claim to bring a summons from the King for my brother to join him in Oxford, and you expect him to make a decision immediately. Is that it?'

'I fear, madam, that it is. Wholly unreasonable, quite indefensible, insupportable, and unjust. That's exactly how it is.'

Again Thomas and Margaret exchanged looks. The monk's frankness at least deserved the courtesy of a considered reply. 'Then so be it. You shall have your decision in the morning. Do not expect it to be the one you would like. I cannot say that you're welcome, but you may sleep here.'

'We'll give you a blanket.' said Margaret.

'Thank you. Your floor will be much more comfortable than the places I've slept these past three days. I shared a barn in Newbury with a blind beggar, two sows, and a family of rats as big as hounds.'

With the blanket, and his bag for a pillow, they left him to sleep on the kitchen floor and went upstairs. Margaret looked in on the girls, then came into Thomas's room. They sat side-by-side on his bed. 'Well, brother. Plundering soldiers, the Queen's monk, a royal summons. Surely this day can bring us nothing more.'

'Other than a visit from Banquo's ghost, I think we're safe. But there'll be no sleep, I fear, until we've come to a decision.'

'The decision must be yours, Thomas.'

'No, Margaret. It must be ours.'

An hour later, they had argued through the conflict of loyalties to country and to family, the threat to the safety of Margaret and the girls, Thomas's own safety on the journey, how Margaret would cope with the shop, what they had heard of Oxford now that the King had made it his capital, and their impressions of Simon de Pointz. Thomas had spoken of his friendship with Abraham Fletcher, Margaret had reminded him of his hatred of the war. They had wondered aloud whether Thomas's skills would be used as a force for good or evil. And they had reached no conclusion. At last, quite exhausted, Margaret said, 'Thomas, I have nothing left to say. You have my support whatever you decide, but, if you choose to go, please do so before the girls are awake. It will be bad enough for them without seeing you leave.' With that, she returned to her room, lay down, and immediately fell asleep.

Thomas, however, tossed and turned until dawn, when, while the house was still quiet, he went down to the kitchen to speak to the priest. De Pointz, too, was awake, and had stoked the oven fire to a good flame. He sat at the table with a cup of water. 'Good morning, Master Hill. How did you sleep?' He was horribly cheerful for such an hour.

'Not at all, thank you, father. And you?'

'The sleep of the just and pious. Have you come to a decision?'

'We have. Although there are two things I hate about this war – the Parliamentarians and the Royalists – it may be that, by being of service to the King, I can contribute to its early end. Or, if not, at least to the saving of lives. And I trust Abraham Fletcher.

He knows my views and would not ask me to come unless he thinks I can help. Be sure of one thing, however. I will never take up arms against Englishmen.'

'That is understood. The King knows it.'

'Good. Then, on that understanding, and for Abraham's sake, I will accompany you to Oxford.'

The priest picked up his bag and emptied its contents on to the floor. 'I am much relieved. To have carried these all the way here and then all the way back, would have been most tiresome.' On the floor lay a hooded habit with a black rope for a belt, the same as the monk himself was wearing, a heavy silver cross on a silver chain, a pair of sandals, and a small bag. He passed the habit and the sandals to Thomas. 'As a Franciscan, I choose to dress as St Francis did. I find the habit comfortable and convenient. For the journey, you'd best be a Franciscan too. God will forgive the deception. If asked, we are returning from Canterbury to Worcester. Wear this cross, and this,' he said, handing over the small bag, 'is for your family while you are away. Please take it.'

When Thomas opened the bag, he saw that it contained a number of gold sovereigns, certainly enough to keep Margaret and the girls fed and clothed for a year or more. 'Thank you. Although I hope I shall not be away for as long as this suggests.'

'I pray not. When will you be ready to leave?'

'We should be away before my nieces are awake. They would be upset to see me go, and that might weaken my resolve. We will breakfast and leave.'

Within the hour they had left Romsey and were on the road to

Andover. The early morning sun was already warm, the baked earth made for hard walking, and Thomas took frequent sips from a leather flask of water, filled from the rain barrel behind the shop. The flask, his razor, a set of clean linen, a translation of Michel Montaigne's Essais, and half the sovereigns, were all he carried. The other half he had left for Margaret. His habit itched like the devil. When he asked Simon where it had come from, the priest grinned. 'The owner was a saintly man, if a little reluctant to wash. I did my best to clean his habit when we'd buried him.' At the hamlet of Tinsbury, they picked up a horse Simon had left there, and a second for Thomas. Simon produced another bag of sovereigns to pay for them. Riding one behind the other, there was little opportunity to talk – a blessing for Thomas, who wanted to be left alone with his thoughts. He tried to rationalise his decision to leave Margaret and the girls unprotected, and to make a dangerous journey to carry out a unknown task for a strange little man who limped and stammered, and who had led his country into a bloody civil war. Would he, he wondered, have done the same for John Pym? No, he would not. Pym did not have an Abraham Fletcher at his disposal and had not been born to the throne. Did that make Thomas a Royalist? Probably, although he would rather be neutral. Did he really hope to shorten the war? That would depend upon what he was asked to do. There were other men perfectly capable of devising and deciphering codes, yet Abraham had recommended him. Why?

Deciding finally that he would find out soon enough, Thomas allowed his thoughts to wander. To the bookshop and the repair work that awaited him on his return, to Polly and

Lucy, whom he had left to sleep, and to his student days at Oxford. He wondered how much the town had changed. Soldiers and courtiers and their trappings no doubt, but surely still the ancient buildings, the Castle, the meadows by the river, the Bodleian Library, the Physic Gardens, the tennis court, the tranquility of the colleges, and, in every inn and tavern, the clamour of opinionated scholars wanting to be heard. At Pembroke, newly built in the middle of the town, he had studied under Abraham Fletcher. Abraham, now well into his seventies, had become a good friend, one of the few with whom Thomas still exchanged occasional letters. It would be good to see him again.

By the time they neared Andover that evening, Thomas knew that he could not have made a worse decision. His chest and back were covered in livid sores, which incessant scratching only made worse, and he was hot, tired, thirsty, and hungry. Unlike Simon, he needed food to sustain him. Simon appeared to be able to go from dawn till dusk on a cup of water and a piece of bread. Thomas offered a silent prayer that some form of dinner would be available in the town. As for the scratching, the previous owner of the habit must have either had skin made of a cow's hide or have actually enjoyed the torture of biting fleas. He would burn the loathsome thing that evening, and find something cleaner to wear. Either that or go naked. Was there a Lord Godiva, he wondered?

No more than half a mile from the town, they heard horses approaching. Simon signalled Thomas to stop, and then to make quickly for a stand of elms fifty yards to their right. They had barely reached cover when the first horsemen appeared. They were Parliamentary cavalry. Thomas held his breath. They were not invisible from the road, and dared not move for fear of being noticed. They sat quite still until the cavalrymen had cantered past. 'I daresay they'd have ignored us,' said Simon, 'but better not to be seen. We'll avoid the town and stay here for the night.'

'Here? Here I see neither food nor bedding. Are you not tired and hungry?'

'A little, perhaps. I'll find us something to eat, and we'll sleep under God's heaven.'

'Excellent, Simon. Poisonous berries and damp leaves. Not to mention this revolting garment, home to families of voracious insects with a particular taste for the flesh of peaceful booksellers.'

'You'd have made a poor monk, Thomas. We're expected to rise above such trivial matters.'

'An empty belly and festering sores may be trivial to you, monk, but not to me. Go and find food. I'll find grass for the horses and then try to dislodge some of the inhabitants of this infernal thing.'

When Simon returned with their dinner in a fold of his habit, Thomas, naked but for his sandals, was thrashing his against the trunk of an elm. 'Take that, you devils. And that. And that. Be gone, and don't come back.'

'English-speaking fleas, are they, Thomas? How fortunate. Here's dinner.' Thomas dropped the habit and inspected his next meal. It looked as if it might kill him.

'God's wounds, what in the name of all that's holy are those?'

'Coprinus comatus, Thomas. Country people call them shaggy inkcaps. Appropriate for a bookseller, I thought. Delicious when roasted like chestnuts over a fire.'

Simon started a small fire and cooked the inkcaps on the end of a stick, while Thomas watched miserably. Still naked, he took a tiny bite of the first one. It was good. He ate four more, washed down with sips of water from his flask. 'Better?' asked Simon.

'A little,' replied Thomas, 'but I still have to put this instrument of torture back on.'

'Get some sticks about a yard long. We'll hang it over the fire and smoke them out.'

An hour later Thomas risked getting back into the habit. It was warm, the smoky smell was not unpleasant, and he was not immediately devoured. Somewhat cheered, he scraped out two places to sleep among the leaves, while Simon, having moved a little away, knelt, and prayed. 'I have prayed for a dry night,' he said later, 'and a flealess one.'

Next morning, they skirted Andover before dawn, and continued towards Newbury. The road here was wider, enabling them to ride side-by-side. Simon was in a talkative mood. 'You haven't asked me much about myself, Thomas. Nothing, in fact. Why's that?' he asked, as they rode.

'You're a Franciscan monk. What is there to ask?'

'Not all monks are the same.'

'Yes they are. They wear flea-ridden habits, eat little, drink less, and pray a lot.'

'Ah, but what if you scratch the surface? Will we all be the same then?'

'Scratch is the very word. Very well, Simon, do tell me about yourself. I suppose you can't always have been a monk.'

'I was born in Norwich. Ours was a God-fearing family. My father was a tailor, prosperous and respected. My mother died when I was twelve. I have two sisters, both older than me. One is a sister of Saint Sulspice in France, the other is married to a farmer.'

'Nothing all that odd, so far. Why did you become a monk?'

'After my mother's death, I turned away from God, left home, and lived on the streets. I begged and stole and learnt how to survive. I got into a fight over a girl, was badly beaten, and left in a ditch. I managed to struggle to the Abbey, where the monks took me in. There I recovered my health and my faith, and eventually became a man of God. Mind you, I still don't much like dogma and ritual. They lack humour.'

'Yet our devout Queen surely insists on all the Catholic rituals.'

'She does, and I'm happy to advise and support her in the way she practises her faith.'

'And you are equally happy to lure a peaceful man to Oxford without confiding in him the truth of the matter?'

'As long as the ends justify the means, and Her Majesty wishes it, I am. A pragmatic approach, I think. Pragmatism and humour. Both essential to a happy and fulfilled life on earth.'

'I do hope that my life on earth is not about to be curtailed. Romsey has its faults, but it's a good deal safer than Oxford by the sound of it.'

'Have no worries, Thomas. You will be under the protection of the King, and quite safe.'

They avoided Newbury and arrived that evening at the village of Chieveley. To Thomas's relief after forty miles in the saddle, they found there a small inn with a room available for travellers, and a simple landlord who thought nothing of a pair of monks arriving at his door. He had no other customers, and fed and watered his visitors and their horses without inquiring as to their business. While they ate, Thomas tried to draw the monk out. 'Why would Abraham recommend me when there must be others in Oxford quite capable of encoding and decoding messages?' he ventured.

For a moment, Simon looked thoughtful. Then, 'Now that we're on our way, I think I can tell you this. Abraham has suspicions about Erasmus Pole's death. He believes it may not have been an accident.'

'Then what was it?'

'He might have been murdered.'

'So I'm to replace a man who might have been murdered? Very pragmatic of you not to tell me that before we left. You'd have returned alone.'

'It was a little deceitful, I admit. I have prayed for forgiveness.'

'Anything else you'd like to tell me?'

'Abraham also had reason to believe that Pole had been passing messages to the enemy. Oxford is full of spies. It would not have been difficult, and he saw everything that came in and out.'

'So why would he be killed?'

'That is a question to which we do not yet have an answer. Abraham knows that you can be trusted, and he thinks you might find out the truth.'

'Does he? Abraham was ever the optimist.'

Thomas slept little that night. Again and again his thoughts returned to what had persuaded him to leave Romsey, his family, his business. Vanity? To be sure, it was flattering to be summoned by the King, but what was really behind the summons? Curiosity? Curious about what? Could he really hope to bring the war to an end? It seemed far-fetched. And what was he going to find there? He had heard stories about the royal household. Only stories, mind you, nothing more.

They set off again at an early hour, intending to cover the twenty or so miles to Abingdon, a small town some ten miles from Oxford. Twice they left the road when they heard horses – both times horses of the King's cavalry – but otherwise saw almost no-one. Even the fields were deserted. 'England has never been so quiet,' remarked Simon, 'at least away from the fighting. People are too frightened to venture out.'

In Abingdon they found another inn with a room, this one busy and noisy. They sat quietly with onion soup and rough bread, and listened to the talk around them. It was about little other than the war. Once their tongues were loosened, the drinkers spoke freely, ignoring the two monks in the corner. 'King or Parliament – do I have to choose?' asked one, 'How can I? Which one will put food on my table and clothes on my back? I don't know.'

'Better stay out of it, then.' replied another, 'Keep mending shoes. It's safer.'

'I'd rather support the King,' offered a third, 'only not this King. A lame Scot who cares nothing for us. It's Queen Bess's fault. No heirs. We should find a better King.'

'Hush, William,' hissed the first man, 'you could lose your head for saying such things. And anyway, where do we find another King? We don't want a Frenchman or a Dutchman, do we?'

For the first time, a large man, black-bearded and deep-voiced, spoke. 'We should do what they're doing in Cornwall. Organise ourselves to defend our homes and families from both sides. Arm ourselves with whatever we can find and frighten off any who approach the town. Kill them if we have to.'

'Jeb, do we really need another army? Aren't two enough?' asked the first man.

'Maybe that's just what we need. Show them what we really care about. Our wives, children, land, homes. Food to eat and ale to drink. Not who sits on his arse in Parliament, nor wipes the King's. That makes no difference to us. Fight fire with fire, I say.'

'And I say we should keep quiet and wait for peace.' said the one called William.

'And what good will peace be if our women have been raped and our homes torched?' demanded Ned, 'Tell me that.'

While the argument continued, Thomas and Simon said nothing. As soon as they had finished the soup, they went up to the room where they would sleep. There was only one bed and the thin mattress was made of old straw, but it was wide enough for two. 'This is a strange war, Thomas, don't you think?' asked Simon, rising from his knees after a long prayer, 'Who wins or loses seems less important than how long it will go on and what will happen afterwards.' Thomas did not reply. He was asleep.

Again they left the inn at dawn, riding side-by-side on a road that widened as they approached Oxford. 'When were you last here, Thomas?' asked Simon.

'It must be eight years ago now. I went to visit Abraham and to attend a college feast.'

'You'll see much changed. The King is in Christ Church, the Queen in Merton, and their households are billeted everywhere.' He hesitated. 'Their presence has sharpened the divide between university and town.'

'In what way?'

'Both the King and the Queen have large households. And there are the soldiers. They all have to be housed and fed. The King urges restraint, but is not always heeded. And his nephews are not easily controlled when they're here. If they weren't Royal princes, Rupert and Maurice would be highwaymen. They exert much influence over the young. The townspeople can be resentful.'

'With good reason, no doubt. The town must be overflowing. And not just with bodies.'

'It is. Humans and animals create waste. Much waste. The drains can't cope.'

Two miles from the town, Thomas's sensitive nose had

already detected the stench of excrement and decay. He shuddered at the thought of what lay ahead. 'And the town itself? Is there much damage to buildings or to the colleges?'

'You'll see for yourself. I thought it best to warn you.'

Soon Thomas did begin to see for himself. They passed through the remains of three deserted villages burnt to the ground as a precaution against siege, and around huge earthworks thrown up as defences. Long poles, sharpened to a wicked point, had been stuck into the earthworks to deter oncoming cavalry, and gangs of bare-chested labourers with shovels and picks worked frantically to build more. It was as if Fairfax, Waller, Ireton, and their entire armies, were all expected within the hour. The ancient city walls had also been strengthened by earthworks, filling in the gaps where the stone had crumbled away. Just outside the wall, they came upon a heap of decaying corpses and a large pit being dug by a gang of women. 'Plague, Simon?' asked Thomas.

'Morbus campestris. Too many people and too much foul water.'

Inside the wall, the streets overflowed with people, and the open sewers with their waste. Thomas put his hand to his face. Damn my nose, he thought, too sharp for its own good. They made their way slowly up St Aldate's towards Pembroke. Soldiers and their horses blocked the way, beggars pleading for alms pulled at their habits, and pigs foraged among mounds of stinking refuse. There were even dung heaps on the street corners. It took them more than an hour to reach the entrance to Pembroke. There they dismounted and led their horses through a side gate and into a small paved courtyard, where a college servant took them. They walked through an arch into the main courtyard and Thomas looked around at his old college. It was unrecognisable. What had once been a neat cobbled yard, surrounded by high stone walls and arched entrances to staircases leading to the scholars' rooms, was a mess of broken furniture, broken bottles, old clothes, and rotting food. Most of the doors around the yard had been pulled off their hinges, windows had been shattered, and a chimney had fallen off a roof, scattering bricks underneath. Thomas saw no scholars. Three officers in the dashing blue uniform of the King's Lifeguards stood talking in one corner, while their swords were sharpened by a grinder with a whetstone. A woman with two small girls, all three wearing ribbons in their hair and fine lace aprons over their dresses, emerged from a doorway and picked their way aross the yard to the main entrance. The officers swept off their feathered hats and bowed low. Courtly manners and high fashion amid squalor and decay. Soldiers for scholars, guns for gowns. Thomas stood and stared.

There was a tap on his shoulder. 'Master Hill?' Thomas turned. 'I thought it was you, sir. Mr Fletcher told me to look out for you. He said you might be a monk.'

'Only pretending, Silas. Father de Pointz is the real monk. Simon, this is Silas Merkin, head servant of the college.'

'Welcome, sirs. I'll show you to your room, Master Hill. It's small and damp, but it's the best I can do. I had to get rid of a young captain to get it for you. Drunken beggar. We've over a hundred in college, including women and children. They've been throwing out the furniture and making beds on the floor.' Silas had never been short of a word or two.

'Now you're safely here, Thomas, I'll say farewell.' said Simon, 'I'll be at Merton with the Queen. I'll call on you soon.'

Silas showed Thomas to a room under a low arch at the opposite end of the courtyard to the one by which they had entered. It was indeed small and damp, nothing like the comfortable room near the main entrance in which he remembered reading and rereading Plato and Aristotle, poring all night over Euclid's geometry, and occasionally entertaining a young lady. Water dripped down one wall to make a small puddle on the floor, the window was cracked, and he would have but a narrow bed, a washstand with a jug of water, a small table, and a hard chair, for company. On the bed, two linen shirts, two pairs of breeches, and a pair of boots, had been laid out. 'Master Fletcher asked me to find these for you, sir. There's clean water in the well by the chapel, and a new privy beside it. We dug the drain ourselves. It runs into the sewers, but now they're blocked, it won't be long before it's overflowing. Soldiers do seem to shit a lot. And here's your key. Be sure to keep the door locked. I'll tell Master Fletcher you're here. He's in his old rooms, thank the Lord. It wouldn't do to move him now, not with his eyes as they are.'

'His eyes, Silas?'

'Yes sir. Didn't you know? Mr Fletcher sees very little now.'

'I didn't know. Thank you for telling me.'

When Silas had gone, Thomas got out of his habit, washed his face and hands, trimmed his new beard with the razor, and put on a clean shirt and breeches. He would call on Abraham immediately.

Chapter 3

Abraham's rooms were directly across the courtyard. Thomas climbed a narrow spiral staircase, knocked on the door, and entered at the familiar sound of his old friend's voice. God's wounds, he thought, I could be sixteen again. Abraham was sitting by the window in a high-backed oak chair. In profile against the light, he looked just as he had fifteen years ago. High forehead, roman nose, back straight. But when he turned his face to the room, Thomas could see that his old friend had aged. His hair and beard were white, and he wore a shawl over his coat. His blue eyes were watery, his skin pale, and two deep lines ran from nose to mouth. The remains of a meal were on a table beside him. 'Is that you, Thomas?' Abraham asked, when he heard his visitor come in.

'It is, Abraham.' he replied, taking the outstretched hand in both of his. 'Do I find you well?'

'Quite well, thank you, except for these.' Abraham pointed to his eyes. 'They see only shadows and shapes these days.'

'I'm truly sorry to hear it. Can you read?'

'Alas, no. It's a curse. How are your sister and nieces? I was sad to hear of Andrew's death.'

'They thrive, thank you. The girls are as bright as buttons. Polly will make someone a very demanding wife, one day.'

'Ha. And your writing? Still persevering, I trust.'

'Still persevering. And still reading Montaigne.'

'That old cynic. I don't know what you see in him.' He paused. 'Thomas, my eyes are one reason why you're here.'

'But not the only reason, I gather.'

When Abraham laughed, his eyes sparkled again. 'What has that monk been telling you? He never could keep his holy mouth shut.'

'Very little, in truth. I hope you will tell me rather more.' Thomas looked around the room. It was little changed since he had last seen it. Simple wooden furniture, oak panelling, a door leading to a small bed chamber, and books. Piles of books on the table and on bookshelves. A scholar's room. A scholar who could no longer read. It was a cruel thing.

'Come and sit near me, so I can see your shape against the light. There's wine in the corner if you're thirsty. At least Silas has managed to keep some of our cellar intact. Brasenose and New have nothing left at all. Their lodgers have had every bottle, along with every piece of plate.'

Thomas found a dusty bottle of claret, poured them both a glass, and sat by the window. 'How's that, Abraham? Can you see me here?'

'Well enough. Now, as time is our enemy, I shall tell you what I can. My old friend Erasmus Pole, with whom I shared lodgings fifty years ago, was the King's chief cryptographer. His position was known to very few. He dealt with all the messages and reports coming in and out of Oxford, and decrypted the intercepted ones. They never amounted to much, but they did keep us informed about our enemy's ciphers – inferior to our own, I'm pleased to say. Until my eyes betrayed me, I helped him whenever he asked me to. It wasn't often. Erasmus was a fine scholar.' Abraham paused for a sip of wine. 'He was also a creature of habit. On Wednesday evenings, he always dined at Exeter. Exeter serve venison on Wednesdays. Alas, Erasmus's taste for it may have been his undoing. Next morning, his body was found in Brasenose Lane on the south side of the college. His throat had been cut, and he'd been robbed.' Abraham took another sip from his glass.

'Such deaths are not uncommon, Abraham.' remarked Thomas quietly.

'Indeed they're not, especially now. I daresay he'd enjoyed the hospitality of the evening, but Erasmus was a cautious man. He would not have walked in the dark down that foul lane. And remember that Erasmus was the King's cryptographer. He had access to almost every order and report to and from the King's commanders. He knew a great deal.'

'As do you, my friend. Yet, happily, I find you alive and well.'

'Happily, you do. But there's another thing. I knew Erasmus as well as any man. In the weeks before his death, something was troubling him. He didn't speak of it, and I didn't ask, yet I'm sure of it. As my sight has deteriorated, so my hearing has become more acute. Interesting how the body works, don't you think? I could hear fear in his voice. Fear, and something else. I think it was guilt.'

'Guilt? But why?'

'I believe his role was discovered and he was being threatened. There are many spies in the town. One of them may have got to him and frightened him into betraying secrets.'

'And killed him when he refused?'

'It's more likely he was killed because they thought he was about to be exposed as a traitor. If so, he would have suffered greatly and would eventually have revealed the identity of the spy.'

'Had they grounds for thinking that he was under suspicion?'

'Possibly. When a message arrived from Lord Digby informing the King that he planned to attack Alton, the town garrison was immediately strengthened. The attack never took place. It looked suspicious.'

The two men sat in silence. Outside they heard the clatter of boots on cobbles, the clash of sword and armour, voices raised, orders being given. 'Who would have imagined it?' asked Thomas, as much to himself as to Abraham, 'Pembroke College a soldier's billet. Our beautiful place of learning turned into this.'

'Thomas, the King trusts almost no-one.' Abraham's voice was suddenly brusque. 'I've persuaded him that you're the best cryptographer in the land, and that I would gladly put my life in your hands. We need you. We want you to take Erasmus's place.'

'Abraham, you know my views on this war,' replied Thomas evenly, 'and on any war. On the journey here, I asked myself again and again why I was coming to take part in something I hate so much. And, when I saw what has become of the city, I very nearly turned round and went straight back to Romsey.

Beggars, soldiers, whores, poverty, destruction, filth. Barely a scholar to be seen.'

'So why did you come?'

'I'm still not sure. The pleasure of seeing you, of course. The vain hope that I might hasten the end of the war. Perhaps even loyalty to the King. He is the King, after all, for all his faults. I would not have done the same if the summons had been from Pym.'

'Of that I am sure, Thomas. But will you do as I ask?'

'For your sake, my old friend, I will. I would not see you embarrassed before the King, and, in any case, I have no wish to climb straight back on a horse for four days. But it's some time since I worked on ciphers. I shall need help.'

Abraham found Thomas's arm and laid his hand upon it. 'And you shall have it. Tomorrow morning I'll take you to meet the King, or rather you'll take me, as I shall need your arm for guidance, and then we'll talk. It'll be just like it used to be.'

'Only a little more serious.'

'Yes. A little more serious. Call for me tomorrow.' Thomas rose to leave. As he did so, he saw the old man's eyes close. He was asleep before Thomas had closed the door.

Thomas, too, was tired. Four days in the saddle and three nights away from his own bed were taking their toll. His shoulders ached and his backside was sore. Back in his tiny room, he lay on the bed and slept.

When he awoke two hours later, he was famished. He splashed his face with water from the ewer, adjusted his dress, carefully locked the door behind him, visited the new privy, and went to find Silas Merkin.

Silas was in his little room by the college entrance. His sentry room he called it. From there, he could see the courtyard and all its comings and goings. Thomas smiled at the memory of trying to slip past him unnoticed with a willing girl from the town. It had not worked. Silas had pounced, the girl had been sent on her way, and Thomas had slept alone. 'Ah, Master Hill. How did you find Master Fletcher?'

'His mind is still sharp, Silas. Would that his eyes were too. Old age can be a terrible thing.'

'I do take care of him, sir. Make sure his food is how he likes it, help him with dressing and washing, that sort of thing.'

'I know you do, Silas, and I thank you for it. He's a good friend and a fine scholar. Now, I'm hungry. Where shall I go for my dinner?'

'I can easily have the kitchen prepare something for you, sir. No need to go foraging.'

'Thank you, Silas. But I need to walk off the stiffness in my back, and I'd like to see the town.'

Silas was a little put out. The kitchens came under his control, and he liked his scholars and visitors to use them. 'As you wish, sir, but do take care. The town is much changed, as you may have noticed. The Crown in Market Street still serves well. You could try there.'

'I will, Silas. And I'll take care.'

Leaving the college, Thomas made his way down the lane and up St Aldate's towards Cornmarket. In the streets, soldiers jostled with townspeople, and at Golden Cross, a noisy crowd had gathered to watch a woman in the pillory being pelted with muck. It must have been stony muck, because blood dripped from her mouth and cheek. 'What did she do?' Thomas asked a young soldier.

'The old hag tried to steal a trooper's breakfast. She's lucky not to be on a gibbet.' the man replied.

Thomas moved swiftly on into Market Street, making for The Crown. Market Street was even busier. Uniformed men and women in rags bargained noisily with the tradesmen hawking their wares from stalls on either side of the street. At least the town's bakers, brewers, and tailors were doing well. The crush of bodies around the stalls forced him to the middle of the street, down which ran a reeking open drain, half-blocked in places with shit and refuse. He took care to avoid being jostled into it, as some had been. On a whim, he continued past The Crown and into Brasenose Lane – the lane Erasmus Pole had walked down after dinner at Exeter. It was a stinking, rough, narrow thing, uncobbled, and with high walls on both sides, dark even at that time of day. Avoiding the worst of the muck, he kept to the middle of the lane, again avoiding the drain that ran down it. He had taken barely ten steps when a foul whore, what was left of her face pitted by pox, emerged from the shadows on his left, and grabbed his arm. 'Looking for company, sir? Meg'll make you stand to attention.' Yellow spit oozed out of her toothless mouth like pus from a boil. Thomas recoiled in horror and pulled his sleeve away. Resisting the urge to turn back to Market Street, he swallowed hard, squared his shoulders, and carried on up the lane. Beggars lined the college wall, some crippled, others diseased. Hands were held out as he passed, and pleading voices raised. He ignored them all. Abraham was right. A cautious old man would not have walked this lane in daylight, never mind at night. At the east end of the lane, where it met Radcliffe Square, a whore was being humped against the wall by a grunting soldier. When the woman saw Thomas, she called out to him. 'Won't be long, sir. Be your turn soon.' He quickened his pace, turned right into the square, and made his way back to The Crown, where he found a corner seat and ordered a bottle of port.

As Silas had said, The Crown did serve well. After a plate of good roast mutton with oysters and radishes, and a sweet apple cream flavoured with ginger and lemon, Thomas felt more himself. Taking his purse from his pocket, he asked the landlord how much he owed. 'How will you be paying, sir?' asked the man suspiciously.

Taken aback at the question, Thomas held up his purse. 'The usual way, landlord. Coins of the realm.'

The landlord grinned. 'In that case, sir, two shillings'll do nicely.' Thomas handed over the coins.

'What other case is there?'

'Ah. You must be new in Oxford, sir. We have to take tickets from the King's men. Tickets instead of coins. Worthless, if you ask me. We'll never see the money.' A woman stoned for stealing a soldier's breakfast. An innkeeper robbed by soldiers who did not pay for theirs. Not the Oxford he remembered.

His belly full and his spirits a little restored, Thomas decided to risk another stroll before returning to his room. He walked down High Street and into Magpie Lane. The crowds had thinned and it was a route he knew well. It would take him past Merton and over Merton Field, from where he would turn towards Christ Church, and into St Aldate's. Ignoring the beggars and the black smoke of coal fires, he reached Merton

Street. He was about to cross the street to join the path leading to the field, when a sudden scream from his right stopped him. Turning sharply, he saw a woman in a yellow gown and a short black cape, beating fiercely with her hand at an attacker. With the other hand she was trying to wrest from him her purse. Despite the scream, she looked unhurt. Indeed, her assailant seemed to be losing the battle quite easily. His shoulders hunched, he was trying vainly to cover his head with his arms. 'You there,' shouted Thomas, hastening to help, 'Thief!' The thief let go the purse and ran. Thomas shouted after him. 'Stop thief. Thief. Stop that man.' But the few people in the street ignored him, and the thief disappeared around a corner.

'So much for Oxford.' said a soft voice behind him, 'Home to King, Queen, army, exchequer, and mint, but apparently not to gentlemen.' Turning, Thomas saw a lady of about his own age, black curls to her shoulders, cheeks flushed, and a little smile playing on her lips. 'Except for you, sir, naturally. I thank you for your assistance, although the wretch would soon have surrendered.'

'I don't doubt it, madam. Are you hurt?'

'Quite unhurt, thank you. It was my own fault. I seldom venture out alone, but I needed space. The college can be so restricting.'

'Why did no-one stop the man?' asked Thomas.

'Alas, sir, the people of Oxford do not all welcome us here. They look out for their own.'

'Then it's fortunate that I too am a visitor. Thomas Hill, madam, newly arrived from Romsey, and visiting my old tutor at Pembroke College.' The deception had been agreed with Abraham.

'A dangerous time to be visiting Oxford, Master Hill.'

'Indeed, madam. He's an old man, and nearly blind. Another year and I might have been too late.'

'I'm sorry. My name is Jane Romilly. I attend Queen Henrietta Maria at Merton.'

'Allow me to escort you there, madam.'

Jane Romilly smiled. She had unusually white teeth. 'Thank you, Master Hill. It's very close, but I should be glad of company.'

At the entrance to Merton, she held out a hand. 'My thanks again, sir. Perhaps we shall meet another time.' Thomas took the hand, bowed, and brushed his lips against it.

'I hope so, madam.' He watched her safely into the college before making his way back to Pembroke. Jane Romilly. An unusual lady, he thought, and an elegant one. Certain to be married. I wonder in what way she attends the Queen. And there was something arresting about her face. He tried to picture it, but could not.

Later, he lay on his bed and thought of the day. Pembroke a soldiers' quarters, blind Abraham, that filthy lane, the poxed whore, Jane Romilly. It came to him just before he fell asleep. Jane Romilly's eyes were different colours. The right was brown, the left blue. Extraordinary.

Abraham was dressed and ready when Thomas called for him. To attend the King, he wore an ancient black wig, a little dusty, and a long black jacket; he carried a broad black hat in his hand.

'Take this,' he said, holding out another wig, 'I'm quite sure you don't have one.' Thomas put it on and took the old man's arm. 'It's no distance to Christ Church. We'll walk slowly. I want to ask you something.' Outside Pembroke, Thomas told Abraham about the attempted robbery of Jane Romilly. 'No-one even tried to arrest the man, never mind help the lady. I couldn't believe it.'

'Thomas,' replied Abraham quietly, 'you and I support the King, but we must accept that feelings in the town are running high. Oxford has always favoured Parliament, and the townspeople have good reason to resent the court and the army being here. They say there are ten thousand men and women in the colleges and the town. Some are even billeted in alms houses. Jesus is full of soldiers, All Souls is an arsenal, and Brasenose a food store. We can't walk in the meadows for artillery pieces. Every day there's pillaging and theft. And not just by the men. The women are worse, especially the Irish and the Welsh, whom no-one understands when they speak that impossible language of theirs. Do you know who your lady was?'

'Jane Romilly, lady-in-waiting to the Queen.'

'I have met Lady Romilly. Sir Edward died at Edgehill.'

'Her husband?' Abraham nodded. 'A widow, then.'

'Yes, and by her dress she would have been marked as a member of the Royal household. That's why she went unhelped. Except by you.'

At Christ Church, they were admitted by the guards, and shown to a chamber near the Great Hall, where the King had established his Parliament. Abraham sat. Thomas stood nervously, trying to remember what Montaigne would have advised. After a couple of false starts, he had it. 'Au plus eslevé throne du monde, si ne sommes assis que sus nostre cul'; 'upon the highest throne in the world, we are seated, still, upon our arse'. The chamber door opened, and a tall man, dressed, like Abraham, entirely in black, entered. He looked about forty and carried a silver-topped cane. 'Good morning, gentlemen.' he said affably, 'Master Fletcher, the King is expecting you. And,' turning to Thomas, 'you must be Master Hill. Welcome. I am Tobias Rush, private secretary to His Majesty.'

'Master Rush.' Thomas offered a small bow. Abraham said nothing.

'If you would follow me, gentlemen. His Majesty is suffering a little this morning. His legs often trouble him. Your audience will be brief.'

They followed Tobias Rush into the Hall, where the King was seated at the far end. Abraham held Thomas's arm. At Rush's signal, they bowed low and walked slowly up its length. The King, surrounded by courtiers, watched impassively. Even sitting, Thomas could see that he was a small man, slight of build; he had a narrow face, and a small pointed beard. His dark eyes showed nothing. He did not rise as they approached. 'Your Majesty,' said their escort, 'may I present Master Thomas Hill, with Master Fletcher, whom you know?' The King held out a limp hand. Not knowing quite what to do with it, Thomas took it very lightly in his fingers, and bowed again. Abraham followed suit.

'Master Hill,' said the King in a gentle Scottish voice, 'We are pleased that you have arrived safely. Your skills come highly recommended, and we have grave need of them. Once Master Fletcher has acquainted you with our methods, we shall depend upon you to render our orders and reports entirely secure, and to reveal the enemy's secrets when you have the opportunity to do so. Have you anything to ask me?' Thomas had not. 'Master Rush will see to your needs. Ask him for whatever you require to carry out your loyal duties.'

'I shall, Your Majesty.'

'Good. Then lose no time. England's enemies must be defeated.' Tobias Rush nodded to Thomas, signalling the end of the audience. The three men took two steps backwards, Abraham holding on tightly, bowed, then turned and left the hall.

Outside, Rush escorted them to the college entrance. 'His Majesty has instructed me to provide you with whatever you need, Master Hill. Are your rooms adequate?' They were not, but Thomas chose not to say so. 'Food, wine, company, you have but to ask.'

'Thank you, sir.' replied Thomas.

'Excellent. We're much relieved that you're here. I never trusted Erasmus Pole and told the King so more than once. I wasn't surprised that his body was found in that vile lane. He was a man of odd habits.' Thomas glanced at Abraham, who was silent. At the gate, Rush shook their hands and watched them turn towards Pembroke. As they did so, two riders, yelling at them to get out of the way, swept past and into the college. Both wore pale blue hats with long feathers, and dark blue coats, festooned with ribbons and lace. 'Sounds like the royal princes.' said Abraham drily, 'Rupert and Maurice. Probably boasting about their exploits in Bristol. If they aren't drunk, they soon will be. The King should send them back where they came from.'

'Who were all those people around the King, Abraham?' asked Thomas.

'I couldn't see them, but the King has a full court. The Master of the Revels was probably there, and William Dobson, the court painter. He's much in demand, I hear. Unspeakably vain, some young men these days. Care to have your portrait painted, Thomas? Rush could arrange it.'

'I think not, thank you. Although it sounds like Tobias Rush could arrange anything. What do you know of him?'

'Rush is not to my taste, but the King relies on him.' replied Abraham, as they entered Pembroke. 'He organises the King's affairs and runs his household. He's skilled at playing on the King's insecurity. He's a clever man, and an ambitious one. Treat him with caution, Thomas.'

'I certainly shall. Now, when shall we start work?'

'This morning. I'll have food and wine sent to my rooms. Silas will escort me. Come in an hour.'

An hour later, they were seated at Abraham's table, a pile of papers before them. 'Since the King came to Oxford,' he began, 'we've been using substitution ciphers devised and developed by Erasmus. The ciphers are based on an eight-letter keyword, changed on the first day of each month. In the final week of the month, Erasmus sent out the first four letters of the new keyword, encoded according to the current keyword, and hidden in the text of the message. Each recipient then sent back four more letters, also encoded and hidden, to make up the full keyword.'

'So each recipient has a unique keyword, which lasts for a month?'

'That is right. It means that we have to know from whom each message has come, but that is easily dealt with. Each message carries the encoded name of the sender, again hidden in the text. Each name has its own code word. If one forgets to include his name, we simply use all the current keywords until we find the right one for the text.'

'There are weaknesses in this, Abraham, as you know. The messages carrying either half of the new keyword might not arrive, and a list of all current keywords and code words must have been kept somewhere.'

'Indeed they were. Inside Erasmus's head. He never wrote them down. As to the other point, we've had no serious difficulties. Process of elimination and a bit of guesswork have sufficed.'

'How many keywords are there?'

'Currently, twenty.' Thomas looked thoughtful. Twenty names with fixed codes, and twenty different half-words each month. Not difficult. Abraham passed Thomas the top sheet of paper.

'This is an encrypted message, received three months ago. If you were the enemy, how long would it take you to decrypt it?'

Thomas looked at it. It was six lines long, each line consisting of about fifty seemingly random letters. 'This is about the right length for a military report, rather than a battlefield order. It looks like a simple substitution cipher, either with a keyword or an agreed cipher alphabet. A simple shift would be too easy, and a cipher alphabet would be written down somewhere, which would make it vulnerable to capture. I'd assume a keyword. With only one encrypted text to work with, perhaps a morning.'

'That's what I thought. Not secure from the attentions of a good cryptanalyst.' Abraham passed over another sheet. 'What about this one?'

Again, Thomas studied the sheet for several minutes. 'This message is shorter. It could be a military order. I guess that there are some coded words. Not knowing the context, I'd go about it as with the first message – frequencies, letter-relationships, vowel indentifications, but if there are codes, it would take longer.'

Abraham smiled. 'Your instincts are as good as ever, Thomas. Now what about this one?'

Immediately Thomas said, 'This is alpha-numeric.' Thomas imagined lines running through each number. 'I think some of the numbers are nulls because there's a pattern to them, but the others could be codes.'

'Excellent. Now, take these and practise your skills on them. Note that they may not all be what they seem.' Abraham passed over the remaining papers. 'Some of these are ours, others were intercepted. All incoming and outgoing messages will now be passed through me to you, for encryption and decryption. Next week you will need to send out the first half of a new keyword. Here is a list of all recipients. Please commit them to memory, and destroy the list.'

'And if I don't, Mr Fletcher? Will I be confined to college?' Abraham could hear the raised eyebrows and the mocking smile, even though he could not see them.

Chapter 4

Armed with sharpened quills and ink supplied by Silas, Thomas set to work, starting with the simple task of memorising the names of the twenty recipients of messages. He used a memory trick Abraham had taught him years ago, and most names surrendered without much of a fight – for Hopton he needed only the 'o's', and for Maurice the 'a' and the 'u'. Within half-an-hour, he had them all.

Next he counted the papers. There were twenty of them. Deciding to tackle them in the order in which Abraham had put them, he took the first one from the top of the pile. Twenty lines of ten letters each, written in a neat hand in brown ink, and with spaces between every four or six letters, covered one side of the paper. Thomas held it up to the light, looking for unusual marks or letter formations. There were none. He smiled. Kindly old Abraham had given him a simple substitution cipher to start with. On a blank sheet, he prepared a table with each letter of the alphabet across the top. Then he counted the number of times each letter occurred in the message, and wrote the number below it. He found that the letters *c, f,* and *p* appeared most often. They would probably represent *e, a,* and *t,* although not necessarily in that order. If he could sort out the three most commonly used letters in the alphabet, he would be on the way to breaking the cipher. As *c* and *p* were preceded and followed by twenty different letters, but *f* by only twelve, *f* would represent *t.* Ignoring the spaces which were merely intended to confuse, there were six instances of double *c's,* but none of double *p's. C* would represent *e,* leaving *p* as *a.*

Continuing with this strategy, Thomas quickly identified ten letters, which revealed the common words *and, a,* and *the,* and parts of other words. With a little intuition and guesswork, he had found the keyword, *advance,* and decrypted the message within an hour. It revealed that Sir John Berkeley, with modest help from Sir Bevil Grenville and Sir Ralph Hopton, had defeated a strong parliamentary force at Braddock Down in Cornwall, capturing cannon and muskets. Reading the plain text, Thomas wondered why Sir John had troubled to have the message encrypted. The gallant knight clearly wanted the King, his court, and all his subjects, to know of his valour and the great victory it had brought. No doubt there had been similar messages from the other two gentlemen.

Thomas moved on to the second paper on the pile. Roughly the same length as the first, this one was also a mixture of letters and spaces. As before, he checked it for hidden signs, found none, wrote out each letter of the alphabet across the top of a blank page, and put under each one the number of times it appeared. When this produced a more even distribution than he expected,

Thomas suspected he was facing a more complex cipher. Twenty minutes later, he knew he was right. Two mixed substitutions had been used alternately, and he had to find both. After another hour, Thomas had identified fifteen letters, which was enough for him to fill in the gaps and render the entire message into plain text. It was an intercepted message, revealing that in March, Sir Thomas Fairfax had been concerned about his troops' morale, and had asked for them to be paid without further delay. The vital word *pay* was represented by four different combinations of letters. As the message had failed to reach its intended destination, however, Thomas assumed that Sir Thomas's troops had remained unpaid.

By the end of the first day, Thomas had decrypted seven complete documents. They were all alphabetic ciphers, using mixtures of single and double substitutions, keywords and code words. His eyes and back ached, his legs were stiff, and he needed refreshment. He was about to go off in search of food and drink, when there was a loud knock on the door. He opened it to find Tobias Rush, silver-topped cane in hand, and, as at court, dressed all in black, outside. 'Master Hill, I find you hard at work no doubt. I trust I'm not disturbing you. I merely wondered if I could be of any assistance.'

Caught off balance, Thomas was less than articulate. 'Master Rush. Good evening. No, no disturbance. I've just finished for the day, and was about to take some air and stretch my legs.'

'In that case,' replied Rush, smiling his thin smile, 'perhaps I may accompany you. You can tell me how you're progressing.' Without waiting for an answer, he turned and strode out into the courtyard. Thomas locked his door and followed. 'I do admire Pembroke.' said Rush, as they picked their way through the debris towards the college gate, 'A lovely building, and attractively small, although I see the officers here have paid scant regard to its care. Alas, it's the same everywhere. Military mess and careless destruction. Typical of soldiers.'

'Yes,' agreed Thomas, 'there is something blinkered about the military mind. It seems able to ignore almost anything other than itself.'

Rush laughed. 'Nicely put, Master Hill. Let us pray that this war is soon over, and the University can resume its former life.' They left the college and turned north up St Aldate's. 'And how does your work progress?'

'It has not been arduous. So far, Abraham has given me quite simple tasks, although I expect them to get harder.'

'Good. Master Fletcher believes that you are the most accomplished cryptographer in England, and the King has put his absolute trust in you. You have a vital duty to perform. If we can anticipate the enemy's movements, while leaving him ignorant of ours, we shall gain a great advantage.'

Thomas hesitated. 'Erasmus Pole was an able man. Has the King not enjoyed such an advantage since the war began?'

Rush stopped and looked hard at Thomas. 'We were never sure about Pole. There were incidents. His loyalty to the King was beginning to be questioned. And the judgement of an elderly man who walked down that foul lane at night must also be questioned.'

'Do you think he was killed there?'

'That's where he was found.' Rush's eyes narrowed. 'Or do you suggest that he was murdered elsewhere and his body taken there?'

'No, sir, I suggest only that I have walked down that lane in daylight, and shall not do so again, never mind at night.'

'Very wise of you. It's a noisome place.'

'Noisome and evil.' Approaching Queen Street, Thomas changed the subject. 'Master Rush, you kindly asked if there is anything you can do for me. I do have one favour to ask.'

'Of course. What is the favour?'

'I should like to let my sister know that I have arrived in Oxford safely, and am quite well. Would you be able to have a letter delivered for me?'

'That will present no difficulty. Messengers are in and out of the town every day. I will find one heading for Winchester or Salisbury, and have him deliver the letter. Romsey, is it not?'

'It is. My thanks, Master Rush. I am in your debt.'

'Say no more about it. Let me have the letter, and I shall deal with the matter at once. Is there any other service I may perform?'

'I think not, sir, but thank you.'

'In that case, allow me to propose a happy diversion from your labours. The Queen is presenting a masque in honour of the King on Wednesday next week. She is fond of masques. Her court, and much of the King's, will be there. You are invited to attend.'

Thomas hesitated. A masque was not his idea of a happy diversion. It would be formal, lavish, and extravagant. He had no suitable clothes, and little to say to members of either court. He tried to think of an excuse. Then he remembered Jane Romilly, lady-in-waiting to the Queen. Perhaps she would be there. 'Thank you, Master Rush. I should be delighted.'

'Excellent. Two o'clock in the afternoon on Wednesday, at

Merton. The masque will be followed by a reception. I will arrange for a suit of clothes to be sent round to you. Their Majesties are most particular as to dress. I shall look forward to seeing you there. Now I shall return to Christ Church. Good day, Master Hill.'

'Good day, Master Rush.' Alone, Thomas turned into Broad Street, intending to follow Catte Street to the High Street, and thence to St Aldate's and Pembroke. It did not take him long to change his mind. Broad Street was more Bedlam than street. Realising that he would have to run a gauntlet of beggars, whores, and pickpockets, he turned back towards Cornmarket. He was not quite quick enough. He smelt the woman before he saw her. Out of a dark doorway she came, another stinking, poxed, toothless, crone, this one with a humped back. She grabbed his shirt and pressed herself against him. 'Good evening, sir. You're a fine gentleman and no mistake. For a sovereign, I'll make you a happy one.' Bile rising in his throat, Thomas wrenched his shirt free, and ran. He kept running almost as far as Pembroke. Outside the gates, he stopped, took deep breaths until he was calm, and walked slowly into the college.

'Good evening, sir. You look a trifle flushed. Are you well?' Silas, keeping watch from his room, had seen him come in. Silas missed nothing. Thomas's face was red and his shirt askew.

'Quite well, thank you, Silas. I should be grateful for a bottle of hock and some dinner. Would you have them sent over?'

Silas looked him up and down. 'As you wish, sir. Nothing the matter, I hope.'

'Nothing, Silas, thank you. The evening is warm. Walking too fast, I daresay.'

Silas looked doubtful. 'Indeed, sir. I'll have the bottle and a plate sent over directly.'

In his room, Thomas took off his shirt and breeches and lay on his bed. They would have to be washed. Waiting for his dinner, he wondered what he had agreed to. Queen Henrietta Maria was known to be fond of masques, and even sometimes appeared in them herself. In London, it was said that the most extravagant of her entertainments had cost over twenty thousand pounds to put on. Twenty thousand pounds. Enough to build two hundred cottages or a hundred schools, feed an entire town for a year, provide for every beggar and orphan....... Before he could add to the list, his dinner arrived, brought by one of Silas's boys. Intending to give the boy a few pence, Thomas reached for his purse on the table. Then he remembered that it was in his pocket. He picked up the discarded breeches, and felt for the purse. The pockets were empty. He looked around the room in case he had been mistaken. No purse. Then he realised. The hump-backed hag had picked his pocket. Silas's boy was not going to get a whole sovereign from the bag hidden under the bed, so he would have to go unrewarded. 'Thank you, young fellow,' said Thomas graciously, 'You shall have a shilling next time.' Unsure whether to be pleased or not, the boy departed.

For two more days, Thomas saw little of the sun. He was determined to decrypt every one of the documents perfectly. When working, he found that he could blot out the clash and clamour outside. Only when he left his room for trips to the privy, to fetch water from the well, or to find food, did he have to face the awful squalor and destruction that had been visited on his old college.

As he always had, Thomas found himself giving each encoder a personality. He could look at a sheet of paper covered in random letters, numbers, and symbols, and after identifying just a few letters could often divine its soul. And, even before starting the decrypting process, he sometimes recognised the hand of the sender. By visualising the man – fat, thin, tall, short – and his traits – tidy, careless, quick, slow – he could anticipate the methods he was likely to use. It was a marriage of science and art that Abraham used to call Hill's magic.

He expected to find the remaining documents encrypted much as those he had already decrypted, but it did not take him long to find Abraham up to his tricks. The old fox had mixed up the documents to conceal their context and chronology, the tenth document surprised him with an unusually high proportion of the letters *a* and *i*, until he realised that it had been written in Latin, there were deliberate misspellings, and some of the texts – the most difficult to decrypt – were combinations of letters, symbols, and numbers. The symbols and numbers were either homophonic substitutions for single words or meaningless nulls, sometimes both in the same message. A word could be represented by more than one symbol or number but each of these could only represent one word. Thomas started with the assumption that the most common letter combinations would have the most numbers or symbols representing them, the least common the fewest, and all those in between would be represented proportionately. This approach was laborious but effective.

By the evening of the third day, Thomas had a pile of twenty plain texts to match the twenty coded ones and his skills had become as sharp as they had ever been. Although Abraham had said that their own codes were superior to those of the enemy, Thomas found little difference between them. They were much the same, and the messages just as tedious. Demands for men and supplies, complaints about the lack of pay, boasts and excuses. It was hard to tell the two sides apart. The most interesting text turned out to be a description, written backwards, of Abraham's favourite wines.

Thomas decided to wait until the morning to deliver the decrypted texts to Abraham. After a walk to the Cherwell and back, and an excellent plate of black puddings with capers and pickled cucumbers, he was undressing for bed when there was a knock on the door. He quickly pulled up his breeches. 'Who is it?'

'It's your favourite monk, Thomas. Simon de Pointz.' Thomas opened the door. 'And I come bearing gifts.' said Simon, handing over the clothes he was carrying. 'These come from Tobias Rush. I do hope they fit.'

'Good evening, Simon. I had thought you might have called earlier, although I have been busy.'

Simon looked at the pile of papers on the table. 'So I see. Have your efforts met with success?'

'Happily, yes. But it was only practice. The real tests will come later. Should I try these on?' holding up the clothes.

'I would recommend it. Queen Henrietta Maria can't help but notice an ill-fitting shirt or coat. She has an eye for such matters.'

Thomas took off his plain breeches again, and tried on the new ones. They were dark blue, loose-fitting, tied at the knee with yellow ribbons, and with bows and rosettes attached to the sides. A pair of white stockings were embroidered in blue and red. Over a fine lace shirt he put on a short pale blue coat with red lining and red ribbons on the sleeves, and, finally, a pair of soft leather boots with silver buckles. Simon, who had watched the process intently, was delighted. 'Master Hill, who would have thought a Romsey bachelor could be turned into such an elegant and courtly gentleman? Their Majesties will share my admiration. And it all fits perfectly. How clever of Master Rush.'

Thomas was doubtful. 'Are you sure, Simon? I feel like a popinjay.'

'Nonsense. You look splendid. Now take them off and put them away somewhere safe. It would be a pity to spill your soup on such finery.'

As Thomas was undressing, he asked Simon if he knew Lady Jane Romilly. 'Of course I do.' replied the priest, 'Lady Jane is a lady-in-waiting to the Queen. A lovely lady, sadly widowed. Why do you ask?'

'I chanced to meet her in the town. Will she be at the masque?'

'I imagine so. The Queen is seldom seen in public without her ladies.' He paused. 'Now I must be away. Wednesday, at two in the afternoon. I shall not be present, as monks and masques do not go well together, but do enjoy the spectacle. The Queen is much looking forward to it.' Soon after Simon had left, Thomas fell asleep wondering whether or not he too was looking forward to it.

Before visiting Abraham the next morning, Thomas wrote to Margaret. He told her that, except for the shaggy inkcaps, their journey had been uneventful, that he was well and comfortable, and that he had met the King. He said nothing about squalor and poverty, nor about the masque, of which he knew his sister would disapprove. He inquired after her health and that of the girls, expressed the fond wish that he would see them all again soon, and entreated her to write back. Lacking a seal, he tied the rolled letter with a red ribbon stolen from his new outfit. He would give it to Tobias Rush at the masque.

Abraham was waiting for him when he called. 'I thought you would come this morning, Thomas.' he said, 'Three days for twenty simple documents seemed about right. Or have any of them defeated you?'

'Happily not, although homophonic substitutions do take time. Here they are.' He put the twenty plain texts on the old man's table.

'I'll have to take your word for it, as I can't read them. Did you learn anything from them?'

'Three things. The science of cryptography has progressed very little in the last fifteen years, military despatches are invariably as dull as a Scottish sermon, and your choice of the Portugese wine was surprising. Isn't it a little too sweet?'

Abraham beamed. 'A little sweet, perhaps. Well done, Thomas. Whatever tiny doubts I had have been banished. Now we can put you to proper work. Take the papers on the table for encoding, please. The first half of this month's keyword is *rose.*

The other halves are on this list, with the owner's name. Please memorise them.' He reached into a pocket, extracted a small sheet of paper, and held it out to Thomas. Next week you'll need to send out your new keyword, and remind them to send theirs. All despatches will go through me. There's no reason for any of our people to know who you are. It's safer that way.'

'Are there any intercepted messages?' Encrypting was easy work; decrypting was what Thomas had regained his taste for.

'No. But be assured that you will see the next one as soon as it arrives. It'll come to me. I'll send word. Now you'd better get back to work.'

'Before I do, Abraham, Tobias Rush has invited me to attend the Queen's masque on Wednesday. He's even provided a new suit of clothes.'

Abraham groaned. 'I don't envy you. The last one I attended went on for two hours, and was quite unintelligible. Something to do with Venus and Neptune. And Cupid, I think. It was hard to know. And the extravagance is unspeakable. Thousands of pounds. No wonder Her Majesty is less than popular in the country. However, Thomas, remember what I said. Tobias Rush is a powerful man, with the ear of the King. You had better go.'

'I will, Abraham.'

Thomas set off for Merton half-an-hour before the masque was due to start. With some difficulty, he had put on his fine new shirt, breeches, stockings, and coat, tied ribbons around his knees, put Abraham's wig on his head, wiped the silver buckles on his boots with a cloth, and made his way through the courtyard to the college entrance. Silas, as always, was at his post. 'Master Hill. I hardly knew you. The Queen's masque would it be?'

'It would, Silas. How do I look?'

'Magnificent, sir. Almost like royalty. Enjoy the masque.'

'Thank you, Silas. I'll try.'

The quickest route to Merton took Thomas up St Aldate's, along Blue Boar Street, and into Merton Street. They were as busy as ever. Remembering the hump-backed hag, he carried no money. He walked slowly, being careful not to be jostled and picking his way around the heaps of butchers' offal and human excrement that blocked sewers and overflowed into the streets. The soft boots did not help. They were a little too big and flopped about his ankles. Concentrating on not tripping into something revolting, he did not notice the sullen stares that followed his progress. Blue Boar Street was the beggars' favourite. Limbless, sightless, diseased men and women lined both sides of it, those with arms holding out their hands and pleading for a penny or a shilling, those without standing guard over tin plates on the ground. A tradesman casually dropped a penny on to a plate in front of a blind man. The blind man heard the coin on the plate, bent to pick it up, and immediately let out a stream of blasphemous curses. The coin had gone in seconds – taken by the one-armed man beside him.

Half way down the street, the abuse started. 'Bit too tall for a Queen's dwarf.'

'Must be one of the King's bed boys.'

'Have a care, sir. Be a shame to spoil those pretty rags.'

Thomas affected not to hear, and managed not to quicken

his pace. It was broad daylight, there were people about, and, for all they knew, he might be armed.

At Merton, he was met by a college servant bedecked in powdered wig, cream stockings, wide crimson breeches, and an embroidered coat. The man wore a pearl and ruby brooch. Two lines of guards armed with muskets and swords stood on either side of the gatehouse. Thomas gave his name and was shown to a seat at the far side of the courtyard. It was bigger than the Pembroke courtyard, but much smaller than Christ Church's. The Queen must have wanted the King to be untroubled by preparations for the day. Thomas nodded politely to the two portly gentlemen on either side of him, noting that compared to theirs his outfit was only just up to standard. The masque was not due to start for another ten minutes, but almost all the seats were already occupied. No-one wanted to risk the embarrassment of arriving after their Majesties. Thomas looked around, hoping to see Jane Romilly. She was not there. Perhaps she was taking part in the masque. He would soon find out. At exactly two o'clock, the King and Queen entered the courtyard from the royal apartments. The audience rose and applauded loudly as their Majesties walked slowly to their seats on a raised dias to Thomas's right. The seats were covered in gold cloth, with gold cushions and gold foot rests. The King, limping slightly, walked with a stick. The Queen, resplendent in satins and pearls, auburn hair curling around her neck, smiled and waved to the crowd. At her heels were four fat spaniels and a dwarf. Thomas guessed he was Jeffrey Hudson, known to be her favourite.

When the King and Queen were seated, a herald called the audience to attention with a blast on his horn, and announced that the masque they were about to see was 'The Triumph of Peace', written by James Shirley, and first performed in London for Her Majesty nine years earlier. With due regard to cost and the sacrifices of her loyal subjects, her gracious Majesty had commanded that this production be made suitable to the present time and place. The entertainment would therefore be modest, and would last but an hour. At this there was more applause, although whether this was in appreciation of Her Majesty's concern for her subjects or the reduced length of the peformance, Thomas was unsure. He took another look around the courtyard. Still no Jane. The masque began.

From The Fellows' Quadrangle behind Thomas, a procession of courtiers entered through a high arch, to joyous acclaim. There were perhaps twenty of them – Thomas guessed at a fifth of the number employed in the London production – fantastically dressed and bejewelled in costumes of crimson, blue, and gold. Having proceeded in stately fashion around the courtyard, they took up station near the gatehouse. These magnificent courtiers were followed by a coach transformed into a golden chariot, and drawn by four matched white geldings in gold and crimson cloths. The chariots carried two lutists, and four singers dressed as celestial bodies. Thomas recognised the sun and the moon, but the other two defeated him. The celestial bodies sang a fulsome eulogy to the King and Queen as their chariots cautiously encircled the narrow courtyard.

Two more chariots, similarly decorated, followed, this time from the direction of the chapel. These, the herald told them, carried the spirits of Peace, Law, and Justice, who descended from the chariots to honour the King and Queen in speech and song.

While they were doing so, a second troupe of courtiers entered the now rather crowded courtyard. These too wore a variety of dazzling costumes and head-dresses. The herald helpfully informed the audience that these performers represented Opinion, Fancy, Jollity, Novelty, Confidence, and assorted other qualities, as well as the customary tradespeople. One of them, whom Thomas thought might be Jollity, was dressed as a morris dancer.

Poems and songs, all declaiming the many virtues of their Majesties and expressing the loyal wish that they be swiftly restored to their thrones in London, occupied most of the allocated hour. The finale, against the backdrop of a windmill, featured an elderly Don Quixote, his plump steward Sancho Panza, and an unnamed knight. Between them, they staged a brief mock battle, much appreciated by the audience. As they left the courtyard, followed by the chariots and horses, the procession of musicians, singers, and courtiers, bowed low to the King and Queen, and waved gaily to the delighted audience. It was hard to be sure but Thomas did not think Lady Jane was among them.

Unsure of what was going to happen next, Thomas waited for guidance. It occurred to him that, despite the Queen's avowed sensitivity to the needs of her citizens, the masque must have cost a tidy sum to stage. Taking his lead from his large neighbours, he rose and wandered into the middle of the courtyard. While their Majesties, beaming and waving, remained seated, an army of servants appeared to clear away the seats of the audience, and to bring out from the college kitchens trays laden with claret and hock, pastries, fruits, sweetmeats, and cakes.

Thomas took a glass of hock and edged round the crowd towards the gatehouse. Not wanting to be drawn into discussion of the entertainment, or indeed of anything else, he planned to slip away unnoticed. He was about to make his escape when, from behind him, a voice he knew at once said quietly, 'Master Hill. I had not thought to meet you in such a place.'

Thomas turned, and took the outstretched hand. 'Lady Romilly. An unexpected pleasure.' She wore a pale blue embroidered skirt, with low neckline and narrow sleeves decorated with royal blue ribbons. Black curls tumbled about her bare shoulders.

'And how do you come to be at the masque, Master Hill?'

'I was invited by Master Tobias Rush. No doubt you know him.'

Jane's eyes narrowed. 'Indeed I do, sir. You are well connected.'

'Not really, madam. Master Rush is acquainted with my old tutor, Abraham Fletcher.'

'I recall that you are visiting him at Pembroke. How is he?'

'Blind, madam, and a little infirm, but his mind is as sharp as ever.'

'And how long shall you be staying?'

'That I am unsure of, madam. There are affairs that may detain me.'

'I see. And what did you make of the masque?' asked Jane, changing the subject.

'I found it, ah, extraordinary.'

Jane laughed lightly. 'Nicely put, sir. I am devoted to Queen Henrietta Maria, a gentle and pious lady, but her masques are indeed exraordinary. She was a dear friend to Master Rubens, you know, and to Inigo Jones, who designed the original set for The Triumph of Peace. Her Majesty takes a great interest in the arts.'

'Your devotion does you credit, madam. But may I ask you a question?'

'Certainly, sir, as long as it's a respectable one.'

'I think it is. What exactly does a lady-in-waiting do?'

Again Jane laughed quietly. 'She waits mostly. Waits for Her Majesty to need her services. Then she attends to Her Majesty's needs, and sees that she is comfortable and content. Sometimes she is also required to attend to the Queen's spaniels.'

'And her dwarf?'

'Mr Hudson, thankfully, looks after himself.'

'Thank you, madam. Was the question respectable?'

'It was. I thought you might ask about my eyes. They are frequently asked about.'

'I had noticed them. Most unusual, if I may say so.'

'I'm fortunate to have been born the daughter of a squire. My father says that, had I been born to a carpenter, I would have been burnt as a witch long ago. No-one in Yorkshire had ever before seen eyes of different colours on the same face.' said Jane, putting out a hand to pick a stray thread from Thomas's coat. As she did so, she noticed Tobias Rush looking at them with interest. 'I see Master Rush is observing us closely, Master Hill. He is a loyal friend to the King, yet he always reminds me of a raven. Black feathers, black eyes, long beak. He stands out in a crowd of peacocks.'

Thomas turned and bowed to Rush, who acknowledged him with a tip of his black hat. 'Master Rush has been most solicitous to me. But I know what you mean. There is something unsettling about him. Do you know anything about him?'

'Very little, except that he's highly regarded by the King. The Queen, on the other hand, does not care for him. I did hear that he comes from humble origins, and that his father was a turnkey in London. If that's true, he's come far.' Jane looked over his shoulder. 'Master Hill, the Queen is signalling. She requires my presence, and, if I'm not mistaken, yours too.'

'Mine? Surely not.'

'Her Majesty takes a close interest in her staff and their friends. She probably wants to know who you are. Come. I shall present you.'

Before the Queen, Jane curtseyed and Thomas bowed. 'And who is this, Lady Romilly?' she inquired.

'Your Majesty, this is Master Thomas Hill, in Oxford visiting his old tutor. We met by chance in the town.' Thomas bowed again. The Queen peered at him. She looked a formidable lady. No wonder some called her 'Generalissima'.

'Master Hill. We welcome you to Oxford, now capital of England, and the seat of its lawful Parliament.'

'Thank you, Your Majesty.'

'Lady Romilly is a loyal servant and a dear friend. He who harms her, harms me. If she is also your friend, be sure to protect her at all times from danger. With your life, if needs must.'

'That I certainly shall, Your Majesty.'

'Good. We are pleased to have met you, Master Hill.'

A third bow, and a cautious retreat. Jane followed him. 'With my life? A little dramatic on so short an acquaintance, don't you think?'

'The Queen is not given to understatement. Do not take her too literally.'

'I shall try not to. Now, if you will excuse me, Lady Romilly,' he said, when they had moved into the crowd, 'I have a letter to give to Master Rush. Then I will slip away. Perhaps we shall meet again.'

'I would like that, Master Hill. You have told me little about yourself. Or about what really brought you to Oxford.' Thomas took his leave with a polite smile.

Rush watched him approach. 'Master Hill, I see you are acquainted with Lady Romilly. A charming lady. How do you come to know her?'

'We met by chance in the street. I was able to render a small service to the lady.'

'How fortunate. A lady to whom many would like to render a small service.'

Thomas ignored the unexpected vulgarity. 'You kindly agreed to have a letter delivered to my sister, sir. Here it is.'

'By all means. It'll go with the next messenger.'

'I'm grateful, sir.' said Thomas, and retreated towards the gate. Tobias Rush was indeed an unusual man. Forbidding in manner, kindly in deed. Scrupulously polite one day, coarse the next. Not an easy book to read.

Having successfully navigated Blue Boar Street, he arrived back at Pembroke to be greeted by an anxious Silas Merkin. 'There you are, sir. Master Fletcher has been asking for you. Wants you to go to his rooms at once. Something important, I fancy.'

'Very well, Silas. I shall visit Master Fletcher the moment I have got out of these garments.'

'You could go as you are, sir. Master Fletcher won't see them.'

'No, Silas, but I shall. I'll go the moment they're off.'

In his rooms, Abraham was waiting impatiently. When Thomas knocked, he was summoned brusquely in. 'Thomas? Back from the masque? Don't tell me about it, please. I can imagine, and you've work to do.'

'Good afternoon, Abraham. Why so urgent?'

'This is why.' said the old man, holding up a rolled document, 'It arrived this morning from London. It was found on a man known to be one of Pym's most trusted messengers, leaving the city at night on the Cambridge road. Quite by chance, the man was apprehended by a troop of our dragoons and thoroughly searched. They found this hidden inside the lining of his hat.'

'What is it?' asked Thomas.

'That is what I want you to find out. It's quite long, and it was hidden. A double precaution. A very fortunate interception, which might be important. Hidden messages often are, more so the longer ones. The messenger was no help. They got nothing out of him before he died. Here it is.' Abraham handed Thomas the roll. 'Can you start at once?'

'I can. I'll give you the plain text in the morning.'

'Good. And, Thomas, be particularly careful. Say nothing to anyone but me. I sense that this may be valuable.'

Chapter 5

Thomas laid the text out on his table, and started counting. On a single sheet there were ten lines of text, made up of four hundred and fifty six letters, forty five numbers, and ninety seven spaces. This intercepted message was not just longer than any other he had seen, the combinations of letters, spaces, and numbers had a different feel to them. Ignoring all spaces which would almost certainly have been inserted at random, the numbers appeared in sequences of three or six. That suggested that they were probably code words, perhaps for names. If so, the text was a nomenclator – a mix of code and cipher – which would make it more difficult to break than a plain cipher, but still breakable. There would be clues somewhere. Despite the length of the text, however, the sender revealed himself not at all. Thomas studied the writer's hand and tried to visualise him. He tried fat and thin, short and tall, old and young. He tried divining the man's nature. Mean, generous, kind, cruel. Nothing. After an hour of staring at the text, the man who had encrypted it remained hidden. Thomas's magic, for once, was not working.

'So much for art,' he said aloud, 'time to try science.' Once again he wrote out the letters of the alphabet across the top of a sheet of paper. Then he counted the number of times each letter appeared in the message. He wrote this number below each letter, and *e, a,* and *t* under the highest numbers; then he examined the juxtaposition of each to other letters, found three instances of double letters, and concluded which encrypted letter represented each of them. He repeated the process to find the letters *i, o, s,* and *r,* and tentatively applied this to the first few lines. For this exercise, all numbers were ignored. The result was nonsense. As he had expected, this was not a straightforward alphabetic cipher, either shifted by a keyword or mixed by a system of substitution. At least two substitutions had been used, perhaps more, and there was still the matter of the numbers. A double or even triple alphabetic substitution would eventually yield to close analysis and a little intuition, but it would take time. And Thomas's instincts were shouting at him that this decryption was going to require all his skills. Hoping that sustenance would bring more success, he put down his quill and went to find food.

Fortified by an excellent mutton stew from Silas's kitchen and half a bottle of claret from his cellar, Thomas lit a candle and started again. This time he attacked the forty five numbers. He still suspected that they were codes for names, but needed to be certain. Assuming that the numbers were actually in sequences of three digits, the sixes being two names together, he found eight separate numbers, of which 769, 574, 852, and 775 were repeated once, and 371 repeated four times. That made a nomenclator almost certain, and decoding 371 would be a huge step forward. After two more hours, however, he had made no further progress. He had identified not a single word from the letters or numbers, and had no more idea what secrets they held than when Abraham had handed it to him. Beyond the facts that a complex system of encryption and encoding had been used and that the message must be important, he still knew nothing about it. Without bothering to undress, he lay down and slept.

Next morning Thomas went first to visit Abraham, hoping his old friend would provide an insight into the problem. He described the text in detail – forty five numbers, four hundred and fifty six letters, and ninety seven spaces. He told Abraham how he had approached the task, the old man nodding encouragingly as he did so, and, finally, he told him that he had learnt nothing. They discussed poly-alphabetic substitutions, nomenclators, variable Caesar shifts, homophonic substitutions, keywords, and code words. At the end of the morning they had agreed only that this was not a message intended to be decrypted quickly, even by someone with the key. It was too complex. So it was not a standard military despatch, and, although important, would not be battlefield-urgent. That made it of strategic rather than tactical value. There was no context, and there were no other clues. They still had no idea what it was about, who had written it, or for whom it was intended. Abraham could tell from Thomas's voice that he was tired and frustrated. 'My best advice is that you put it away for today. You have routine messages to encrypt and decrypt. Why not deal with those? Hill's magic might return with the dawn.' Taking heed, Thomas spent the afternoon on the daily despatches, and the evening with his friend Montaigne. He fell asleep thinking of Polly and Lucy, and of Jane Romilly, the lady with the eyes.

The next three days were spent on the intercepted message. The marks on the paper had become his enemies. He tried a variety of double and triple alphabetic substitutions, he tried assuming that all the numbers were meaningless, that they hid keywords, that the message was in Latin, that it had been written backwards, and he even guessed at a few possible keywords to create alphabetic shifts, such as *parliament, oxford,* and *protestant.* The guesswork was futile without at least some facts, and he knew it. He gave it up when Montaigne tapped gently on his shoulder, and whispered in his ear, 'Thomas Hill, have I taught you nothing? Rational thought is greatly superior to intuition. Think, don't guess.'

On the fourth morning he went again to see Abraham, and again reported his lack of progress. Abraham tried to be encouraging. 'Thomas, you have made progress.' he said, 'You know a good many things that this cipher is not.'

'Indeed. But if have to eliminate all the things it is not before discovering what it is, I shall be even older than you when I finally do so.' Abraham laughed, and then voiced the thought that both had so far left unspoken. 'Could we be facing Vigenère, Thomas?'

'It's possible, of course, although the numbers must also be serving some purpose. Have you heard of a square used with numerical codes?'

'I haven't, but that doesn't mean they don't exist. If the numbers are word codes, the cipher will work just as well if they are ignored.'

'Abraham, a Vigenère cipher has never been broken, with or without word codes.'

'I know. Trust a Frenchman to come up with such a diabolical thing. Tedious to encrypt, tedious to decrypt, and proof against even you, Thomas, unless you can divine the keyword.'

'I can try, Abraham, but you know it'll take a miracle.'

Abraham was thoughtful. 'Perhaps not. Look again at the numbers. Could they be telling us which rows on the square to use? If so, the cipher would still be secure against anyone unfamiliar with Monsieur Vigenère.'

'Very well. I'll assume it's Vigenère, and try the numbers again. Prayers thrice daily, Abraham, please. I shall need them.'

That evening Tobias Rush visited again. All in black, silver-topped cane in hand, he called to tell Thomas that his letter had been safely delivered to Margaret. 'Was there a reply?' asked Thomas, hopefully.

'Unfortunately, no. The courier had to reach Southampton by dusk and could not afford to wait.' said Rush. 'No doubt your sister will find a way of writing back, however. Do let me know when she does.' He paused. 'And how did you enjoy the masque?'

'Masque? Oh, the masque. Remarkable. A remarkable entertainment.'

'Indeed. Their Majesties have unerring eyes for beauty. And speaking of beauty, how did you find Lady Jane? Well, I trust?'

'Quite well. A delightful lady, and an unusual one.'

'You refer to her eyes, I imagine?'

'In part, yes. They are striking. But not just her eyes. She's a lady of spirit.'

Rush changed the subject. 'How goes your work, Master Hill?', looking casually around the room. The encrypted papers were underneath others on the table. Just as well, thought Thomas, although I must be more careful in future. Abraham had insisted on absolute secrecy, even from Master Rush. He dissembled. 'Routine matters only. Not much has changed since last I worked with codes. I would wish for something more interesting.'

'Oh? Have the enemy not offered you anything at all appropriate to your skills?'

'Not as yet, sir.'

'Be sure to let me know if they do. The King has impressed upon me my duty to assist you in any way that I can. I would not wish either of us to disappoint him. Now, I shall bid you good day.' And he was gone. Odd how he's here one minute and gone the next, thought Thomas, and how he changes the course of a discussion. A hard book to read and a hard bird to cage.

Work on the numbers began before dawn. If this was a Vigenère square, the King's enemies would assume that its secrets were safe, and would see no need to change their plans. The square itself had remained unbroken for nearly a hundred years. Thomas began by writing out the square. Across the top of a page he wrote the letters of the alphabet in lower case, and in a column to the left, the numbers 1 to 26. Then, in the first row, under each letter he wrote in upper case the letter that followed it alphabetically – a shift of one. He continued this, each row having one additional shift, until the whole square was complete. So his first row began with *B*, his last with *A*, and each letter across the top had twenty six letters under it. Twenty-six possible substitutions for each letter. A Vigenère square.

Then he wrote out the forty five digits at the top of the message. For some time, he sat and stared at them. Apart from the duplications, he saw no patterns. If the numbers were indicating the rows of the square to be used for decrypting, any number above 26 must be either a null, or have some other function. Proceeding on this basis, he divided the digits into arbitrary one and two digit numbers and tried decrypting the first line according to the twenty rows indicated by his selection. When the word '*dog*' appeared, he thought he was on to something. But when the following words turned out as *ktlo, bqicms,* and *xpd*, he knew that the dog's appearance was no more than chance.

All morning Thomas sat at his table, the encrypted page, sharpened quills, inkpot, and a pile of blank papers before him. The pile of blank papers diminished as the floor became covered in used and discarded ones. Just as well Abraham had laid his hands on a good supply. By the time his stomach started complaining, however, he had achieved very little. Nothing, in fact, except the growing certainty that these numbers did not hold the key to the rows. He had tried adding and subtracting, transposing the digits of the higher numbers, multiplying and dividing – all to no effect. Apart from 'dog', not a single plain word had appeared from the text. It was a bad start. He did not need the unwelcome complication of code words, tricks, or traps. What he did need was a clue to guide him to the key. And he needed fresh air and company.

Emerging into the daylight, Thomas was greeted by a beautiful late summer day – dry and windless. The Pembroke courtyard was still a military dump, young officers and their women still lounged about doing very little, and the stench of human waste was still sickening, but the sky was cloudless and the sun warm. Thank God one was permanent and the other, God willing, merely temporary. Perhaps very temporary if he could break the encryption.

Having visited the kitchen, which was as obliging as ever, he left the college, turned south into St Aldate's, made his way to Christ Church Meadow, working his way between long lines of mortars and cannon, and thence towards Merton. Food and sun did much to lift his spirits and by the time he reached the Merton entrance he was feeling brave enough to call on Lady Romilly. In the college courtyard, golden chariots, white horses, singers, and lutists, had been replaced by a large troop of the Queen's guard, ready to challenge, and, if necessary, dispose of, unwelcome intruders. When their captain asked Thomas his business, he gave his name, mentioned Simon de Pointz, and asked for Lady Jane Romilly. He was escorted to the Warden's lodgings, which the Queen and her court had taken over, and told to wait outside. Merton showed signs of the war – soldiers and their paraphernalia, guns and powder, arms and armour – but it was nothing like Pembroke. The Queen and her ladies would not have allowed it.

When Jane appeared, black curls framing her face, dressed today in pink and blue, she was distinctly flushed. 'Master Hill. A surprise. I was quite unprepared. Had we made an appointment?'

'No, madam, and my apologies for surprising you. I was walking in the meadow, the day is warm, and it occurred to me to call. Would you care for a stroll through the Physic Garden? I hear it is lovely at this time of year.'

Jane hesitated. 'I'm not sure. Her Majesty is at her toilette. She may need me afterwards.'

'If the question is not treasonable, how long does Her Majesty's toilette take?'

'Perhaps an hour more.'

'Then let us enjoy the sunshine for exactly fifty five minutes.'

'That would be delightful.' said Jane, taking his arm, 'Not a minute more, though.'

Outside Merton, they passed a young woman pulling a hand cart. On it was a body wrapped in a dirty sheet. She was heading for the south wall, and, beyond it, the communal grave Thomas and Simon had seen when they arrived. Thomas put his hand to his face. The body was not a new one. Jane crossed herself and looked away. 'Another widow,' she whispered, 'The disease is everywhere.'

'Too many people in too small a space.' replied Thomas, 'It seldom occurs in the countryside.'

They took the path by the river towards the garden. It was lined by willows, and bullrushes and sedges grew along the banks. Jane bent to pick fleabane. 'The Queen loves gardens. She hates to see the gardens in the colleges destroyed. Do you know what this is, Master Hill?'

Thomas examined the fleabane. 'A white and yellow flower of no particular distinction?'

'Tush. Daisy Fleabane is its common name. More properly, Erigeron Strigosus.'

'Madam, you're as learned as Simon de Pointz. Are all the Queen's staff instructed in botany?'

Jane laughed. 'It's as well to know a little. The Queen herself is very knowledgeable. Thomas, can you not call me Jane?'

'If you wish it, Jane, I can. You're very fond of the Queen, are you not?'

'I am. She's a gracious lady with a deep love of nature and art. The more extravagant masques I put down to her rare artistic temperament. The King is devoted to her, as I believe the country would be if they knew her better. Her faith tells against her. In that, she is uncompromising.'

'The country is suffering, Jane.' said Thomas delicately.

'Indeed. The Queen knows it.' She paused. 'Thomas, can I entrust you with a secret?'

'Of course.'

'The Queen is expecting a child in the spring. Her physician has just confirmed it.'

'Why is it a secret?'

'She fears the reaction of the people.'

'The people will know soon enough.'

'She will go to France for her confinement, and return with the child.'

'Let us hope they return to peace.'

When they reached the Physic Garden, Jane asked about Thomas's family, and he about hers. She told him that when Sir Edward had died at Edgehill, she had returned to her family home in York, and joined the Queen's court when she arrived there from Holland. In July she had travelled with the Queen to Oxford. They had been accompanied by three thousand men and a hundred wagons. The Generalissima had proved herself a most persuasive recruiter. She spoke of the Queen's hardiness on the journey and her kindness to a young woman recently widowed. She spoke, also, of her husband, whom she had known since they were children, and of her fear that she would now never have children of her own. Thomas told her about Margaret and his nieces, about his time as a student in Oxford, and about his interest in books and philosophy, just managing not to mention Michel de Montaigne.

The garden was tended by a dozen gardeners in leather breeches and straw hats. It, at least, had so far survived the ravages of war. Jane and Thomas walked between tidy beds of lavender and violets, and around a patch of mallows. Jane bent to pick St John's Wort. 'And how do you occupy yourself in Oxford, Thomas, when you are not with Master Fletcher?' she asked.

'Abraham has given me work to do. It keeps me busy.'

'May I inquire what work it is?'

Thomas sighed. 'Jane, this is awkward. My work is known to very few – the King, Abraham, Simon de Pointz, Master Rush. I should not tell you.'

'I have entrusted you with a secret, Thomas. Can you not entrust me with one?'

He was unsure. Abraham's censure or Jane's approval. He chose the latter. 'I studied mathematics here, as well as philosophy, and developed an interest in codes and ciphers. Abraham and I enjoyed trying to defeat each other with new ones. When the King's cryptographer died, Abraham recommended me to take his place. I encrypt and decrypt despatches coming in and out of Oxford.'

'Somehow I knew you would be doing that kind of work. Scholarly and solitary. Is it difficult?'

'Not really. Military messages tend to be short and direct. Not too difficult.'

'And what about messages intercepted from our enemies? Do you see those?'

Thomas hesitated. Abraham had been insistent. Tell no-one and trust no-one. As he had with Tobias Rush, he dissembled. 'I do, but they're rare, and generally dull. Supplies, pay, horses, that sort of thing.'

'Still, I can see that your work is important, and you must be very good at it or the King would not have given you the responsibility. You will take care, Thomas, won't you? The Queen says that Oxford is full of spies, and the King trusts almost no-one. I imagine you would be in danger if your work were known.'

'I shall certainly take care, Jane. As should you. I might not be at hand next time you start an unseemly brawl in the street.'

Back at the Merton entrance, Thomas took his leave. 'Call again, Thomas, please.' said Jane, disappearing into the college.

Chapter 6

But it was more than a week before Thomas was able to call again. The next morning, Tobias Rush paid him another visit. This time he did not bother with pleasantries. 'Master Hill,' he said briskly, 'Kindly make ready to travel. The King wishes you to accompany him to Newbury, where he will join forces with Prince Rupert.'

'Is the King expecting to fight?'

'It is likely. We have information that the Earl of Essex, with at least fourteen thousand men, is also marching there from Gloucester. We must reach the town before he does. You are to be responsible for the security of the King's despatches.'

'When do we leave?'

'By noon. The King's Lifeguards of foot and horse are assembling on Christ Church meadow. Present yourself there within the hour. I shall be accompanying you to Newbury.' And with that, Rush hurried off.

Newbury, which Simon and he had avoided on the way to Oxford. Strategically important, Thomas supposed, either for an attempt by Essex and Fairfax to take Oxford, or for a Royalist attack on London. Otherwise, a modest town of no great merit or distinction, which he had visited several times to buy books. Fourteen thousand of the enemy against how many of us? he wondered. Would he be obliged to carry arms? God forbid that he might have to use them. Simon had said that the King knew that he would never take up arms against Englishmen, but in the heat of battle would the King care? Would he care himself? A sword in the stomach for Thomas, or a musket ball in the eye of the other fellow? He might be about to find out.

It took Thomas very little time to be ready. He packed his few spare clothes, quills, his sharpening knife, and papers, into his bag, and hid the encrypted message under his shirt. It felt safer there. He did not want to leave it behind, and he might have time to study it some more. His box of quills he wrapped in a shirt. When he arrived, a light rain was falling, and the meadow was a muddy mass of soldiers, tradesmen, women, horses, wagons, supplies, ammunition, and cannon. He could discern no semblance of military order, nor of anyone attempting to impose any, and he could make little out of the incessant clash and clamour of an army preparing to march. Soldiers stood in small groups, apparently waiting to be told what to do, grooms tried in vain to keep their horses calm, while lines of townsmen and women, supervised by young officers, loaded each transport with as many crates and boxes as it would take. As long as they had insisted on payment in advance, the butchers and bakers of Oxford were in for another quick and substantial profit. Thomas stood under an elm on the north side of the meadow and watched.

By the time the King and his entourage arrived, some form of order had miraculously appeared, and His Majesty, enthusiastically greeted by his guards, rode a grey stallion to the front of the lines. He wore a gleaming breastplate, carried a heavy cavalry sword, and acknowledged the cheers with a regal wave of his gauntleted hand. On horseback, his lack of height was less obvious, and he looked cheerful and confident. Thomas, unsure where to go or what to do, stayed where he was and waited for instructions. They came from Tobias Rush. While the Queen was bidding a fond and very public farewell to the King, Rush appeared quietly beside him. 'Master Hill, if you would make your way to the main gate of Christ Church, you will find a carriage waiting for us. I will join you as soon as the King has departed.'

Wondering how Rush had found him, Thomas edged his way around the meadow, and up the path between Christ Church and Corpus Christi, to the Christ Church gate. The carriage that awaited him was painted in royal blue, emblazoned in gold with the King's coat of arms, drawn by four matched black geldings, and driven by a magnificently uniformed coachman, whose assistant, equally magnificent, sat beside him. Inside, the seats were padded and covered in soft red leather. While the army trudged over mud, splashed through ankle-deep puddles, twisted its ankles in ruts and holes, and took its rest in dripping hedgerows, Master Rush and Master Hill would travel to battle in comfort. Thomas wondered whether the King intended to ride bravely at the head of his men, or to abandon his stallion for the comfort of a royal carriage.

It was not long before two college servants appeared carrying between them a large chest, which, with the help of the coachmen, they manhandled on to the coach. The chest was closely followed by its owner. Tobias Rush, angrily telling them to make haste and allow him room to board the carriage, swept them aside with his silver-topped cane and sat down with a sigh opposite Thomas. 'I do so dislike travelling.' he said, 'And with this rain, the journey will not be pleasant. Luckily, I know a tolerable inn in the village of Drayton, where we'll spend the night. It's about ten miles from here. Tomorrow we'll continue to Newbury, another eighteen miles or so.' Rush eyed Thomas's small bag. 'Is that all you've brought, Master Hill? We may be away for some days.'

'Master Rush, it's all I have.' replied Thomas sharply. 'I was not permitted to bring anything more to Oxford and have not been inclined to make purchases here, with the prices three times those in Romsey.'

'In that case, feel free to ask for anything you need. I will arrange for it.' Rush smiled his thin smile, then called to the coachman. 'Let us be off. We must be away before the army sets off, or we'll be trapped amongst them.' Thomas heard the coachman snap his long whip, and they were off, bumping and lurching over the cobbles. They left Oxford by the south gate, passed through the town's defences and round three huge burial pits, and were soon on the road to Newbury. Somewhere behind them, the King and his Lifeguards marched to battle.

Conversation in the carriage was difficult, and little was said until they approached Drayton, when Thomas asked about his duties. 'If we face Essex,' said Rush, 'despatches will be coming in and out all the time. Orders to our commanders, their reports, and intelligence from our observers as to Essex's movements. Some will be encrypted. And there is always the chance of interceptions. If they are to be of any use, you will have to decrypt them imediately. Otherwise the moment will pass, and any advantage will be lost.'

'Do we know what ciphers they will use?'

'We don't, but, like ours, they will perforce be simple. In battle there is no time for complexity. Please give some thought to the ciphers you will use, and advise me of them. I will communicate them to our commanders in the field.'

'As you wish, Master Rush.' replied Thomas, thinking that a simple alphabetical shift might be best suited to a simple military mind. Certainly not Vigenère squares.

At Drayton, the carriage pulled up outside Rush's inn. The carriage driver's assistant jumped down and opened the door for them. Thomas picked up his bag and was about to step out of the carriage, but Rush would not hear of it. 'The men will take your bag, Master Hill. Leave it for them.'

'It's only light.' protested Thomas, 'I can easily manage it.'

'Nonsense. That's what servants are for. They'll bring it with mine.' Reluctantly, not wishing to make a scene, Thomas put down the bag and alighted. The innkeeper emerged, all smiles and hand-wringing, to greet them.

'Gentlemen, welcome to The Crown. Your rooms are ready and your dinner is being prepared. The stables are at the back.' Rush nodded and strode into the inn. Thomas followed him. A fire had been laid in the hearth, the floor had been swept, and the tables wiped clean. There were no other customers. The innkeeper had been warned. Tobias Rush did not like unwelcome company or unnecessary discomfort. While Rush supervised the unloading of his chest, Thomas was shown upstairs to a small room. There was a straw mattress on the bed, a woollen blanket, a bowl for washing, and a jug of water. It was clean enough, smelled only slightly of mice, and was superior to either of the inns he and Simon had sampled on their journey from Romsey.

The coachman's assistant soon arrived with his bag. 'Here you are, sir,' said the young man with a grin, 'Not too heavy. We can't get the chest up the stairs, so it'll have to spend the night downstairs by the fire, same as us. Master Rush isn't too happy about that.'

Thomas thanked the young man, and opened the bag. He knew at once that it had been tampered with. His box of quills was no longer wrapped in the shirt, and a corner of one sheet of paper was slighly torn. Either the coachmen had been looking for coins, or Master Rush had seen fit to conduct a search. For what? wondered Thomas. Doesn't he trust me? No, it was probably the coachmen. Too bad they had found no coins. He decided to say nothing, but to keep the encrypted message with him at all times. That, if nothing else, should not fall into the wrong hands.

The innkeeper had certainly made an effort with their dinner. After bowls of hot vegetable soup, they were served a good rabbit pie with pickled cucumbers, and a sweet apple tart with cream. While Thomas tucked in happily, washing the meal down with half a bottle of claret, Rush ate and drank little. And he would not be drawn by Thomas's questions about himself. He admitted to having been born and brought up in London, but that was about it. Nothing about his family, his education, or his home. By the end of the meal, Thomas had given up, and turned the conversation, instead, to the battle that lay ahead. 'If Essex has fourteen thousand men,' he asked, 'will he outnumber us, or we him?'

'I believe the King will have the advantage in cavalry numbers, and his enemies in infantry. As to artillery, about the same. Much like Edge Hill.'

'Were you at Edge Hill?' asked Thomas, surprised. He had not thought of Rush in battle.

'I was, as a member of His Majesty's household. But for Prince Rupert's cavalry who preferred to chase a broken and fleeing rabble rather than wheel and charge at the rear of the enemy centre, we should have enjoyed a great victory. As it was, we could only claim one.'

'It was certainly reported as a victory in the newsbooks.'

Rush smiled. 'Yes. For that, I must take some responsibility. The King insisted upon as glowing a report as I could write. The truth, however, is that the battle was inconclusive. Many are.'

'On that we agree.' said Thomas, 'Inconclusive and pointless. Much suffering, little progress. Will we never learn?'

'Who knows? For now, our task is to win. When the King is back in London, we will turn our attention to the future. There is much to do to secure England against our enemies, and to expand our influence and interests overseas. Sugar, cotton, and tobacco from the Caribbean islands and Virginia, spices from the East Indies, slaves from Africa. The opportunities for wealth and prosperity are limitless, as long as we have the courage to take them. If we don't, the French and the Dutch will.'

'How will we do it?'

'The navy. A strong navy is the key. If we control the trade routes, we control the trade, and, if we control the trade, we control its sources. The Americas, Africa, India. We must build a navy that cannot be challenged by our enemies.'

Thomas did not respond. He had never thought much about such matters. Rush clearly had. Abraham had called him an ambitious man. Ambitious and clever. Looking to the future, and ready to take whatever opportunties came his way. Not a man to be trifled with.

Dinner over, the coachmen settled down by the fire with Rush's chest between them, while he and Thomas retired to their rooms. Tomorrow they would reach Newbury and prepare for battle. Before he fell asleep, Thomas replayed the dinner conversation in his mind. The King will have the advantage in cavalry, Rush had said, and his enemies in infantry. No 'we' or 'they'. An oddly dispassionate manner of speaking. Intellect rather than emotion. A clever man.

They set off again at dawn and covered the eighteen miles to Newbury in a little over two hours. Outside the town they were met by a troop of dragoons who had been sent to meet them. From their captain, they learnt that Prince Rupert and his cavalry had arrived two days earlier to find the town already occupied by Essex's quartermasters, busy arranging provisions for the parliamentary army. The Prince had wasted no time in taking them prisoner, and had taken control of the town. The bulk of Essex's army was still twenty miles away, having marched from Gloucester, and intending to return to London. On the way, the Prince's cavalry had overtaken them.

Their carriage passed through the cavalry's encampments, proceeded into the town, like Oxford heaving with soldiers and their equipment, and were led to a large house by the market square. There the carriage stopped and they were shown inside by the captain. 'This house has been requisitioned for you, Master Rush. Sir Francis was happy to oblige.'

Rush looked around. 'It will do well enough, captain. Master Hill and I will base ourselves here. Have the men bring my chest in. And Master Hill's bag.'

It will do well enough to be sure, thought Thomas, admiring the high ceiling and tall windows. The walls of the entrance hall were covered with paintings, including a sumptuous Rubens nude, and two portraits by Van Dyck, which he took to be of the owner of the house and his wife. This Sir Francis was a man of wealth, a man who would have much to lose in the event of a parliamentary victory in this war. No wonder he had been ready to offer his house to the King. Having taken his bag from the coachman, Thomas climbed a magnificent curving staircase, more family portraits covering the stair wall, and found a bedroom with an elegant window looking out over the square. He threw his bag on the four poster bed, and deposited himself into a large padded library chair. Admiring the room, the thought occurred that even war might have its good side. It was nothing short of luxurious. Velvet curtains, an embroidered silk cover on the bed, a collection of miniatures on the walls, a handsome fireplace, the padded chair, and a fine rosewood writing table. Then he caught himself. It was a disgraceful notion. Nothing could excuse war and there was nothing good about it. And he had work to do.

He laid the encrypted message out on a writing table and concentated on it once more. There it was.

URF UBD HE XQBTF KGA OEMD RRFUOTLC WMG LRB WHT R XHGORKZ IO KPW769
WA MQFV BVMF HPL ZFTD RVV57 4SEWMFREJ VGL SVKMGE 852 GTSC WZTD QE
TIJG IVL GJT RA KDOE IK EOJAAQLV GGJR MQU IOIGSI GRQF HBFZG JGY
ALG EE OLWEEA GJR YIFS1 82AEL2 64SGE SC AAD ZVY JP KP WXR JB JTN XBZ77
5XNW WJBS LA LWAK371 EAIH TPA AD RVV BAP TWPVV AGDN WWJ URR VUT
IW EW HTI QCT WY QDT37 1IE852 769UMHT RKC CONT WSGV WMG IEN DJEE KW
IHV ZW PNU EAIH371 ZV GJR YIFSS NQ DA BV NGGCVL LD SVMC IRLKW DN
KMJ BS WINDU IITAE KW42177 5OX LCIVK IJM LXMV IFS PCI UT FFZ
SEPI MZTNJQGCOW3 71E ZDWZTD QE SZGJ GYB LD 574SKIFS RVIV N GFL
OX LC QFV WV AZPLCJJX NX IF TNU BG IHZA OP RJWGC

Twenty six possible encryptions for each of the four hundred and fifty six letters, plus forty five numbers, and ninety seven spaces. A cipher that had never been broken. Where to begin? He made another effort to envisage its encrypter, this time with more success. He saw a small man, precise in dress and manner, a pair of spectacles perched on his sharp nose, and a cap on his head. He sat in a dark room, working by the light of a single candle. This man would work carefully and make no mistakes. He might well use the square, he might use codes, but he would not use nulls or misspellings, which would offend his sense of order. What sort of keyword would he use? Nothing random, nothing too complex. A Latin word, perhaps, or a religious one, or something historical. Or a million other things. Use your head, Thomas. There's no future in playing guessing games. Concentrate on the cipher. There must be a way.

He gazed idly out of the window at the toings and froings in the square below. It was a square full of noise and bustle, and the hubbub of a town preparing to defend itself. Officers about their duties, soldiers about theirs, tradesmen about their businesses, fascinated children standing in huddles around the square, noise and movement and excitement. The King and his army were coming to Newbury, and there was to be a great battle. A great battle in which Thomas would have a part to play. That reminded him that he needed a keyword. Not too long for the sake of speed, not too short for the sake of security. Five or six letters, with no repeats. It came to him. MASQUE. Perfect. He would tell Rush the keyword for all incomng and outgoing despatches would be MASQUE.

When Thomas ventured back downstairs, intending to take a stroll around the town, he was met by Rush, hurrying in through the door, cane in hand. 'Master Hill, there you are. I have word that the King will arrive this evening, and the bulk of the army tonight. We believe that Essex's vanguard will not arrive until tomorrow, so we shall have the adantage of him. Kindly remain here until I give you further instructions.'

'I was about to take a walk around the town.'

'That will not be possible. You're safer here, and you might at any time be needed. Is your room comfortable?'

'Very comfortable, thank you.'

'Is there anything you need?'

'Some ink, if you please. Nothing else.'

'It will be arranged. Have you decided upon a cipher?'

'I have. A simple alphabetical shift, using the keyword MASQUE.'

Rush's smile was as thin and humourless as ever. 'Very appropriate. I will inform the King and our commanders.' And with that, he was off. Here one minute, gone the next, thought Thomas again. A busy bird, with a nest to build and food to gather. An odd man, but I'd rather be with him than against him.

Unfortunately, Sir Francis, for all his interest in art, was not a literary man, and there was not a book to be found in the house. Thomas had little to do but make himself at home and await events. Having been admirably fed and watered by Sir Francis's cook, he sat by the window in his bedroom, staring at the encrypted text, and thinking about Jane Romilly. The lady with one brown eye and the other blue. A lovely lady, witty and charming. A widow, still young, and childless. Margaret would like her, and the girls would appropriate her as their personal property. That is, if she ever cared to meet them. Mind you, she had asked him to call again. That was surely a good sign. Once he got back to Oxford, he would call immediately. Another stroll in the Physic Garden perhaps, or a walk by the river. He would find a book on flowers and plants, and delight her with his knowledge. Mother Nature herself would provide the way to the lady's heart.

News of the King's arrival came from Tobias Rush that evening. 'His Majesty is housed safely in the town, and the army, as expected, will be in position by tomorrow morning. There is every chance that Essex will also arrive during the night, and, if so, the King intends to join battle tomorrow.'

'Have I any instructions?'

'Remain here for now. I will escort you to your station in the morning. You and I will be with the King and his personal guard at the rear of the lines. From there, you will deal with all despatches, taking instructions only from the King or from me.'

'Very well, Master Rush. I shall be ready.'

Thomas slept badly, tossing about on the four poster bed until dawn. On the eve of battle, he was nervous. He could only guess at what it would be like actually to witness a battle, but he knew he would see blood and carnage, and a good deal of it. He wondered how he would react, and how his brain would work in the heat of the moment. Would he have much to do? Would he make mistakes? If he did, would they matter? Would they win? If they did not, what would happen? A hasty escape, capture, death? He wondered, too, if all soldiers lay awake on the night before a battle. If they did, there would be two very tired armies facing each other in the morning. The Earl of Essex and Prince Rupert had both marched from Gloucester, and the King from Oxford. Every man must already be weary and footsore, not to mention cold and wet. A sleepless night, and they would scarcely have the energy to draw their swords or lift their muskets. Although that might not be such a bad thing. Everyone too exhausted to fight, and anxious to get home as soon as they could. Take up your weapons, men, and follow me to London. Wives, sweethearts, warm beds, and strong ale, await us. Could it happen?

It could not. Thomas was up, dressed and breakfasted, when Rush arrived to fetch him. 'It is as we expected.' he reported, 'Essex's army arrived during the night and has taken up position outside the town. He cannot reach London without facing us. The King is determined on a victory which will greatly set back the cause of parliament, and open the way for an attack on London. Follow me, Master Hill, and we will join His Majesty.'

They rode straight to the King's station, on a low hill behind the Royalist lines, from where they had an excellent view of the surrounding country. The King sat in full armour on his grey stallion, his heavy cavalry sword resting across its back. His Lifeguards surrounded him, one of them holding aloft the King's standard. An heroic figure with a righteous cause. Or so the King made it look. Staring fixedly into the middle distance, His Majesty acknowledged neither Thomas nor Rush. Thomas could not even guess what was going through the royal mind, but he hoped it was more than the fixed smile on the royal face suggested.

From their vantage point, Thomas saw four ranks of infantry in the centre of the line, with massed cavalry on either wing, the whole army stretching across perhaps as much as a mile. Facing them, the enemy army was formed up in similar fashion. He supposed that Prince Rupert would, as usual, have the honour of being on the right, which would put Sir John Byron on the left. There streams and hedgerows marked the fields below a ridge upon which Essex had placed a detachment of musketeers. When he looked closely, Thomas could see that the enemy opposite Rupert also occupied higher ground. That seemed very odd. The Prince had arrived here first, with plenty of time to secure the high ground, so how did the enemy come to hold it?

There was no time to dwell on the matter. Before a shot had been fired, Rush handed him a despatch to be encrypted and delivered to all commanders. As there were five of them, five copies would be needed. The despatch was from the King and informed them that the infantry must hold firm against the expected enemy advance, while both wings charged forward to outflank them. With these tactics, the day would surely be theirs. Using the keyword MASQUE, Thomas quickly encrypted the order, made four more copies, and handed them to Rush. Five messengers on five horses galloped off to deliver them. Each commander had an aide to make the decryption, and they too would have to work fast.

It began slowly. Essex's infantry, firing as they went, advanced steadily towards the King's musketeers. As ordered, the musketeers returned fire, but did not advance to meet them. The lines on both sides thinned as the parliamentary infantry approached. It had not before occurred to Thomas that, in battle, it was the screams of the wounded which were most terrible. The dead simply fell and lay still. A cannon fired, and Thomas, to his horror, saw three heads detached from three bodies by the shot. He turned away and vomited. More cannon fired, and more men fell, headless, armless, disembowelled. One file of infantrymen, struck by a cannon shot, fell like skittles. Thomas wanted desperately to look away, but found that he could not. Then Rush appeared beside him and handed him a second order. It was for Sir John Byron on the left wing, and instructed him immediately to take the ridge, known as Round Hill, which lay before him. Wondering how Sir John was going to manage this, given that his cavalry would have to find a way over a muddy mess of fields and ditches, before they could even think of attacking the hill, Thomas dutifully encrypted the order and sent it off. Having seen the carnage already being wreaked on the cavalry by Essex's men hidden among the trees and hedges below the hill, he thanked God that he was not with Sir John.

As the air grew black with smoke and thick with the smell of gunpowder, Thomas could hear the battle, but could see very little of it. Muskets and cannon fired, men bellowed and shrieked, and horses screamed. Only occasionally did the clash of swords and the thrusts of pikes appear briefly through the smoke. At times it seemed to Thomas ghostly and unreal. But these were real men, real weapons, real wounds, real deaths, real war. Noise, pain, fear, confusion.

Somewhere on the right, Prince Rupert must have charged at the enemy, and might have broken through to attack from their rear; and on the left, Sir John Byron's cavalry was probably being destroyed as it struggled towards the hill. With the battlefield all but invisible, however, there was no way of telling how they were faring, or even if they were still alive. Thomas half expected a troop of parliamentary infantry suddenly to emerge out of the smoke and shoot him. He could not even see the King, and the King would not be able to see the battle.

The first report came from Sir John Byron. It was in clear text and respectfully begged to inform His Majesty that his friend Lord Falkland had been killed. Falkland's death would be a cruel blow to the King, who was known to be fond of him. The second came from an aide of Prince Rupert and was encrypted. The cavalry had broken through the enemy ranks and was engaged in attacking the infantry from their rear. They had been temporarily stalled, however, by strong resistance on the part of the parliamentary pikemen and musketeers. It did not sound good.

During the morning, more reports came in, some encrypted, others not, and more orders were issued. Thomas worked diligently away, trying in vain to ignore the crash of cannon being fired and shot finding its target. Through the smoke, he caught only glimpses of the fighting, and could best judge the battle's progress by the contents of incoming reports. The Earl of Carnarvon was reported killed, as was the Earl of Sunderland. Two more cruel blows. On it went on all morning, cannon balls crashing into ranks of infantry, cavalry horses shying away from raised pikes, wheeling, trying again, and shying again, and musketeers picking off targets from the safety of hedgerows and ditches. Through all of it, Thomas carefully encrypted the King's orders for despatch to his commanders, and when necessary, decrypted their reports. In one hour several might arrive, in the next, none at all. As far as he could tell, by noon neither side had achieved much, other than a severe reduction in their numbers.

In mid-afternoon, the cannon at last began to grow silent and the air to clear. On the far right, Thomas could see that Prince Rupert had failed to break through the enemy infantry and had withdrawn to his original position. Both infantry centres had done the same, and only the remains of Lord Byron's cavalry, still well short of Round Hill, was fighting in the fields below it. Everywhere, bodies and bits of bodies lay bloody and mangled on the field, spent muskets and broken swords amongst them. The walking wounded were being helped to safety by their colleagues, those without hope being left to die where they had fallen. Thomas, horrified, could only stand and stare, until Rush hurried up and handed him another order. Thomas forced himself to encrypt it and sent it off. He barely noticed that it instructed Lord Byron to withdraw immediately and return to the King's headquarters.

By evening, it was over. The King had departed the field, and Tobias Rush had accompanied him. Thomas watched bodies being stripped and carted away for burial, exhausted soldiers, their hands and faces blackened by powder, staggering off in search of water, and bewildered horses, many fearfully wounded, wandering forlornly among the dead. Some found a stream from which riderless horses were drinking, and lay down on their bellies in it. In one day, thousands had died, hundreds more would die, and many more had lost arms, legs, and eyes. After a day of hacking each other to pieces, would either side, he wondered, claim victory? Unable any longer to think clearly, he wandered off in the direction of the town.

By the time he reached the house by the market square, Thomas, too, was exhausted. He had wielded neither musket nor sword, he had suffered no wound, he had never been in real danger, and he had had enough water to drink. Yet his back and neck were knotted with tension, he was filthy, his head ached from the powder, he could barely speak, and his hands were shaking. God alone knew what state the fighting men were in. He clambered up the staircase, fell on to his bed, and passed out.

When he awoke twelve hours later, his head still ached, his throat was still sore, and he was still filthy. He held out his hands; they at least were steady. Rising with difficulty from the bed, he stripped off his clothes, retrieved the encrypted massage which fell from under his shirt on to the floor, and did his best to wash off the worst of the dirt and powder. In his bag he had the change of clothes provided by Silas. He put them on. Then he went to see what news there was.

Downstairs, Tobias Rush was in the entrance hall, busily supervising the two coachmen who were carrying his chest outside. 'Master Rush,' said Thomas hoarsely, 'what news is there?'

Rush looked up sharply. 'Master Hill, good morning. The King leaves within the hour for Oxford, and I am to travel with him. You may have my coach. Prince Rupert will stay in Newbury until Essex leaves. If he marches towards London, the

Prince will pursue him. Our troops will follow us to Oxford.' Rush's voice seemed unaffected by the smoke.

'What of the battle?'

'There is little to report, other than heavy casualties on both sides.'

'Can we claim victory?'

The thin smile. 'Alas, no. Even I would be hard put to write an account of a victory, even Pyrrhic. If Essex does reach London, however, he might very well claim one.'

'Master Rush, may I ask another question?'

'You may, of course.'

'How did we allow the enemy to occupy the high ground on both wings? Shouldn't we have taken it before they arrived?'

For a moment, Rush was silent. 'I too have pondered that. One does not care to comment on military matters, but one does wonder about some form of deception.'

'What sort of deception?'

'False intelligence, perhaps, or an intercepted message. Either might have led the Prince to believe that we held the ridge, until it was too late to act.'

'Surely that would be unlikely.'

'Who knows? But enough, Master Hill. I must join the King. My carriage is at your disposal. We will expect you in Oxford within a day or two.'

Well, I suppose it's possible, thought Thomas, when Rush had gone, although the Prince drunk and incapable is more likely.

They covered the thirty-odd miles to Oxford in a single day. Thomas did not care to stop overnight, and urged the coachmen to make all speed. After the horror of Newbury, he wanted to see Jane, and he wanted to get to work on the message. If he could break the cipher, he might shorten the war. A shorter war would mean fewer widows and orphans, fewer deaths, and fewer lives pointlessly wrecked. The Battle of Newbury had given him new purpose. He must break the cipher.

Chapter 7

Can there be such a thing as an unbreakable cipher? thought Thomas, sitting again at his table, the encrypted text before him. Monsieur Vigenère thought so, and so far, he was right. Twenty six possible substitutions for each letter, determined by an agreed keyword, from whose own letters the encryption row was taken. If the key word were 'thomas', a single letter in the text might have been encrypted according to any of the rows starting with *t, h, o, m, a,* or *s.* It would not respond to analysis of frequencies. Yet the more he thought about it, the more Thomas's logical mind could not accept the concept of an unbreakable cipher. That the square had not yet been broken did not mean it never would be. There would be a way. And even if this message had been encrypted using Blaise de Vigenère's square, he would find it.

Putting himself in the shoes of an encrypter, he wrote down five repetitions of his keyword 'thomas', and, underneath them, his 'message' in plain text.

T H O M A S T H O M A S T H O M A S T H O M A S T H O M A S

O N E E Y E I S B R O W N Y E T T H E O T H E R I S B L U E

Then, using the square he had already constructed, he encoded the second line according to the letter above it, which indicated which row of the square to use. This gave him a third, enciphered, line:

H U S Q Y W B Z P D O O G F S F T Z X V H T E J B Z P X U W

The recipient of this message would decrypt it by reversing the process, as long as he knew the keyword, or the sequence of rows to be used, which could, less securely, be communicated by numbers. But the numbers having proved time-consuming and unhelpful, Thomas had decided that they were codes and that he would return to the letters. Two things stuck out from his encryption. Double letters were coincidental and would be no help in decryption, and any letter encrypted according to the letter *A* would appear as itself. Without knowing if there were any *A*'s in the keyword, this too was unhelpful. He also noticed, however, that the sequence of letters *BZP* appeared twice, because they happened to coincide twice with the plain text letters *ISB*. A thought struck him. He knew why *BZP* appeared twice because he knew what the keyword was. In a Vigenère square, single letter repetitions were meaningless, but repetitions of sequences might not be.

For an hour he pondered the question. The answer did not leap at him like Archimedes in his bath, it crept up slowly. If he just knew the length of the keyword it would be a start.

Common letter sequences, such as 'the', 'and', and 'tion', would have been repeated in the text, and would sometimes have coincided with repeats of the letters of the keyword, thus leading to repetitions in the encrypted text. If he measured the distances in letters between each repeated sequence, he should be able to calculate the length of the key word. In his 'message' *BZP* were letters seven to nine, and twenty five to twenty seven. So there were eighteen letters between the start of the first sequence and the start of the second. His keyword, *thomas*, had six letters. Twenty four was divisible by six. The letters of the keyword had been repeated three times before meeting the same plain text sequence of letters again. It was a matter of simple arithmetic. Then an awkward thought occurred. Eighteen was also divisible by one, two, three, nine, and itself. Not so simple after all. Time for another stroll. He locked his door and set off.

Outside Pembroke, Thomas turned left towards the ancient castle. Head down, he barely noticed the beggars and whores who infested this part of the town. Jumbles of letters and numbers tumbled about in his mind, as if trying to make some sort of sense but never quite managing it. He walked round the castle and back towards St Ebbe's. Could he find the length of the keyword from repeating sequences of letters, and, if so, how could he usefully use it? He felt the vague stirring of an idea.

He did not see the coach until it was too late. It came thundering up Littlegate, swerved at the intersection with Pembroke Street, knocked him off his feet into a blocked drain, and thundered on up St Ebbe's. Dazed and bruised, he lay on his back in the drain, wondering what had happened. Then he passed out. When he opened his eyes, he thought he saw the long face of Tobias Rush peering down at him. He closed them again. 'Master Hill, are you hurt?' It even sounded like Rush. 'I happened to be passing and saw you here. Did you fall?' Cautiously, Thomas opened his eyes again. It was Rush. His shoulder ached, his head throbbed, and he was covered in shit and slime. Unsteadily, he got to his feet. Rush helped him up. 'How fortunate that I was nearby. After surviving Newbury, a fatal accident would have been most regrettable. Can you walk to Pembroke?'

'I think so.' replied a shaken, evil-smelling, Thomas.

'Good. Permit me to accompany you.' He gave Thomas his arm, and, together they walked slowly to the college gate. There, Rush, having confirmed that he was not badly hurt, left him, and silver-topped cane in hand, hurried off towards Christ Church. Thomas struggled to his room. For once, Silas was not on sentry duty so he did not have to undergo an inquisition. He reached into his pocket for the key. It was not there. He tried the other pocket. Not there either. 'God's wounds,' he said out loud, 'it's in that dung-filled drain. And it'll have to stay there.'

He returned to find Silas back at his post. Having offered a feeble lie for his condition and for the loss of the key, he was begrudgingly given another one. 'I keep three keys for each lock, sir. One for the gentleman, one for me, and one spare. Now you've lost yours, I've got no spare until I can get another made, and only the good Lord knows when that will be. The forges are all busy sharpening swords and shoeing horses.' Inside his room at last, he stripped off his foul clothes, sluiced himself down with water from the ewer, and tried to examine his shoulder. It hurt, but he could see no signs of a wound. Just bruised probably. His head still ached and his vision was a little blurred. In no state to resume work, he lay down and slept.

When he awoke, it was pitch dark. His lips were swollen and his mouth felt like goatskin. He groped for a candle, lit it, and tipped the remains of the water down his throat. Then he lay down again. Knocked down by a rampaging coach which did not trouble to stop, found by Tobias Rush who happened to be passing, left to make his own way back, and his key lost in a drain. It was a strange place for Rush to be – one of the foulest in the town. He thought about Rush. Abraham and Jane had both warned him about the man. Clever and ambitious, they had said, and with the ear of the King. There was something sinister about him, too, although in time of war there must be many just as sinister. Nevertheless, although it was probably just the deranged ramblings of his dazed mind, he would take more care, and before leaving his room or opening the door to anyone, he would find a place to hide his papers.

At dawn, the vague idea stirred again. In a longer text, there would be more than one letter sequence repeated. If he took the letter-measurements between all repeated sequences of the same letters, he should find a common factor, suggesting the length of the keyword. To test this theory, he started by counting the number of different repeated sequences in the text, ignoring those of less than three letters. He found eight of them – seven of three letters and one of four. He could not be entirely sure that he had not missed any, but eight should be enough for a test. Then he counted the letters separating each repetition of each sequence. The results he wrote on a table, with the sequences in the left column, the letter-distances he found for each in the second column, and the numbers three to twelve across the top row, working on the assumption that the keyword would be more than two and less than thirteen letters long. The eight repeated sequences had respectively twenty, thirty five, forty five, fifty, sixty five, one hundred and ten, three hundred, and three hundred and seventy letters separating them, so he marked with a cross the intersections of rows and columns which were divisible by each number from three to twelve. Only the number five divided into all eight separations. The keyword must have five letters.

So delighted was he at the first hint of progress, that Thomas almost forgot to hide his papers before hurrying to tell Abraham. In such a tiny room, there were few opportunities for concealment. Under the wash stand or in the bed would not do. Nor would the pile of stinking clothes on the floor. He pushed the bed aside and tapped the floorboards. As he had hoped, one was loose. He prised it up and put the papers into the space beneath. Then he tapped the board down again and replaced the bed. Not perfect, but the best he could do. He locked his door and went to give Abraham the good news.

Expecting to be summoned straight in, he knocked loudly on Abraham's door. When there was no response, he knocked again. Still no response. He tried the door, which was locked. Odd. Perhaps Silas would know where he was. He found Silas at his post. 'Silas, Master Fletcher's door is locked and he appears to be out. Do you know where he is?'

'No, sir. Master Fletcher never goes out unaccompanied, and I haven't seen him today. Perhaps he's asleep.'

'Have you a spare key to his rooms?'

'I have, sir,' replied Silas suspiciously, 'but I'd prefer not to lose it. If you don't mind, I'll come with you and unlock the door myself.' He took a large bunch of keys from a drawer and followed Thomas to the room. They knocked again, but there was still no response. Silas found the right key and unlocked the door. Thomas entered first, and gasped. The room had been ransacked. Every one of Abraham's books had been torn from its spine and thrown on the floor. His chair and table were in pieces, and his few clothes and other possessions were strewn about everywhere.

Thomas called out. 'Abraham? Are you here?' There was no reply. They went cautiously in, and tried the door to the small chamber where Abraham slept. It was unlocked. Thomas entered. On the blood-soaked bed lay the naked body of the old man. His face and chest bore the signs of torture, his eyes had been gouged out, and his throat cut. Thomas's stomach heaved. He put his hand to his mouth and closed his eyes. Silas looked past him into the chamber, and vomited. For several minutes neither man could speak. Both stood with hands on knees, trying to breathe. Thomas was the first to recover. 'What manner of human filth could have done this? And why?'

Silas, too, was recovering. 'I'll fetch the coroner, sir. You'd best stay here.'

'Be quick, Silas. The coroner must see this at once.'

When Silas had gone, Thomas sat on the floor by the door. His old friend, a gentle man who had never harmed a soul, and had helped many, foully murdered in this monstrous, sickening, obscene, way. His tears flowed and he howled in anguish. God in heaven, how could any man commit such an act? What could drive a man to inflict such suffering on another? Why take the eyes of a man who could not see?

For an hour, Thomas barely moved. The strength had gone from his legs and his mind was numb. He sat staring at the room and thought of nothing. He was still on the floor when Silas returned with the coroner, a fussy-looking little man, with a red-veined face and a pair of pince-nez perched on his nose. Thomas took a deep breath and rose to meet him. 'Henry Pearson, sir, coroner. You must be Master Hill.'

'Thomas Hill, sir. An old student of Master Fletcher, and an old friend.'

'Did you find the body?'

'I did. Mr Merkin was behind me.'

'Have you left everything as you found it?' The coroner was brusque.

'I've touched nothing. The body is in the bed chamber.' Pearson bustled past him and into the chamber. When he emerged, he was ashen.

'Master Fletcher suffered greatly before he died. Judging by the state of rigor mortis, I would say he has been dead for six or seven hours.'

'So he was murdered in the night?'

'That is my opinion. Have you any idea why anyone would do this?'

Thomas had no intention of disclosing Abraham's position, or his own, to Henry Pearson, coroner or not. 'None, sir.

Abraham was a quiet, scholarly man. I can conceive of no reason for this barbarity.'

'Have you seen anything suspicious?' he asked Silas.

'No, sir.' replied Silas firmly. 'Both college gates are locked from midnight to six in the morning. Anyone wishing to enter must ring the bell. I only let them in if I know who they are.'

'Then the murderer was already in the college before you locked the gates. Either he's still here or he must have slipped out again this morning. Have you been at your post all the time?'

'Yes, sir, except when I came to unlock the door for Master Hill.'

'Then if he left, that was when. He would have been watching, knowing that sooner or later the door would be found locked. Alternatively, he is living here.' Pearson changed direction. 'You say the door was locked. Could the murderer have had a key?'

'No, sir.' replied Silas firmly. 'Master Fletcher had his key. I have the other two.'

'Could one have been stolen, and later returned?'

'No sir. I'd have noticed. I check all the keys every morning.'

'Then either Master Fletcher opened the door to his murderer, or the door was unlocked. The murderer took his key and locked the door when he left. Master Fletcher probably knew the man.'

'Not necessarily, Master Pearson.' pointed out Thomas, 'Abraham Fletcher was blind. He could have opened the door to a stranger without knowing it.'

'In that case, he would have been an easy victim and the

murderer's motive will be more difficult to establish. Had he any relatives in Oxford?'

'Not as far as I know, sir.' replied Silas, 'He never mentioned any.'

'A pity. You'd be surprised how many murderers turn out to be wives, husbands, and sons. Did he have any enemies?'

'I can think of none.'

'Alas, Master Hill, it seems he had at least one. One who was searching for something. What could that have been?'

'I doubt it was money. Abraham was not a wealthy man.'

'It looks more like a document or information of some kind. The murderer must have hoped to find it in a book. What subjects did Master Fletcher teach?'

'Mathematics, philosophy, and a little divinity.'

'What might be secret about those?'

'Very little. He was just an elderly scholar, who loved books and learning.' Thomas was getting cross. He was feeling the strain of answering the coroner's questions and of having to lie. He did not know who the murderer was, but he was quite sure about the motive. It was about ciphers, and, most probably, the one under Thomas's floorboards. But he could not risk telling the coroner that.

'And why would he have been tortured?' The little man was persistent, as coroners usually were.

'Master Pearson, I really have no idea.' said Thomas, 'Abraham Fletcher was my friend. This has been a terrible shock, and I would like to go now.'

'Before you do, sir, someone will have to come to my house formally to identify the deceased. I will have the body taken there as soon as I have inspected the room.'

'I will come tomorrow.' said Thomas, 'May I go now?'

'You may, sir. I know where you are if I need you.'

In the courtyard outside, Thomas was horrified to find a curious crowd of soldiers. The coroner must have been recognised, and word spread around the college. Soon it would be around Oxford. He wondered if that was the murderer's intention. Ignoring the stares and whispers, he hurried past the soldiers and across the yard. His fellow lodgers had never taken any notice of him – to them, he was just another scholar doing nothing for the King – and he hoped it would stay that way.

Thomas opened the door to his room, and stared at it. In the time he had been at Abraham's room, it had been entered and searched. The bed had been turned upside down, the papers on the table thrown on the floor, and his clothes shredded. The Essais were in small pieces. Whoever had done this knew what he was looking for. Thomas pushed aside the bed and opened the loose floorboard. The message and his workings were still there. With more time, the intruder would doubtless have found them. He replaced the board and sat on his chair. The room reminded him of the bookshop after the soldiers had wrecked it. For some time he sat and thought. Erasmus Pole and Abraham Fletcher cruelly murdered, run down by a coach in the street, a message encrypted with a Vigenère cipher, and his room ransacked. What in God's name had induced him to come to Oxford? He went to fetch Silas.

Silas too was horrified. 'Master Fletcher, and now you, sir.' he said, 'As well you weren't here, or….' . He stopped himself just in time.

'Did you have a spare key made, Silas?'

'No, sir. It was only yesterday you lost it.'

'And you've had yours on your ring at all times?'

'I have, sir.'

God's wounds. Surely not. Had his key not disappeared down that stinking drain, after all? He thought about it. The unexpected visits, the solicitous questions, the accident. 'Silas, please send a boy for Father de Pointz at Merton. Ask him to come at once.'

'At once, sir.'

'And, Silas, tell no-one about this. It would only complicate matters.'

If Silas was surprised, he did not show it. 'As you wish, Master Hill.'

When Silas had left, Thomas made no effort to put the room back together. He wanted Simon to see it.

Simon arrived within the hour. News of a murder in Pembroke had already reached Merton, and he had come as quickly as he could. 'What's been happening, Thomas?' he asked, 'We hear there has been a murder. Is this connected to it?'

'It is. And it's Abraham who's been murdered. Murdered and tortured. Simon, his eyes were cut out. How could any man do such a thing?'

Simon crossed himself. 'Someone who wanted something badly enough, and thought Abraham had it. Poor Abraham. He was a good man. I grieve that he suffered. I shall pray for his soul.' He paused and crossed himself again. 'When did it happen?'

'The coroner thinks it was during the night. The door wasn't forced. Abraham let his own murderer in.'

'And this?', indicating the ruined room.

'When I was at Abraham's room.'

'Then the murderer did not find what he wanted in Abraham's room and came here to look for it. Did he find it here, Thomas?'

'Thankfully, he did not. I have it safe.'

'And can you tell me what it is?'

Thomas retrieved the message from its hiding place and handed it to Simon. 'This is what he was looking for. Three pages encrypted with a Vigenère square. A cipher thought to be unbreakable.'

'A Vigenère square?'

Thomas patiently described Blaise de Vigenère's square with its twenty-six possible encryptions of each letter of a text, rendering analysis of individual letter frequencies useless. Only a possessor of the keyword could decrypt a Vigenère text, and the cipher had remained unbroken for over seventy years. He told Simon how the message had come to him, and that he was sure it contained information vital to the outcome of the war. 'Texts which use the square are laborious to encrypt and decrypt,' he explained, 'so it's seldom used for military purposes. This message is hiding something the King needs to know, and his enemies will do anything to prevent him knowing. That's why Abraham died.'

'If you're right, Thomas, you're in grave danger. You certainly can't stay here.'

'Simon, I believe I know who killed Abraham and Erasmus

Pole. Or at least who had them killed. I think it was Tobias Rush.'

'How do you know this?'

Thomas told him about Rush's visit and the questions about his work. He pointed out how easy it would have been for Rush to gain entry to Abraham's room by pretending to be on the King's business. And he told him about the 'accident' and the loss of his key. He guessed that when Rush had seen that Thomas had not been killed by the coach, he had taken the opportunity to remove the key from his pocket. Simon listened carefully.

'And there's another thing. I've walked down the lane where Erasmus Pole was found, and I don't believe he would have been there at night. He was murdered elsewhere and his body left in the lane. The coroner wouldn't have bothered with just another dead body there. What's more, both Pole and Abraham had their throats cut. The same method of killing, and the same killer.'

'Thomas,' said Simon when Thomas had finished, 'It may be that Rush is a traitor and a murderer. I for one would not be altogether surprised. But all you have is evidence. Evidence, not proof. If the King is to be persuaded of the guilt of one of his closest advisors, absolute proof will be needed. He trusts Rush implicitly.'

'And how are we to get proof? The man's cunning and devious. Proof will not be easy to come by.'

'We'll have to think of a plan. Meanwhile, we must find you a safe haven. Rush will be even more dangerous with the King away.'

'I didn't know the King had left Oxford again. Where is he now?'

'I don't know. A secret rendezvous somewhere. Her Majesty is despondent. She always fears the worst when the King is away. It's her nature.'

'So what do you propose?'

'When it's dark, we'll slip out of Pembroke and go to Merton. You can stay in my rooms tonight. Even Rush wouldn't dare enter the rooms of the Queen's priest without permission. Until then we'll stay here.'

'I have to visit the coroner tomorrow morning to identify Abraham's body.'

'In that case, I shall accompany you there. Then we'll think of a way to get you home.'

'Simon,' said Thomas, 'There's one more thing. I've made some progress on the cipher. Given time, I think I may be able to decrypt it. I must stay here until I have. And, in any case, Rush's long arm will certainly reach Romsey. I'm safer here.'

'What about your family?'

'I worry for them day and night. I've had no word from them. Rush offered to have my letter delivered to them, but I doubt it ever got there. Yet they're probably safer without my being there. If Rush's men came calling for me, they would all be in danger.'

'If that's what you want, Thomas. We'll stay here until dark. Would you care to show me the cipher and what you've been able to do?'

Better to keep the mind occupied, thought Thomas, as Simon well knows. 'Very well. I'll explain.'

It was a long afternoon. When darkness eventually fell they left the room together, taking only the message and Thomas's papers. The courtyard was empty and Simon diverted Silas's attention while Thomas slipped out, then joined him outside the gate. Even Silas must not know where Thomas was going. They walked quickly to Merton, taking care to keep their distance from anyone passing in the street. At Merton, Simon took Thomas to his room in the little quadrangle behind the chapel, and left him there while he went to arrange food and drink for them and to find a pallet for Thomas's bed.

Thomas slept little. The image of sightless, eyeless, Abraham, his chest and face bloody, his hands tied and his throat cut, had imprinted itself on his mind. It was a different sort of horror, and even more terrible than that he had seen at Newbury. Abraham had been his friend. He might have admitted knowing about the message or he might not. It was of no account. The old man had suffered beyond imagining, and Thomas could do nothing about it. He could only grieve. If he could have left that night and returned safely home, he would have gone without hesitation. The Oxford he knew had disappeared, Abraham was dead, the country was tearing itself to shreds. He longed for home and family.

Simon, too, slept little. He asked Thomas to repeat the account of his being knocked down in the street and found by Rush, and he asked about the questions relating to Thomas's work. He gave Thomas the impression that he knew something more, something not even Abraham had known. He did not say what, and Thomas lacked the will to ask. The monk would tell him if he wanted to.

Next morning, they left Merton for the coroner's house. In order not to attract attention, Simon walked well behind

Thomas, and kept an eye out for danger. At the corner of Cornmarket and Ship Street, where the coroner's house stood, Thomas suddenly stopped and ducked into a doorway. Not knowing why, Simon did the same, and waited until Thomas emerged before going on. Thomas waited for him to catch up. 'It was Rush, Simon. I saw him leaving the coroner's house.'

'Did he see you?'

'I don't think so. He was hurrying.'

'Good. Well, you'll have to visit the coroner or he'll be suspicious. I'll wait outside for you.'

When Thomas knocked on the coroner's door, it was opened immediately. Henry Pearson was waiting for him. Without saying a word, he led Thomas to a back room, empty but for a low table on which lay Abraham's body, covered by a grey cloth. Pearson raised the cloth. 'Do you recognise this man?' he asked briskly.

'I do. It's Abraham Fletcher.' Pearson replaced the cloth and ushered Thomas out of the room. Indicating for Thomas to follow him, he opened the door to another room and went in. This too was a room bare of furniture but for a small desk and two chairs.

'While you are here, Master Hill,' said Pearson, 'I have some questions to ask you.' He remained standing and did not offer Thomas a chair.

'Very well,' replied Thomas, 'although I believe I have told you everything I know.'

'That we shall soon ascertain. I have examined the body and established the cause of death as the severing of the deceased's windpipe with a very sharp blade. The cut was clean. Before he died, his face and chest were cut with the same blade, and his eyes removed, probably also with the same blade. The eyes were not at the scene of the murder. There are marks on his wrists consistent with their being tied with rope, no doubt in order to restrain him. There are also signs that a rag or cloth was stuffed into his mouth to prevent his crying out.' Thomas felt his knees give, and reached for a chair to steady himself. The coroner ignored his distress. 'Can you confirm that you were the first to find the body?'

'I can. Silas Merkin and I.'

'Quite. You used Merkin's key to enter the room?'

'We did. When there was no answer to my knock, I fetched him.'

'Were you surprised that there was no answer?'

'I was. Abraham was blind, but his hearing was good. And he seldom left his rooms.'

'Why were you calling on him?'

'Abraham taught me mathematics and philosophy. He was a good friend and a fine scholar. I came to Oxford to visit him before he died. We spent the mornings together discussing philosophy and books.' It was the story they had agreed.

'I see. And how long have you been in Oxford?'

'I arrived some four weeks ago.'

'Indeed? A long visit.'

'I enjoy Oxford, even in time of war, and I enjoyed Abraham's company. I am unmarried. I saw no need to hurry home.'

'Where is your home, Master Hill?'

'I live in the town of Romsey, in Hampshire.'

'A long journey, not to be lightly undertaken.'

'Long enough. The more reason not to make it again too soon.'

'I believe Master Fletcher was killed during the night before he was found. Perhaps six hours earlier. Where were you at that time?'

'Asleep in my room, naturally.' Thomas was fast losing patience. 'Master Pearson, do you suspect me of this unspeakable crime? For the love of God, Abraham Fletcher was my friend.'

'So you say. I am of the opinion that the murderer resided in the college. A stranger would have been noticed.'

'The college is full of soldiers and their families. Which of them would want to kill an elderly scholar, and why?'

'Why, indeed? The motive is as yet unclear, but I have received information that Master Fletcher performed certain services for the King. Services important to the conduct of the war. If this became known to a traitor, he might have been in danger.'

And I know who you received it from, thought Thomas. Tobias Rush, a murderer and a traitor. 'I know nothing of such matters.'

'I have also been informed that you were recently found drunk in the street.'

'Drunk in the street? Nonsense. I was knocked over into a shit-filled drain by a coach which did not stop. I was quite sober.'

'Were there any witnesses to this?'

'I expect so. There were people in the street. Someone must have seen the coach.' Someone did. Rush.

'Thomas Hill, a coroner's jury will be summoned to

examine the death of Abraham Fletcher. I have no doubt that the jury will reach a verdict of murder. I also have no doubt that you had the means, and probably the motive, to commit this awful crime, and that the jury will send you to the Court of Assizes, to stand trial for murder. Meanwhile, while I conduct further investigations, you will be held at Oxford Castle. Guard!'

At the coroner's command, two guards who must have been waiting outside, threw open the door. 'Bind the prisoner and take him immediately to the castle. He is to be held there until I order his release or transfer elsewhere.' Thomas's hands were tied and he was marched between the guards out of the house. He searched frantically for Simon. At first he could not see him and was almost panicked into calling out. Then the monk appeared briefly from behind a wall, signalled that he had seen him, and disappeared again. He must have feared that they were being watched.

At the castle, the coroner's guards told the gatekeeper their business, and they were escorted through the castle yard to a thick oak door on the other side. The gatekeeper unlocked it, and Thomas was manhandled into a dingy guard room, where a pox-scarred man with a huge belly sat eating a chicken leg. His guards handed their charge over to the fat gaoler. 'Room for a small one? Shouldn't be here long. He'll be off to the Assizes for murder.'

'We'll fit 'im in somewhere.' replied the gaoler, through a mouthful of chicken. 'If 'e's a murderer, we'd better chain 'im.' He took an iron ring attached to a short chain from a row hanging on the wall, and locked it round Thomas's neck. 'That'll keep 'im out of trouble.' The guards left, and Thomas was led by the chain to a flight of stone steps which spiralled up the ancient tower of the castle. The steps were so narrow that the gaoler could only just squeeze himself up them. The iron ring was rusty and cut into Thomas's neck, and his hands were still bound. From inside low doors leading off the steps at intervals came the sounds of men and children in pain. This tower was where prisoners-of-war, convicted criminals, and men awaiting trail, were all thrown in together. The prison made no distinctions. The stench of filth and death was overpowering. At the fourth door, the gaoler stopped. He unlocked the door with a key from a bunch tied to his waist, pulled Thomas inside, kicked something out of the way, and forced Thomas to his knees. He fastened the chain with a lock to another chain hanging from the wall, unbound Thomas's hands, and left. The door clanged shut, and Thomas was in darkness.

Chapter 8

The blackest night could not hide the pool of shit and vomit in which Thomas was sitting, nor the noxious slime that ran down the wall behind his back. His stomach heaved, and he added his own contribution to the pool. As his eyes adjusted to the meagre light from a tiny window high up on one wall, he began to make out the shapes around him. They sat, chained as he was, around all four walls of the cell, and unchained, back-to-back in the middle. In a space no more than twenty feet by fifteen, he counted forty bodies, including three that were so small that they could only be children, not one of which could move a muscle without sloshing about in a sea of muck. No-one spoke, or even raised a head to look at the new arrival. Some were moaning, a few weeping, most were silent. Chained or unchained, every prisoner sat, knees up and head down, in whatever space he could get. There was scant room to stretch a leg, never mind lie down. Not that lying in six inches of piss and shit held much attraction. Thomas looked to his right, and, with a shock, saw that the thing the gaoler had kicked out of the way was a body. A dead one. And as the cell became clearer, he realised that it was not the only dead body. There were certainly four others, and might have been more. It was hard to be sure. He rested his head on his knees and closed his eyes. Smell, sound, and touch, he could not avoid. Taste and sight, he would try to. It was at least something to concentrate on.

After a while, the door was unlocked and the fat gaoler waddled in. He grabbed a boy by the hair and dragged him outside. The boy went without a sound. Again, no-one showed the slightest interest or said a word. For all they cared, the boy might be going to the gallows or on his way home.

They cared when he was brought back, however. They heard his screams coming up the steps and they saw him tossed like a doll into the cell. Holding his hands out in front of him, the boy sat and howled. For the first time, someone spoke. 'Shut up, boy, or I'll snap your neck.'

'They burnt my hands.' wailed the child, 'They tied leaves and twigs between my fingers and burnt them.'

'Piss on them. That'll cool them down.'

Thomas had heard of this. The governor's fire, it was called. Torture for pleasure, and on a boy of no more than ten. Gradually, the boy's howls became sobs, then stopped altogether. He slumped to the floor and lay still. The first voice spoke again. 'If I 'ad a knife, I'd eat the little bugger.'

'Me, too.'

''E's only a runt. Wouldn't be enough on 'im to go round.'

God in heaven, thought Thomas, how in the name of everything holy did I get here? He knew, of course. It was the very unholy Rush. The man had bribed the coroner. With the King away, he thought he could get away with anything. First Pole, then Abraham, now him. Whatever was in it, Rush wanted that message. Simon must keep it hidden until he got out of here and could work on it again.

Sometime later the door to the cell was unlocked and the fat gaoler came in again, this time carrying a heavy-looking cudgel. A younger man, who might have been his son, followed with two loaves of bread, which he threw on the floor. 'Dinner time.' croaked the gaoler, 'Eat up. Too skinny and you'll go slow on the rope. And be grateful. Remember I 'ad to pay for it from m' own pocket.' Even before the gaolers had left, an unchained boy leapt on a loaf and sunk his teeth into it. He had barely done so when he was knocked aside, and the loaf grabbed by a large, black-bearded man, whose arms were just long enough to reach it. No-one else got a bite, and Thomas did not see where the other loaf went. It hardly mattered. He was not yet hungry enough to take a mouthful of stale, shit-covered bread.

He sat against the slimy wall and let his mind wander. He saw gangs of men, serfs and slaves, digging out the foundations of this place, lowering down stone and bricks and timbers on ropes, clambering down rickety ladders to dig and build foundations, and watching a great castle slowly emerge. They had built well. The castle and its tower had stood for five hundred years. How many men had died in it? How many had died in this very cell? If it stood for another five hundred years, how many more would die here? He wondered who had designed the castle, where the stone had come from, where the iron had been forged. He wondered how long it had taken to build and how many men had toiled on it. Gazing at the stone walls, he wondered about the mason who had built it. Was he tall, short, fat, thin? How did he speak? Did he have a family? How old was he when he worked here? What tools had he used? Realising that he was doing just as he did when faced with a new cipher, Thomas smiled and tried something else. Starting from the top left corner, he began counting the stones in the wall. He counted along the rows, noting that the odd numbered rows began with a small stone, and the even-numbered ended with one. The same occurred where a row met the door. He counted two hundred and sixteen stones in the wall. Building a wall must be like decrypting a cipher. It had to be done stone-by-stone. One stone out of place, and the wall would be weak, and would fall. One mistake in a decryption, and the system would fail. Lay a strong foundation, take careful measurements, and lay one stone carefully on top of another. Check your work regularly. Stone building and decryption. Much the same.

By the following evening, Thomas was starving. No more bread had been brought by the gaolers, and no bodies removed. His stomach was racked with cramps, and he longed to stand or stretch his legs. But whenever he tried to, his legs were grabbed and twisted until he moved them back. He tried to think about the cipher. He saw letters and stones, shapes and patterns. He saw de Vigenère's square as a rippling wave and as a wall of stones. He knew that something important was eluding him, but lacked the strength to search for it. He fell into a sleep which was not a sleep. He saw shapes and heard noises, but he could not tell whether they were real or imagined. He no longer noticed the stench, nor the sounds of men retching and defecating. His world began at the wall behind his back and ended at his toes.

Sometime that night, the door was opened and the fat gaoler came in again. He unlocked Thomas's chain and pulled him roughly to his feet. Thomas immediately fell, and was hoisted up by his arm. He struggled to stand. 'You've a visitor, 'ill. Downstairs.' Thank God. Simon, or even Jane. The gaoler tied his hands with a short length of rope, and led him by the chain around his neck through the door and down the stone steps to the guard room. ''ere 'e is, sir. I'll be outside.' Thomas went in and heard the gaoler lock the gate behind him. In the room were a small table and two chairs. On one of them sat Tobias Rush.

'Master Hill.' said Rush, not bothering to stand. 'I'm greatly distressed to find you here. Do sit down.' As always, Rush was all in black, hand resting on the silver-topped cane. Thomas sat. 'News of your arrest reached me only yesterday. I came as soon as I could.' It was a lie. Thomas stared at him and said nothing. Rush continued. 'Master Pearson, the coroner, tells me that there is evidence against you for the murder of Abraham Fletcher. I could scarcely believe it, and told him so. Absurd, I said. Why would Thomas Hill murder Abraham Fletcher?' He paused. 'Did you murder Master Fletcher, Thomas?' You know I did not, Rush, because you did, thought Thomas, saying nothing. Rush's voice turned menacing. 'Nothing to say? Then let me assist you. The coroner believes that the murderer resided in the college. An intruder would have had difficulty hiding and would have been noticed. His inquiries have turned up nothing to suggest this. On the contrary, he is certain that the murderer was well known to Master Fletcher. As to motive, the culprit was obviously looking for something, and was prepared to kill to get it. I wonder what that could have been. Have you any idea, Thomas?' Still Thomas remained silent. 'No? Let me remind you that you are suspected of a murder for which you have no alibi, and for which you had the means, and, very probably, the motive. Whatever secret Abraham Fletcher was guarding, it would have been dangerous to someone, and who is to say that that someone isn't you? Oxford is full of spies and traitors to the Crown. The coroner suspects you of being one of them.' Thomas stared across the table at the black eyes, and saw the evil in them. Again Rush's voice changed. 'Thomas, this is foolishness. If you tell me everything, I can help you. I have influence with the King. If you know why Master Fletcher was killed, I urge you to tell me. Otherwise.......' Thomas rose and went to the door. Rush exploded in fury. 'You stupid little man. Tell me what you know, and you may live. Stay silent and you will die. You have my word on it.' Thomas ignored him and rattled the gate. It was opened by the gaoler. 'Take him up,' yelled Rush, 'and make him suffer. I want the truth out of him.' Hands still tied, and neck in the iron ring, Thomas was dragged up the steps to the cell. The gaoler locked him back into his place and left without a word.

Thomas tried again to concentrate on the wall. He could not do it. His mind was not working. He needed food and water. Without them, the vague idea would stay vague. He shut his eyes and dozed.

'On yer feet, 'ill.' ordered the gaoler the next morning, 'You're a popular little bugger. You've got another visitor.' After the same procedure with the chain, Thomas was led roughly through the door. He could barely stand and the light outside the cell hurt his eyes. He stumbled down the steps to the guard room, expecting to see Rush. A figure was standing by the gaoler's table. He squinted at it. It was Jane.

'Bring two chairs, man, and be quick about it.' she snapped at the gaoler, 'You've been well enough paid.' He lumbered off to find chairs. Jane came to Thomas and took his bound hands in hers. 'Thomas, I weep to see you like this. Have you been harmed?' Thomas shook his head. The gaoler brought the chairs and they sat. 'I wish to speak privately to Master Hill.' Jane told him, 'Return in half-an-hour.' As soon as the gaoler had disappeared up the steps, Jane untied his hands. From under her shawl, she produced a bottle, half a chicken, and a small loaf. 'I thought you might need these.' Thomas smiled. 'Eat first, then we'll talk.' Thomas drank ale from the bottle and ate a chicken leg.

'Thank you, Jane.' he croaked, 'I'm sorry you see me like this, but it's even more of a pleasure than usual for me to see you. However, I do not recommend prison for an invigorating visit.'

Jane smiled. 'Your old wit, Thomas. That's good, and much needed. We hear that six thousand men died at Newbury, and the King grieves greatly for the loss of his friends, especially Lord Falkland. His mood is sombre.'

'It was pointless, Jane. Thousands more widows and orphans, and for nothing. '

'I know. For nothing. As Edward's death was for nothing.' She paused. 'Thomas, Simon has told me about Erasmus Pole, about Abraham Fletcher's murder, about your room being searched, and about your lost key. We too suspect Rush.'

'He came here yesterday, hoping to find out what I know. Having had me sent here, he offered help and he made threats. Would an innocent man do that? If I had a shred of doubt, I have none now. The man's a murderer and a traitor.'

'I am sure of it. But he has the ear of the King, and it would be foolish to move against him without proof. Have we any proof?'

'No. We have evidence and we have our instincts, but we do not have proof. Not yet.'

'Not yet?'

'Jane, has Simon told you about the message?'

'Not a particular message, no. I know about your work, because you told me. That's all.'

'Then, for your own safety I shall not tell you either. However, there is a slight chance that if I can escape from here, I will be able to furnish proof.'

'Thomas, the coroner's jury will assemble in three days. In the absence of the King, Simon is trying to persuade the Queen to sign an order for your release. The Queen is always reluctant to act without the King's agreement, and would prefer to wait until he is in a more receptive mood. That might be too late. If the coroner's jury send you for trial at the Assizes, even the King would hesitate to intervene.'

Thomas reached for her hands. 'Then we must hope for the Queen's assistance. Rush is a vile murderer, a torturer, and a traitor. He must be exposed.'

The half hour was almost up. Jane retied Thomas's hands. As they heard the gaoler's footsteps on the stones, she leaned forward and brushed her lips against his. 'Simon will bring news as soon as there is any. I shall be thinking of you.'

'And I you, Jane. Thank you for coming.'

Back in the cell, fortified by the food and water, Thomas tried again to trap the elusive thought that somehow linked the wall and the cipher. He counted the stones again, and pictured the mason. Neither helped. He stared at the wall, willing it to speak to him. For a long time, it remained silent. Then, without warning, it spoke. The patterns made by the rows of stones jumped out of the wall. He could see it clearly. It was the patterns. There were four distinct vertical columns of stones, each one with a pattern of its own. Half-stones and whole stones in the first column, and whole stones attached to one or the other in the second column. Each column different, all four of them making the whole. All day, he studied the rows of bricks and thought about how he would use what he had at last realised to break the cipher. The Vigenère square could be broken. He was sure of it.

The fever started that night. He was racked by cramping pains, his head was on fire, and his joints ached. He sat shivering until morning, unable to prevent his stomach and bowels voiding themselves, until, too weak to sit, he slid down the wall and lay on his side, his head resting on his dead neighbour and his legs pushed up into his stomach by the man in front. For a day and a night he lay there, slipping in and out of consciousness, barely aware of where he was, and lacking the strength to move and the will to live. When the gaoler came in with bread, he was kicked in the back, and heard a voice say 'finished'. He knew then that it was over.

An hour later, he did not hear the commotion outside the cell door, and he did not see the door open and the iron collar removed from his neck. When strong arms lifted him from the floor, he opened his eyes and tried to focus. He saw a face he recognised and heard a voice he knew, but could not place them. The effort was too much. His eyes closed and he passed out.

Chapter 9

On a glorious June day Margaret and he had taken the girls for a walk to the water meadows outside Stockbridge. They were bright children, especially interested in nature and words. Both were blond, with their mother's brown eyes and dimpled chin. They set out their dinner under an oak tree near a narrow stream, normally clear and shallow, but on that day running faster and deeper than usual from the recent rains, and brownish from mud that had slipped from the bank. Sometimes they saw trout in the stream, but not that day. It was too muddy. Margaret and he put out a cold chicken, small loaves she had baked herself, cheese, butter, apples stored since the autumn, and a dish of early raspberries. There was apple juice for the girls and bottles of sweet elderberry wine for them.

After they had eaten, Thomas entertained the girls with a game he had invented for them. He spelt out a new word, and they had to find its meaning. They could ask him ten questions and then had to make a guess. That day, the first word had been arboreal. It was a difficult one, they did not guess it, and he had to explain it to them. The afternoon was warm, and they dozed under the oak tree. The girls were old enough to play by themselves for a while, and they would be woken if they were needed.

It was cooler when Thomas managed to open his eyes. He could not see the girls, so he called for them. There was no reply. Margaret came immediately awake. They called again and again, and walked up and down the bank of the stream. Surely it was too shallow for either of the girls to have been in danger, even if they had somehow slipped in. They walked back and forth calling the girls' names. Still there was no reply. Margaret began to panic. 'Thomas, where are they? They wouldn't run off. Someone must have taken them. They've been taken. Please God, no. Who would have taken them? Thomas, who would have taken them?'

'Hush, now, Margaret. They haven't been taken. They've wandered off and will be back soon. We'll wait here a while.' But he too was worried. This had never happened before.

They stood together under the oak tree, taking it in turns to call out, and scanning the meadow and hedgerows for a glimpse of the girls. There was neither sight nor sound of them. Suddenly a shower of twigs landed on their heads. They looked up expecting to see red squirrels in the tree. There were indeed squirrels – two of them – but they were blond not red, with brown eyes, dimpled chins, and big grins. Margaret was furious. 'Come down at once, you two. What are you doing up there? We were worried. Didn't you hear us calling?'

The girls climbed out of the tree. 'Of course we heard.' said Polly, 'You were asleep, so we climbed the tree.'

'Yes,' said Lucy, 'we wanted to be arboreal.'

Margaret did her best to be cross. 'Arboreal, indeed. That's the last time you play your uncle's games, if they give you ideas like that.'

He winked at them. 'I'll think of a better word next time. Something safer. Terrestrial, perhaps.'

'That's enough, Thomas. Gather up the things, girls, and we'll go home.'

Thomas woke and called for Margaret. His room had been changed. His bed was against the wrong wall and the window had been covered. Why had she covered his window? He struggled off the bed and stumbled to the window. It was not there. He looked about. Where was the window? He saw a door. It was locked. He rattled the handle and called again for Margaret. There was no answer. He lay on the cold stone floor and passed out.

When he woke again, he was on the bed, a thin blanket over him. He was hot. He threw off the blanket and immediately started shivering. He retrieved the blanket and lay on his side with his eyes open. The shivering stopped, and he was hot again. His mind registered a fever. Images of the castle and the cell came back to him. Gaol fever. Where was he now, and how did he get here? Why was he alone? He reached out a hand to a small table beside the bed and lifted a cup to his mouth. Cold water dribbled between his cracked lips and down his chin. He held on to the cup and managed a few more sips. Then his eyes closed.

While Thomas slept, Simon de Pointz came quietly into the room, carrying a wooden chair. He felt Thomas's forehead, wiped it with a damp cloth, and sat down on the chair. He smiled and said a short prayer of thanks. Boyish but for his lack of hair, Thomas Hill, at no more than five and a half feet tall, philosopher, cryptographer, and pacifist, was not a man to be taken lightly. By the grace of God, he was going to survive. The monk was still sitting by his bedside when Thomas awoke again. He handed Thomas the cup of water and helped him drink. 'There you are, Thomas,' he said quietly, 'and looking a little better. Best stay on the bed, though. I found you on the floor yesterday.'

Thomas had no recollection of the floor, or of anything much else. 'Simon? Where am I?'

'You're in a safe place. An Abbey near Botley. The Abbot is an old friend. The monks know they have a visitor, but even he doesn't know who you are. They won't trouble you.'

'How long have I been here?'

'This is your third day. Are you hungry?'

Thomas realised that he was. 'Ravenous.'

'Then I'll fetch something for you. Stay on the bed unless you need the bucket. It's in the corner. I don't want to have to scrape layers of shit off you again.'

Simon was back in a few minutes with soup and bread. With a little help, Thomas managed to swallow some of each, and immediately felt stronger. His arrest and the castle cell came back to him. 'When did I last eat?' he asked.

'I can't be sure,' replied Simon, 'but at least four days ago.'

'What was it? Gaol Fever?'

'Probably. We got you out just in time.'

'How did you do it?'

'Jane Romilly persuaded the Queen to sign a paper ordering your release. It might or might not have been lawful, but it impressed the gaoler, and he had little choice but to obey.'

'Is Jane safe?'

'Quite safe. Rush won't risk the Queen's anger.'

'And Rush?'

'Furious. He's got half of Oxford looking for you, but he won't find you. Even the Queen doesn't know where you are.'

'And what now?'

'Now you stay here until you're fully recovered. The message is safely hidden, as are your papers. Tell me when you're ready to resume work on them.'

The message. The Vignère cipher. Abraham. The cell. Stones in the wall. An idea. What was it? Thomas could not remember. It would come to him later. 'Simon, is there any way I can get a message to my sister? The letter I entrusted to Rush will have got no further than his fire. After he'd read it, of course.'

Simon looked doubtful. 'It won't be easy. Since Newbury, it's hard to know which side is where. And bands of clubmen are attacking them both. The roads are much more dangerous than when we came here. Still, I'll try to think of something. Now rest again, Thomas. I'll come back this afternoon.'

The pattern of Simon's visits continued for two days. Morning and afternoon, he came bearing food and news and to observe the patient's progress. He brought a copy of a new Oxford newsbook, Mercurius Rusticus. 'There you are, Thomas,' he laughed, 'you'll enjoy that. Full of careful scholarship and excellent writing.' Of course, it was nothing of the kind, being little more than satirical attacks on high-minded puritans and their ill-disciplined soldiers. It could just as well have been written by high-minded puritans about ill-disciplined royalists, as most of the London newsbooks were. Verborum bellum. A war of words. There was much on the so-called 'Rules of War', an expression that had always struck Thomas as absurd. There were no rules, or, if there were, neither side took any notice of them unless it suited them to do so. A town was sacked and burnt. One man killed another. A woman was raped and her child slaughtered. War was not a game of tennis. The loser could not protest that the winner had broken a rule, nor did the winner have to play a point again. His opponent was dead. C'est tout.

Obeying Simon's request to stay in his room, Thomas spent the time thinking about Margaret and his nieces, reading a Bible given to him by Simon, staring at the plain white walls of his room, and trying in vain to remember the idea. On each visit, Simon also brought a cup of water, into which he had mixed equal amounts of camomile, sage, and garlic, claiming that this was an ancient cure for all manner of diseases, including morbus campestris. Complaining that the brew tasted revolting and would do him no good at all, Thomas dutifully forced it down, and by the morning of the third day, was strong enough to accompany Simon around the walled garden of the Abbey. Dressed once again in a plain brown habit and leather sandals, he carried an elm branch as a walking stick. Hooded monks worked away in the garden, carefully tending beds of herbs and flowers. They took no notice of Simon and Thomas. 'Is this where that noxious brew of yours comes from, Simon?' asked Thomas, as they walked.

'It is. And, noxious or not, it has got you back on your feet. We monks might seem unworldly, but we know a thing or two. Which reminds me, I have found a way to get a letter to your sister. Write it today and it will go tomorrow with a troop of the Queen's guard, who are riding to Exeter. Her Majesty will be travelling there to embark for France. The guard are preparing the route for her, so that she will be inconveniencd on her journey as little as possible. One of them will make a short detour to Romsey to deliver the letter. If there's a reply, he will bring it back to Oxford. But be careful what you say. Confine yourself to telling her about your excellent health and the splendid company you keep. Messages can always be intercepted.'

Intercepted messages, thought Thomas. Yes. 'Thank you, Simon. If you can provide paper and ink, I'll write a letter this evening.' They walked slowly around the garden, which was enclosed by a high wall. The wall was old, its bricks and mortar brown and moss-covered. Near the gate, however, a short section had recently been repaired. It stood out against the rest of the wall, and caught Thomas's eye. The bricks were new and had been correctly laid so that the vertical lines of mortar between them did not meet. One row began with a whole brick, the next with a half, so that after two bricks in each row, one could make out four distinct vertical patterns. Thomas's memory stirred. 'You'd better bring plenty of paper and ink, Simon.' he said, 'And please bring the message and my working papers. I may need them.'

As instructed, Thomas confined his letter to Margaret to assurances about his own welfare and to earnest inquiries about her health and that of the girls. He promised to return home soon. The town, the castle, the message, and the Abbey, would have to wait until he did so. Abraham's foul murder he might never tell her about. Having finished his letter, he turned to the message. It had not, unfortunately, magically decrypted itself, and there it lay before him, challenging him to reveal its secrets. Forty five digits – he guessed fifteen numbers of three digits each – four hundred and fifty six letters, separated by ninety seven spaces, occupying ten lines on one sheet of paper. And possibly hiding something of grave importance to the outcome of the war.

He looked again at his own text:

ONEEYISBROWNYETTHEOTHERISBLUE

and its encryption, using THOMAS as the keyword, as

HUSQYBZPDOOGFSFTZXVHTEJBZPXUW

There were the repetitions of BZP, coinciding wth ISB in the plaintext, and there was the gap of eighteen letters between the start of the first sequence and the start of the second.

He turned back to the encrypted message. The numbers would have to wait. He would gamble on their being codewords, and therefore outside the encryption of the rest of the text. There were the seven repeated three-letter sequences – RFU, WHT, QFV, RVV, EKW, IFS, WWJ – and one four-letter sequence – WZUD, which he had marked by putting a line under them. The letter-distances between all repeating sequences were divisible by five, one, and themselves, but by no other number. One letter only would have meant a single shift and could be discounted. But there might be more repetitions. Finding them was laborious work and he could have missed some. If his theory was right, however, and his simple test suggested that it was, the distances between any unnoticed repetitions would also be divisible by five, and would be repeated in the plaintext, albeit with different letters.

Or could repetitions occur by some other means? He experimented with his own random sequences of letters, encrypting them using the Vigenère square and with keywords of different lengths. In ten separate sequences, just one repetition of three letters occurred in the encryption which did not coincide directly with a repetition in the plaintext. In this one instance, different sequences of letters in the plaintext had been encrypted using the same letters of the keyword. Deciding that nine out of ten was good enough, he christened the odd one out 'cuckoo', and ignored it. The keyword used on the intercepted message had five letters, and he would proceed from there.

That evening, Simon came to collect the letter to Margaret. As usual, he brought food from the Abbey's kitchen, which they shared, and grim news from Oxford. New taxes were being levied on the townspeople, and the colleges were being forced to supply new regiments to defend the town. Even the college servants were not exempt.

The mention of college servants reminded Thomas of Silas Merkin. He must try to contact Silas. 'Not actions likely to endear the King and his court to the people.'

'Indeed not. The Queen, too, is despondent. Her mood, as ever, reflects that of the King.'

'And Jane? Have you seen her?'

'I have. She is well, and asks after you. An admirer, Thomas, I fancy.'

'Come now, Simon, I hardly think so. We get on well. Nothing more.'

'Well, Jane would like to visit you. I'm reluctant to arrange it because she would learn where you are, which might be dangerous for her and for you. She's probably being watched, and Rush must on no account learn of your whereabouts. '

'It would cheer me greatly to see her, Simon. Can you not think of a safe way for her to come?'

'If you wish it, I'll try. But do not raise your hopes. Rush's men are everywhere.'

'And what of dear Abraham, Simon?'

'The coroner released his body today. He will be buried in two days' time at the Church of St Barnabas, just outside the west wall. He liked the place. The funeral is set for ten.'

Thomas was silent. He felt guilty for not having grieved properly for his old friend, and now he could not attend his funeral. He would have to mourn in private. 'Here's the letter, Simon.' he said, handing it over, 'God willing, it will arrive safely, and that there is a reply.'

The next morning, Simon did not visit, and Thomas's breakfast was brought by an elderly monk who could see little and said nothing. When he had eaten, Thomas laid the encrypted message out on the table and studied it again. It was still the same:

URF UBD HE XQB TF KGA OEMD RRFUO TLC WMG LRB WHT R XHGORKZ IO KPW769 WA MQFV BVMF HPL ZFTD RVV57 4SEWMFREJ VGL SVKMGE 852 GTSC WZTD QE

TIJG IVL GJT RA KDOE IK EOJAAQLV GGJR MQU IOIGSI GRQF HBFZG JGY ALG EE OLWEEA GJR YIFS1 82AEL2 64SGE SC AAD ZVY JP KP WXR JB JTN XBZ77 5XNW WJBS LA LWAK371 EAIH TPA AD RVV BAP TWPVV AGDN WWJ URR VUT IW EW HTI QCT WY QDT37 1IE852 769UMHT RKC CONT WSGV WMG IEN DJEE KW IHV ZW PNU EAIH371 ZV GJR YIFSS NQ DA BV NGGCVL LD SVMC IRLKW DN KMJ BS WINDU IITAE KW42177 5OX LCIVK IJM LXMV IFS PCI UT FFZ SEPI MZTNJQGCOW3 71E ZDWZTD QE SZGJ GYB LD 574SKIFS RVIV N GFL OX LC QFV WV AZPLCJJX NX IF TNU BG IHZA OP RJWGC

And still it revealed nothing of itself. Having been intercepted nearly two weeks ago, it might, in any case, no longer be useful – a thought he quickly put aside. His job was to decrypt this text, whatever it turned out to be.

Proceeding on the assumptions that it had indeed been encrypted using a Vigenère square and that the keyword consisted of five unrepeated letters, Thomas wrote out each of the letters that would have been encrypted using the first letter of the keyword. Ignoring all numbers and spaces, he began with the first letter, U, followed by the sixth, D, the eleventh, B, and each following fifth letter, until he had listed ninety two letters. In a text of four hundred and fifty six letters, the first letter of the keyword would have been used ninety two times, and the other letters ninety one times. It was painstaking work and easy to make a mistake. He worked slowly.

Next he added up the number of times each letter had been used. He found that the frequencies ranged from ten (T) and eight (D, G, I, J), to none at all (F, M, O, Y, Z). He allowed himself a small smile. This distribution looked promising. The letter E would almost certainly be represented by one of the letters appearing most often, and the others would also represent common letters such as A, O, I, and T. He looked again at his square. If T represented E, the alphabetical shift dictated by the first letter of the keyword was fifteen. This would mean that the voids would represent Q, B, D, J, and K. Apart perhaps from the D, that was entirely plausible. And when he checked the other frequent letters, T emerged as a near certainty for E. If D represented E, for instance, the shift would be twenty five places, I would represent J, and J would represent K. Even allowing for the possibility of the word KING being in the text, eight appearances each of J and K was very unlikely. He would assume that the absence of D was an anomaly, and settle for T representing E – a shift of fifteen places. If he was right, the first letter of the plaintext was F – a shift of fifteen places from the first letter of the ciphertext, U, and, most important of all, revealing that the first letter of the keyword was P. So far so good. Monsieur Vigenère was smiling. He turned to the second letter.

Again he wrote out all the letters in the ciphertext which had been encrypted, this time by the second letter of the keyword, counted the frequency of each, and applied the same logic to the result. It made nonsense. If any of the most frequent letters represented E, there would be no R's, three Q's and two X's, in the second letter sequence. Thomas threw down his quill, splattering ink on his papers, and cursed. Either he had been wrong all along, or he had made a mistake in writing down the letters or in counting them. He checked his counting. It was correct. He cursed again. He would have to work his way laboriously through the text to search for a mistake. But not before he had had a rest. He lay on the bed and closed his eyes.

When he opened them again, it was dark. He lit a candle and returned to the text. He rewrote the second list of letters, starting and ending with R. When he compared it to the original list which had proved useless, his mistake was obvious. In the seventh line, he had missed the double S and jumped from listing the second letters to listing the third. The first jump had caused all the rest to be wrong. No wonder the letter distribution had been chaotic. Montaigne spoke sternly. 'If only talking to oneself did not look mad, no day would go by without my being heard growling to myself "You silly shit"'. 'Merci, Monsieur' replied Thomas.

The first glimmers of light were appearing through the barred window above his bed. Astonished that he had slept for so long, he undressed, splashed his face with water, and put on the habit and sandals he had worn in the garden. Taking the elm branch for a walking stick, he slipped quietly out of the door and into the courtyard of the Abbey. He could hear voices in the chapel, but saw no-one. All at prayer, no doubt. A prayer for Thomas Hill would be welcome, if only the monks knew who he was. The key to the monks' door within the huge Abbey gate was in the lock. Thomas let himself out, and turned east towards Oxford.

Within the hour, having passed only a milkmaid and two boys gathering mushrooms, he saw the steeple of the Church of St Barnabas above a small copse of oaks. He was hungry and thirsty. With no money for food, he would have to rely on nature. A narrow stream ran alongside the copse. Lying on his stomach on the bank, he could just reach the water, and, with cupped hands, slake his thirst. He took a small pebble from the stream and put it in the pocket of his habit. In the copse, he found blackberries. Water and berries for breakfast. Not as good as Margaret's bread with cheese and eggs, but it would have to do. He found a comfortable place from which he could watch the church unobserved, and sat down to wait.

The church bell started ringing as the funeral procession approached from the direction of the town. It was a small gathering – just Silas Merkin and three others carrying the coffin, a handful of elderly mourners, and Simon de Pointz. Thomas slipped the pebble under his foot, took up the elm branch, and limped around to join the back of the procession as it entered the graveyard. No-one appeared to notice him. He kept his hood on and his head down, and when they reached the grave in which Abraham Fletcher would be laid to rest, stood a little back from the other mourners.

The service was mercifully brief. Some prayers and a few words from the parson, before the coffin was lowered into the grave. Abraham, sensible, unsentimental Abraham, would have approved. Thomas turned to leave. Better to be away before the others. He limped back down the path towards the graveyard gate. Glancing up, he saw two men, both armed, standing just outside it. Rush's men, without a doubt. He could not turn back without drawing attention to himself, so he continued on down the path, hoping that the two men would take no interest in a limping monk.

As he approached, however, one of them called out. 'Good morning, father, a sad day. Was Master Fletcher a friend?' Thomas said nothing. These men would have his description, and to reply, he would have to raise his head. The man spoke again. 'I asked if Master Fletcher was a friend. Do you not answer a civil question?' With no idea what else to do, Thomas stayed silent and kept limping towards them. The two men stepped in front of the gate and barred his way.

A hand gripped his shoulder, and a voice behind him said, 'You must forgive Father Peter, gentlemen. He's deaf as well as lame. He and I were old friends of Master Fletcher. I will see Peter safely home.' Rush's men shrugged, and let them pass. Simon kept a firm hand on Thomas's shoulder until they were well out of sight and out of earshot. Beyond the copse, they stopped and Simon released his grip. Thomas bent to remove the pebble. 'For the love of God, Thomas, what do you think you're doing? Rush himself might have been here.' Simon was furious.

'It was necessary.'

'Necessary? Necessary to be arrested and hanged? Or necessary to be thrown back into that cell?'

'I was released on the orders of the Queen.'

'Thomas, you know perfectly well that that won't stop Rush finding a way of silencing you. You acted rashly.'

'Then I apologise. My confinement is irksome. I needed to see the sky and to hear voices.'

'In that case, I will accompany you back to the Abbey. You can look at the sky while listening to my voice.'

As they walked, Simon described the mood at court. Following the death of so many loyal friends at Newbury, the King was still suffering from a deep melancholy, which the murder of Abraham Fletcher had only made worse. His Majesty now saw treachery behind every smile and a spy in every room. Rush had protested about Thomas's release, claiming to have proof absolute of his guilt, while the Queen had insisted on her faith in Jane's assurance of his innocence. Rush had demanded to know where Thomas was hiding, and did not believe that the Queen had not been told. In his present state of mind, there was no telling what the King might do. 'Did I tell you,' asked Simon as they reached the Abbey gate, 'that Rush's father was a gaoler in the Tower? The story goes that he took a bribe to let a wealthy merchant, accused of treason, escape, and used the money for his son's education.'

'How do you know that?'

'We monks have ways of knowing things, Thomas, and we like to gossip. It's our besetting sin.'

'What else do you know about him?'

'Only that, as a young man, he studied at Cambridge and was friendly with Hampden and Pym, both scholars at Oxford. Hampden, of course, is dead, and Pym, they say, hasn't long to go. Let us hope that they are soon joined by their old friend.'

'A trifle unchristian, Simon, don't you think?'

'No, Thomas, I do not think. The man's evil. He should be in hell. And if you decrypt the message and provide proof that he's a traitor, the sooner we'll send him there. Have you made any progress?'

'As a matter of fact, I might have.' replied Thomas, trying not to sound smug. 'I shall know for certain by this evening.'

'Good. I shall call tomorrow morning. I trust you'll be able to tell me more then.'

Back in his room, Thomas started again on the second keyword letter. Two letters stood out in his list – R and E – both with ten appearances. He would assume one of them represented E. He started with R. If R represented E, the shift was seventeen. That would mean that the voids – J, K, X, Y, Z – would represent

A, B, O, H, and I. Impossible. Suddenly, however, it was obvious. The uncommon letters J, K, X, Y, and Z represented themselves, and E represented E. The shift was twenty six, and the second letter of the keyword was A. So the second letter of the text, R, was itself. He had the first two letters of the keyword, P and A, and the first two letters of the text, F and R.

The third letter was easy. With fourteen appearances, V had five more than the second highest, E. And if E represented itself again, the keyword would start with an unlikely PAE. When he checked the voids with the shift of seventeen dictated by V, there were no oddities. He settled for V as E, which gave him the third letter of the keyword, R, and the third letter of the text, O. FRO.. had the look of FROM. He moved speedily on to the fourth letter.

This one also looked easy. With eleven appearances, I was the most frequent letter, followed by A and Q, with eight each. He tackled I first. It worked. With I's shift of eight, the voids would represent uncommon letters. Better still, it would make the fourth letter of the text M, and the first word FROM, as he had hoped. Thomas now had four letters of the keyword – PARI. 'I do hope it's PARIS,' he said out loud, 'Monsieur Montaigne would be much amused.'

It took longer than Thomas expected to find out. In the fifth sequence, neither G, with thirteen appearances, nor W, with eight, could represent E. The voids were too unlikely. He tried D and L, both with six. Neither worked. So he tried the other way around. If the keyword was PARIS, the fifth letter of the text, B, must represent J, a shift of eighteen. Using PARIS, he quickly decrypted the next three letters of the text, DHE, revealing OHN. This message had been sent by a man named John.

Thomas was half way through decrypting the whole message when the old monk brought his dinner. He gobbled it down without noticing what it was, and resumed his work. After another hour, he was able to write out the full text, putting his assumptions about the code numbers in brackets:

FROM JOHN PYM TO COLONEL CROMWELL OUR LATEST APPROACH TO THE [KING]
HAVING BEEN SPURNED AND [LONDON] DEFENCES NOW SECURE [OXFORD] PLAN WILL BE CARRIED OUT AS SOON AS POSSIBLE. YOUR VICTORY AT GAINSBOROUGH
STRENGTHENS OUR HAND. [182?] AND [264?] ARE BUILDING UP THEIR STRENGTH.
[775?] INFORMS US THAT [QUEEN] WITH CHILD AND MAY LEAVE SOON FOR FRANCE.
IF WE STRIKE WHILE [QUEEN] IN [OXFORD], [KING] MUST ACKNOWLEDGE OUR INFLUENCE THERE AND WITH [QUEEN] IN OUR HANDS WI LL BE FORCED TO SEEK TRUCE ON TERMS FAVOURABLE TO [421?]. [775?] WILL ADVISE TIME AND PLACE FOR APPREHENSION OF [QUEEN] WHO WILL BE BROUGHT TO [LONDON]. STAND READY. GOD WI LLING WE SHALL BRI NG AN END TO THIS WAR SOON.

He guessed from the context that the numbers 769 and 371 were codes for the King and Queen, and that 574 and 852 were London and Oxford. 182, 264, and 421 probably did not matter much. The critical code was 775. If it could be shown who 775 was, the traitor and murderer would be revealed. A pity the letters of his name had not been encrypted with the cipher. He would wager his life that they would spell out RUSH.

Thomas sat and stared at the message. No wonder it had been encrypted with the Vigenère square, complicated further by numerical codes, and hidden in the messenger's hat. Simon was due in the morning, but if the Queen was in danger of being abducted to London, should he hurry immediately to Merton? If he did, would he be admitted? And if he were, would he be heard? He decided that the Queen would be safe in her lodgings at Merton, with the college gates closed and guarded, and her own Lifeguards on watch. Anyone attempting to apprehend her would surely do so when she had left the college.

Sleep was out of the question. He made careful copies of his decryption and of the encrypted message, replicating as best he could the encrypter's hand. It was something he always did when making a copy, just as he always tried to find a way into the encrypter's mind. Then he lay on the bed and waited for dawn. One eye is brown yet the other is blue.

Chapter 10

A loud knock on the door signalled the arrival of Simon bearing breakfast, and accompanied by another, shorter, monk. 'Good morning, Thomas. Here's your breakfast, and a letter from Romsey. I do hope you've recovered from your exertions yesterday.' Simon was always unspeakably cheerful in the early morning. He handed Thomas the letter. 'And we want to know how the work is going. Have you made progress?'

'We?' asked Thomas, looking pointedly at the other monk who had so far kept his face hidden under his hood.

'Ah. Of course.' Simon nodded to his companion, whose hood came off to reveal a serenely smiling Jane Romilly.

'Good morning, Thomas. We thought to surprise you, although the disguise was necessary to gain access to the Abbey. The Abbot would not approve of a lady visitor.'

Torn between Jane, the letter, and the decrypted message, Thomas blathered. 'Lady Romilly. Jane. An unexpected pleasure. How are you? Well, I trust. And the Queen? Is she well?'

Jane raised an eyebrow. 'The Queen's spirits are low, but she is well, thank you. As am I.'

'Good, good. Excellent. That is a comfort. It's well that you've come. I have news. The message is decrypted. Here it is.' Thomas passed his decryption to Simon, who read it twice, and handed it to Jane.

'The brackets, Thomas? Guesses?' asked Simon.

'Guesses, yes, from the context. 182 and 264 could be any of their commanders, and 421 may be Parliament. They matter little. It's 775 we need to know.'

'We know it's Rush.' said Jane.

'We do, but this is not proof. Rush would just laugh at it.'

'Are you quite certain of the decryption, Thomas?' asked Simon.

'Quite certain. The idea I mentioned worked.'

'Then, proof or no proof, the Queen is in grave danger of being abducted. We're lucky they haven't already tried, if this is their plan. The King must be told at once. Jane and I will leave immediately.'

'Why me?' asked Jane, 'You'll travel faster without me, and I can add nothing to the task. Go alone, Simon, and I will wait here until you return.'

'Leave you here? The Abbot would never speak to me again if he found out. A lady alone in the Abbey. My soul would be in mortal danger. Yours too, I daresay.'

'Nonsense, Simon. Your soul is quite safe, as mine shall be. Thomas will make sure of it, won't you Thomas?'

'Certainly, I will. Go, Simon, and return as soon as you've warned the King and Queen. I'll show Jane how a Vigenère cipher works.'

'Very well. Lock the door after me. And be here when I return.'

'Read your letter, Thomas,' said Jane, when Simon had gone, 'and then we'll eat.'

Thomas broke the seal and read the letter. It was short and direct. Margaret thanked him for writing, albeit belatedly, and was glad to learn that he was in good health. She and the girls were also well, but missed him greatly. Lucy asked if he would be home for her birthday in October. The town had been quiet since he left. News of the war arrived daily, occasionally something about the King and Queen in Oxford. And, finally, she had received two unsigned letters advising her to take great care of herself and her daughters in these troubled times. The hand was untutored and the grammar poor, and she had dismissed them as the work of some troublesome mischief-maker. Still, she hoped they would see Thomas soon. They all sent fondest love.

Uncertain quite what to make of this, Thomas read it out to Jane. 'I'm sure it's no more than a local man with his eye on a handsome widow. While you're away, perhaps he's hoping to persuade Margaret that she should take a husband. Can you think of anyone who might do that?' she asked.

'Several, but I'm not so sure. Margaret wouldn't have mentioned it unless she had some concern.'

Jane rose and took his hands in hers. 'Be calm, Thomas. Margaret and your nieces merely want to see you safely home. We must deliver you to them just as soon as we can. Now let us eat our breakfast, and then you can show me this fiendish square that has brought so much grief.'

'Why are the Queen's spirits low, Jane? asked Thomas, as they ate.

'Her Majesty's mood is a mirror of the King's. When he laughs, so does she. When he is despondent, so is she. When he is anxious, his stammer gets worse, and that makes him angry. Then the Queen is angry, and the mood at court is black.'

'Was it Newbury that so affected him?'

'Partly, yes. The carnage, they say, was fearful, and he lost many friends. Falkland especially he mourns. And Essex has reached London with most of his army intact. Newbury was a disaster. Three thousand men lost, and for nothing. But there has also been news from the north. The Scots have signed Pym's Solemn League and Covenant. They have promised military support against the King in return for a guarantee of no interference in the Scottish Church, and reforms to the Church of England. Her Majesty is particularly vexed, and the King now expects the Scottish Covenanters to march south in the new year. For a Scot, it is doubly hard to bear.'

'And it could alter the course of the war. If the King has to strengthen his defences in the north, his forces will be greatly stretched. Parliament will seek to take advantage. I fear we'll see a good deal more bloodshed next year.'

'If only a peace could be negotiated. Talks have been going on for months, yet that is all they are. Talks. And, by all accounts, ill-tempered talks. Ill-tempered talks, and no listens. Talks without listens achieve very little, Thomas, don't you think?'

'I do. And I think you should be a writer, Lady Romilly. You have a way with words.'

'And what should I write? Plays, essays, philosophy?'

'You should write poetry. Lady Wroth's poems have become quite popular, and I'll wager this war will find more ladies putting quill to paper. Love, war, death, misery – the very stuff of poetry. Why not try your hand?'

'Would you be my tutor, Thomas? I should need guidance.'

'Naturally. That is exactly why I suggested it. Shall we begin at once?'

'We shall.'

Three hours later, tutor and pupil, arms and legs entwined, awoke in the narrow bed. The first lesson had proved so good that Jane had insisted upon a second, declaring it afterwards to have been even better. Thomas rolled off the bed and stretched. 'You're an excellent pupil, Lady Romilly. Alas, however, I have neither wine nor sweetmeats to offer you. Instead, would you care for instruction in the matter of the Vigenère cipher?'

'If I must, Master Hill.'

'Then perhaps we should clothe ourselves. The monk has seen my naked form before, but not, I trust, yours. He might be laid low with guilt.'

'How did he come to see you naked, Thomas, if I may ask?' inquired Jane, wriggling into the borrowed habit.

Thomas told her the story of their journey, dwelling at length on the flea-infested habit and the shaggy inkcaps. 'Fortunately, my dear, I am made of strong stuff, and survived the journey unharmed. Otherwise, you would have been robbed in the street, might never have seen the inside of Oxford gaol, and would certainly never have dressed as a monk.'

Jane stuck out her tongue. 'Nonsense. The robber would have run off in fear of his life, I had planned to visit other and more deserving friends in the gaol anyway, and I find this habit quite comfortable. I might well have acquired one for special occasions.'

'And I might yet be King.'

Thomas told her about ONE EYE IS BROWN YET THE OTHER IS BLUE, and how it had led him to realise that Monsieur Vigenère's square was not one cipher, but as many ciphers as there were letters in the keyword. 'Just as well my eyes aren't green.' was all Jane had to say on the matter. Thomas's lesson in decryption she found less interesting than his earlier efforts. The fiendish square soon forgotten, they sat together on the bed and waited for Simon. 'Now that you have decrypted the message, perhaps the King will send you home.' she said. Thinking of the lady sitting beside him, Thomas did not reply.

By the time Simon arrived, they were both starving. 'Have you brought food, Simon?' demanded Jane, when Thomas let him in, 'It's been a long time since breakfast, and studying the French cipher is hungry work.'

'I have not. Your stomachs will have to wait. The King wishes to see Thomas immediately, and we must leave at once. There are horses waiting.'

'What does he make of the decryption?' asked Thomas.

'He fears for the Queen. Other than that, he said little.'

'What about Rush?'

'I did not see Rush.'

'Shall we tell the King what we know about Rush?'

'No. It would be too dangerous.'

Thomas gathered up his papers, carefully rolling up the original message, his copy, and his copy of the decryption, and tucking them inside his shirt. Within two minutes they had left the Abbey and were on their way.

They rode first to Merton, where Simon escorted Jane, still in her monk's habit, to her rooms, and returned at once to take Thomas to Christ Church, where the King awaited them. They were shown into a receiving room in the Deanery, now the Royal Palace, where they waited for the King to appear from his private apartments. When he entered, they bowed their heads. Thomas looked up and flinched. An unmistakable figure, all in black, his face hidden in shadow, stood behind the King.

'So, Master Hill.' His Majesty said quietly. Thomas had noticed that the King's voice was never raised. Perhaps it had to do with his stammer. 'And where have you been hiding, since I returned from seeing loyal friends die in a just cause? We have been most exercised by your disappearance, and the good Master Rush has had to make other arrangements for the security of our messages.'

Thomas glanced at Simon, who nodded. 'I have been at the Abbey near Botley, Your Majesty. Father de Pointz ensured that neither the Abbot nor the monks knew who I am or why I was there.'

'And why, pray, did you choose to hide in an Abbey?'

Before Thomas could reply, Simon spoke for him. 'If I may, Your Majesty, Master Hill was near death when he left the gaol, and had to be nursed back to health. The monks have a number of excellent remedies, which proved efficacious. He also needed solitude in order to work on the intercepted message. Happily, in that too he was successful.'

'So it seems.' said the King, stretching out his hand to take a paper handed to him by Rush. 'And a most alarming message it is. If true, my dear Queen is in grave danger. I have already ordered that her guard be doubled, and that she stay within the walls of Merton at all times. If false, it must have been designed to cover up some devious plot. Be sure that, if that is the case, we shall uncover its nature and punish the traitors behind it.'

'Your Majesty,' said Thomas, 'The message was given to me to decrypt by Master Fletcher. As you are aware, until he was foully murdered, all intercepted messages were passed to Master Fletcher. If it is false, its contents must have been intended to be revealed. Yet it was encrypted by means of a cipher that is seldom used, and which, until now, neither Master Fletcher nor I believed had ever been broken. It was also hidden. Its writer did not want it found or decrypted.'

'It may or may not have been hidden. Master Rush will trace its source. He will find the man who brought it to Oxford, and any others through whose hands it may have passed. No doubt, his interrogations will reveal their guilt or innocence in the matter. However, you too, Master Hill, as Master Rush has pointed out, are not above suspicion. We trusted Master Fletcher, but we can all be deceived. He might have been deceived by you. What have you to say to that?'

'Your Majesty, Abraham Fletcher was a good man and your loyal servant. As am I. I make no pretence of liking this, or any other, war, and I wish to see it over. If I can hasten the day when it ends justly, I shall be content. I have no reason, no reason whatever, to act against Your Majesty's interests.'

Rush stepped forward. 'With Your Majesty's permission. Master Hill, the coroner had grounds for suspecting you of the murder of Abraham Fletcher. As you rightly say, a foul murder. When I visited you in gaol, you spurned my offer of help. I wonder why. And when, through the kindness of Her Majesty, misplaced kindness in my opinion, you were released, you hid. Furthermore, you now ask His Majesty to believe that you have broken a cipher which has remained unbroken for nearly a hundred years. A trifle far-fetched, is it not?'

'All ciphers can be broken. This one was no different. It needed but a stroke of fortune to set me on the right road to breaking it. Would Your Majesty care for me to show you how?'

The King was growing impatient. 'Not now. The Queen is safe under guard at Merton. For the present, that is what matters. Father de Pointz will return to the Queen's service, and you, Master Hill, will be confined here in Christ Church. Master Rush does not believe your story, the Queen, plainly, does. We will think presently on what more is to be done. You will not leave the college grounds for any purpose. If you do so, you will be branded a traitor, and treated accordingly. Now leave us.'

Thomas and Simon bowed, turned, and left the room. Thomas was immediately flanked by two of the King's Lifeguards. 'You know where I am, Simon.' he said. 'Be sure to visit, and bring Jane with you. His Majesty said nothing about visitors.'

'I shall. And send word if you need me.'

The guards led Thomas through an arch into a small courtyard behind the Hall. They entered one of the dorways that opened on to the courtyard, and climbed two flights of stairs. There a door was opened with a key produced by one of the guards, and Thomas was ushered in. The guards left without locking the door. So much for being sent home. Thomas inspected the room. The King must have ordered it prepared for him. It was spacious and comfortable, with a writing table, chairs, bookshelves, a fire laid in the grate, and a window which looked out on to the courtyard. A bed stood against the wall farthest from the door. One stinking cell, one Abbey, and two colleges. Four places to rest his head so far. He wondered if there would be a fifth.

The papers went under the bed. When he left the room, they would go with him, so that no intruder would find them. He had nothing else but the miserable clothes he stood in. The monks had done their best to clean them, but four days in Oxford Castle had taken their toll. His precious copy of Montaigne and the small bag of money were long gone. He would send a message to Jane for clothes. Until then, he could do little but read, think, and walk in the college grounds. Not that the grounds were at all alluring. The main courtyard housed a cattle pen, and two others acted as stables. As well as overblown army officers and obsequious courtiers, he would have humble grooms and cowmen for company. And Rush. He would be here, lurking like a hungry black crow with its eye on a nest of fledglings. Prenez garde, Thomas, this crow won't let you fly away again.

Luckily, his predecessor must have been a scholarly man, interested in ancient history. There was plenty of reading on the shelves of the room. Plutarch and Tacitus, Homer and Cicero. Thomas spent the rest of the day in his room with them. But while his intellect was occupied, his imagination was not. Margaret must have been much alarmed by the threatening letters even to have mentioned them. An untutored hand, she had said. Jane had suggested a local admirer. Thomas doubted it. Untutored hand or not, it could only be Rush. Threats to two innocent children. Monstrous. And almost certainly just to get rid of Thomas. Yet, with Rush, one could not be sure. The threats might be carried out just for the pleasure of it. This was a man who had foully murdered Erasmus Pole and Abraham Fletcher, had tried to murder Thomas by having him run down in the street, then had him thrown into a cell from which he had been fortunate to emerge alive, and was plotting to have the Queen taken prisoner and used as a pawn in this cruel, needless, war. And, worst of all, he had the ear and trust of the King. Without undeniable proof of the man's guilt, Thomas could say nothing. The King would simply assume that he was trying to divert attention from himself, and have him hanged as a traitor. Thomas Hill against Tobias Rush. Not much of a contest.

Jane arrived that evening with a bundle of clothes and a bottle of claret. 'Why am I forever visiting you with food or drink, Thomas?' she demanded, 'Prisons, Abbeys, college rooms, where next, I wonder? And you never have any suitable clothes. Try these.'

Thomas took the bundle and removed his ragged shirt.

'Would that I could visit you, Jane. Alas, His Majesty has seen fit to keep me here until he makes up his mind whether or not I'm a traitor.' he said, pulling a new linen shirt over his head.

'I know. Simon told me. And if it wasn't for the Queen, I daresay you'd be back in the castle. Much as he trusts Rush, the King finds it impossible to go against her wishes. Remember she brought three thousand men with her to Oxford. The King thinks she's a goddess.'

'And I have you to thank for persuading her that I'm innocent. Otherwise, I daresay I'd be dead.'

'Entirely innocent of all crimes, you are, Thomas. Innocent of all wordly matters, you are not. If you have finished trying on those clothes, I suggest you take them off and try a little of this excellent claret. I shall do the same.'

Some time later, Thomas sat on the bed, his back to Jane. She reached out to trace the line of his spine with her finger. 'The Queen will soon be departing for Exeter. When she does, Simon and I must go with her. And you will be left to face the King and Rush, alone. Is there anything we can do before we go?'

'Not unless you can force a confession out of Rush, my dear. There is just not enough evidence against him.'

'The Queen dislikes him as much as we do, but I don't think she believes he's a traitor. She has too much faith in the King's judgement.'

'Then I shall have to take my chances. Perhaps Rush will make a mistake.'

'Perhaps he will. Now, Master Hill, kindly escort me to the gate. It's time I attended the Queen.'

They dressed quickly. Thomas put the papers under his new

shirt, and they walked down to the heavily guarded gate. As they approached, two guards stepped forward and blocked their path. 'That's far enough, Master Hill. We have orders to make sure you stay inside the college.' said one of them, his hand on the hilt of his sword.

Jane glared at the guard. 'In that case, Thomas, I shall bid you farewell here. As long as I may be permitted to pass?'

'Our orders are for Master Hill, madam. Master Rush only wants to be informed of his visitors, who may come and go as they please.'

'Then be so good as to inform Master Rush that Lady Romilly has visited Master Hill, and was pleased to find him in excellent condition.'

The guard raised an eyebrow. 'That I will, madam'.

The King's summons came the next morning. Master Hill was to attend His Majesty in the Great Hall at once. Thomas made ready, the papers again inside his shirt, and left immediately. The King sat in his customary place at the far end of the Hall, and Thomas approached in the manner in which he had been instructed. The King clearly enjoyed observing his subjects like this. Otherwise he would meet them in his apartments. He sat quite still, and waited. As before, he was surrounded by courtiers, including Rush, and, as before, he spoke quietly. 'Master Hill, I am persuaded by Master Rush that it would be wise to demand from you a description of the cipher you claim has never before been broken, and an explanation of the manner in which you broke it.'

Thomas had been half expecting this. 'That I will certainly do, Your Majesty, if you wish it. However, since I do not believe that there is anyone else in England who has the means to break the cipher, I suggest, with respect, that an understanding of the decryption technique would be best kept to as few as possible. It may yet prove as great an asset as a loyal army.'

The King took a moment to consider this. 'Very well. You will demonstrate the cipher only to Master Rush and to me. We will begin at once.' While servants brought paper and ink, and all the courtiers but Rush left the Hall, Thomas took out his papers, and laid the square he had written out and the original message, on a table beside the King's seat. He began with the square.

'This is a Vigenère square, Your Majesty. The letters of the alphabet form the top row, and the numbers one to twenty-six the first column. A message is encrypted by use of a keyword, which dictates the encrypted letter which will replace each letter of the text. The intercepted message I decrypted used the keyword PARIS. Thus, the first letter of the message, F, was replaced by U.' He traced with a quill the column headed by F to where it intersected the row starting with P. 'The second letter of the message, R, was replaced by itself, because the second letter of the keyword is A.' He pointed to the first letter of the final row.

'What is the point of encrypting a letter as itself?'

'Unless the receiver of the message knows the keyword, Your Majesty, it is as good an encryption as any. Without the keyword, he cannot know, or even guess, that the letter A appears in it.'

‘And how did you discover that the keyword used in this message was PARIS?’ asked Rush.

Thomas explained how he had realised that the square created a number of mono-alphabetic ciphers, rather than a single poly-alphabetic one, and that he had found the length of the keyword, and thus the number of ciphers, by analysing the frequency of repeated letter sequences.

The King did not immediately grasp the importance of this. ‘And in what way did this lead you to a succesful outcome?’ he asked suspiciously. Thomas explained the theories of frequency analysis, and how he had applied them, once he had identified the five ciphers in use.

‘I was fortunate, Your Majesty, in that, in a text of this length, there were sufficient letters in each cipher to make analysis by letter frequency viable. Even then, it was not entirely straightforward. The fifth letter of the keyword, S, gave me the most difficulty.’

‘Master Rush, do you understand this?’ asked the King.

‘I do, Your Majesty. Master Hill’s explanation seems to me to be plausible, although one wonders why, if he was able to decrypt the message with comparative ease, the cipher has remained unbroken for so long.’

‘Prison walls, Master Rush.’ replied Thomas sharply, ‘Prison walls led me to the solution. When one has nothing to do but sit on an excrement-covered floor and stare at a stone wall, it helps to concentrate the mind. I recommend it to you.’

Rush ignored the remark. ‘This is the original message is it not? Did you make a copy?’

‘I did.’

'Then perhaps we may have it. We should keep both original and copy in a safe place.'

Thomas handed the copy to Rush, who examined it closely, as if looking for differences. With a smile, he placed it on the table beside the original. 'Your Majesty will see that both original and copy were written by the same hand.'

The King peered at the papers. 'It would seem so. How do you account for this, Master Hill?'

'When decrypting a message, it is my habit to put myself, as far as I can, in the shoes of the encrypter. Thus I try to copy his hand.'

'Then you have done it as well as any forger.' said Rush, 'His Majesty might find it difficult to believe this claim.'

'By your leave, Your Majesty,' Thomas replied, 'If Master Rush would write a sentence or two in his own hand, I will reproduce it, so that you are unable to tell the two apart.'

'What would you like me to write?' asked Rush.

'Let us try 'One eye is brown yet the other is blue'. That should be sufficient.'

Rush wrote the sentence and passed the quill to Thomas. With a quick glance at Rush's script, he wrote a copy underneath. It was an exact match. 'This proves only that, in addition to his other crimes, this man may be a forger, Your Majesty.' Rush spat out the words. The King looked thoughtful.

'You are a man of many talents, Master Hill. I would not want you for an enemy, and I would like to be convinced, as the Queen is, that you are a friend. Until I am, however, you will remain in Christ Church. Master Rush will conduct further inquiries.'

And how exactly will Master Rush do that, wondered Thomas, on his way back to his rooms, Threats? Torture? An accident? All three? If only he knew. One eye is brown yet the other is blue. The eyes of a lady soon to be accompanying the Queen to Exeter and thence to France. A lady much too beautiful and accomplished to be but a bookseller's wife. And yet, and yet…

Chapter 11

Even in times of trouble, the King and his household did not believe in stinting themselves, and for two days, Thomas enjoyed the offerings of the King's own cooks, labouring day and night to keep His Majesty happy. Breakfasts of buttered eggs and lamb cutlets, and dinners of roasted venison and beef, washed down with excellent wines purloined from the college cellars, did their best to keep his spirits up. The meals were brought to him in his rooms by a young kitchen boy, who must have been told to say nothing to the gentleman he was serving. Even Thomas's polite inquiry as to the boy's name was met with blank silence. They were a strange two days. Imprisoned in the college, suspected of treason and murder, yet dining on royal food and drinking royal wine, both served by a silent boy. Neither Jane nor Simon visited, and he spent most of his time with the ancients.

The King's summons came on the third morning. A guard escorted Thomas to the Hall, where the King waited with his courtiers around him, the Master of the Revels and the Court Painter among them. Just what we need, thought Thomas, dancing and portraits. Enough to frighten away any musketeer. To Thomas's surprise, Rush was not there. 'Master Hill, it appears that your skills are needed once more. Another message has been intercepted.' said the King, waving a paper at him. 'It was hidden in a sword case, and captured near Reading. With Master Rush away on important business, it has been delivered to me. Kindly tell me what you make of it.'

Thomas took the paper from the King's outstretched hand. The message was short – only two and a half lines – and written in a hand he did not know. He quickly counted the letters. There were one hundred and thirty four. No numbers and no spaces. No clues at all. 'Other than that it is short, Your Majesty,' he replied 'I can tell you nothing. I shall need time to analyse it.'

'Time, Master Hill, is one thing we do not have. The Queen will soon leave Oxford, and this message must be decoded before she does. She must not be put in any danger. How long will you need?'

'That depends upon the cipher used. If it is the Vigenère square again, I will have to find the keyword. In such a short message, that may be difficult. There may not be any repetitions, and the frequencies of letter sequences are unlikely to be helpful. There are too few of them.'

'And if it is not the square? What then?'

'Then I should be able to break it within a day.'

'In that case, you will attend us here tomorrow morning. We shall expect good progress, Master Hill. Pray remember that you are not a free man. The contents of this message must be revealed.'

'I shall do my best, Your Majesty.'

The King lent forward and spoke softly. 'Yes, Master Hill, I have no doubt that you will.'

Thomas laid the text out on the table in his room.

XZFMGMAYTDSXPMFMMVNLAJCLTSDVWXLPTICVIPSUGZSRSAAKOAWVIOJ
WBVEMWBVRPFNUFGSVTEHZWLEAVEVAILMDPIXBFEMWKLTTHOCACAVS
RXKBYOAAINAXLQEIHLZLCIAWES

One hundred and thirty four letters, in two and a half lines. Not much to go on, but he had faced worse. He held the paper up to the light of his window. The paper was good quality and the hand was an educated one. He could see no distinguishing marks or hidden symbols. It had been hidden in a sword case, which suggested that the decrypted text would be simple and direct. Senders of hidden messages did not expect them to be discovered, and did not usually bother to obscure their meaning, other than with a cipher. With luck, this one had been encrypted by means of a simple alphabetic substitution cipher or a keyword. He would start with those.

The word LEAVE, in the middle of the second line, leapt off the page. The letters EAV of LEAVE were also followed by EVA. That too might or might not be significant. And he noted the repetition of WBV and the four instances of double letters, but no other particular instances of letters appearing together. Partially coded messages were not unkown, especially if they were also hidden, and, if this was about the Queen, the word LEAVE might very well appear. But there were no other plain words. Why would one word alone appear unencrypted? It might be genuine, a trick, a mistake, or a coincidence. Or it might tell the receiver what the keyword was. He tried that first. Ignoring the second E, he tried a cipher alphabet starting LEAV, and continuing W, X, Y, Z, B, C …… It did not work. LEAVE was not a keyword dictating an alphabetic shift. He put LEAVE to one side.

To find a keyword or a simple shift, he would have to analyse the letter distribution. He counted the frequencies. At first glance, the distribution was encouraging. Without LEAVE, there was a single Q, two each of J, U, and Y, nine each of M and V, and twelve A's. Concentrating on the high numbers, he set about finding the most common letters E, A, and T. When that did not work, he tried the lowest numbers, looking for the least frequent letters, J, Q, X, and Z. That too did not work, and serious doubts were creeping in. If the sender of this message had used nulls or mis-spellings, the decryption would take longer, and the King would not be happy with longer. He tackled nulls first, trying every fifth, tenth, and twelfth letter, and re-analysing the distributions without them. From experience, he knew that these were the most likely places for nulls. It was long and tedious work, and it got him nowhere.

The long day turned into a long night. Every effort to pin down just one encrypted letter had failed, and Thomas was losing heart. Eight hours of toil had achieved nothing. By midnight, he had tried every form of frequency analysis he could think of, from single letters to sequences and juxtapositions, he had tried assuming the text included nulls and deliberate misspellings, and he had even tried guessing keywords which might have dictated an alphabetic shift. Nothing had worked. He went to bed exhausted, dreading tomorrow's meeting with the King and knowing that he would have to turn his attention, once again, to Monsieur Vigenère's square, and this time he would have to do so without knowing the length of the keyword. The text contained but one repetition, and one was not enough.

The King was in no mood for explanations or excuses. 'So, Master Hill, am I to understand that you have made no progress whatever?' he asked, impatiently tapping his stick on the floor.

'Other than the elimination of simple ciphers, I fear so, Your Majesty.' replied Thomas, trying to keep his voice steady. 'This message has been encrypted by a very cautious man indeed. He hid it, encrypted it with some complex method, and, I rather think, protected it further with tricks and deceptions. I can find no useful repetitions or clues.'

'So what is to be done?'

'I shall try Vigenère's cipher again, and the more unusual multi-alphabetic ciphers, Your Majesty. All ciphers can be broken. It just takes time.'

'As I have already advised you, Master Hill, of time we have little. We shall meet again here tomorrow morning. If you are not able then to advise me of progress, we will be forced to consider other options.' Thomas managed a tiny bow, followed by a swift retreat. This quiet little man, with his pointed beard, his limp, and his stammer, could be more threatening than any hectoring bully.

Simon was waiting for him when he returned to his room. The monk was sitting by the window reading The Iliad, a glass of Thomas's wine beside him. Apart from the habit, he looked for all the world like a contented teacher of classical literature. 'Ah, there you are, Thomas.' he said jovially, when Thomas walked in. 'An excellent claret. I do hope you don't mind my helping myself.'

'The claret I do not mind, Simon. It is your unspeakable cheerfulness at this hour of the day that I find offensive. Especially as I have just come from an uncomfortable meeting with the King.'

'Uncomfortable?'

'Most uncomfortable. Here I am, unable to leave the college for any reason, still under suspicion of murdering my old friend Abraham Fletcher and betraying secrets to the enemy, and now expected by the King to decrypt a message which so far has shown not the slightest inclination to be decrypted.'

'A new message? Is it our French friend, again?'

'I had hoped not, but I fear so and this time probably with extra protection. And the King wants it done immediately. He's reluctant to let the Queen leave Oxford without knowing what it says.'

'Naturally. No wonder your temper is short this morning. And what of Rush?'

'Not present. Away on the King's business. Or pretending to be. That's why the message has come to me. How is Jane?'

'Very well, and I bring you her greetings. The Queen has

kept her busy preparing for their journey, or she would have visited by now.'

'Return her greetings, please, and say that I hope her duties will allow her to call soon.'

'I shall. Now, what about this message? Can I be of any assistance?'

Thomas thought for a moment. A willing listener was always helpful. 'Perhaps you can. Fill the other glass, and let us examine the problem together.'

Thomas took the message from under his shirt and set it on the table. 'As you can see, it's short. Only one hundred and thirty four letters.'

'And no numbers, this time. Does that mean no coded words?'

'Not necessarily, although we shall assume that to begin with.'

'Is there any significance in the lack of spaces?'

'I doubt it. It might signify a different sender to the last one, or it might be the same sender disguising himself. There's no way of telling.'

'So what now?'

'Now we make a copy of the message, so that we can both study it. We are looking for clues. I have found only one repetition, WBV, but look again. It's easy to miss them. Here's my list of the letter frequencies. Concentrate on the most frequent and the least frequent. See if you can find any oddities. Note the word LEAVE in the second line. I can find no significance in it. Perhaps you can. I'm going to try possible Vigenère keywords.'

The copy made, both men set to work. Simon looked for clues, while Thomas tried LEAVE, and PARIS as keywords. When neither worked, he tried LONDON and Simon tried ROME. 'I know you'd like it to be ROME, Simon,' said Thomas, 'so try it, although I doubt they'd use it. It's too short and too Catholic.' One bottle of claret became two, food came and went, and still they had made no progress. By mid-afternoon neither of them had come up with the slightest sliver of a clue as to the method of encryption. Simon was the first to call a halt. 'Thomas, I'm not used to this type of work. I've been backwards and forwards over this damnable message and it has made my head ache. Shall we take a stroll?'

Thomas looked up from his page of numbers and letters. 'Odd, that. Praying used to make my head ache. Come on then, monk. A little air may help.'

With Thomas confined to the college, there was nowhere much to stroll other than round and round the big quadrangle in the middle of which noisy cattle waited to be milked or eaten. 'Are you really a Franciscan monk, Simon?' asked Thomas suddenly.

'Now that's an odd question.' replied Simon, 'Why would you think otherwise?'

'The words you used about yourself. Pragmatism and Humour. Not very monkly words.'

'Not all monks are dull recluses. I choose to live in the same world as you. I find both qualities useful.'

'And you don't behave like a monk. You travelled to Romsey to fetch me, disguised me as one of your own, protected me from Rush, and brought Jane to visit me in the Abbey.'

'Were these not monkly actions, Thomas? Except, perhaps, for the last, and even that was an act of kindness to you both. Even a monk knows worldly love when he sees it. Rest assured, Thomas, I am a monk.'

'As you wish.' They made another circuit of the quadrangle. 'Now, this accursed message. We'd better break it or I may not be anything much longer. This is what I think. We've tried everything I know and achieved nothing. I'm sure it's Vigenère again, this time without code words.'

'Why would the numbers have been omitted?' asked Simon.

'The strength of codes is that they can be quickly decoded by the intended recipient. In the case of the square, they also make the frequency analysis harder by reducing the number of letters in the text. This is a very short message, probably containing tricks. If the keyword has, say, five letters, there will be no more than twenty seven letters in each encryption. Too few to be much use, although I shall of course try.'

'And do you see Rush behind it?'

'I do. He's no fool. He suggested to the King that I show them how the decryption of the last message worked, he's realised that, unless it is very long, the length of a keyword can be worked out, and he's inserted nulls or mis-spellings or both, to throw unwelcome hounds off his scent. Why otherwise would the encryption be as it is? Rush wrote this message, it may well concern the Queen, and we must discover its contents.'

'What about the word LEAVE?'

'It must be a coincidence. When it came up, the encrypter left it there to confuse further. Such things happen. I'll leave LEAVE alone.'

'So a long night of counting letters and looking for vowels, is that it, Thomas?'

'It is.'

'I would gladly offer to help, but the Queen will expect me for her evening devotions.'

'Of course. I'm used to working alone.' They came to the college gate. 'Now be off with you, and please ask Jane to visit soon.'

'I shall. Goodbye, Thomas. I'll offer a prayer for you.'

A long night it would be. Thomas sent for more candles and adequate sustenance until morning. Each letter distribution would have to be counted and analysed separately. He would start with a four letter keyword and work his way up to eight. The chances of its being longer were remote. Too complicated and time-consuming to encrypt and decrypt. If he learnt nothing from that, he would have to look for nulls, just as he had before, only this time in the context of the square. He'd need Simon's prayers, or the meeting next morning with the King would not be a happy one.

It started badly. The first letter of a hypothetical four letter keyword yielded four I's, four T's, and six voids, and the other three letters produced similar distributions. Quite useless. Five and six letter keywords were no better. Shapeless distributions, offering no clues as to where the most common and uncommon letters hid. After fifteen separate counts, Thomas started making mistakes. He had to rewrite the list of letters produced by the third letter of a seven letter keyword, and miscounted twice. It was time for a short rest.

He was woken by a hammering on the door. Bleary-eyed

and thick-headed, he struggled off the bed and opened it. A guard stood outside. 'Master Hill, the King awaits you. Make haste, if you please.' God's wounds, he'd slept for five hours. There was no time to wash or dress. The King would have to receive him rumpled and unshaven. He stuffed the message inside his shirt, and followed the guard to the Hall.

After the usual preliminaries, Thomas stood before the King. And Tobias Rush stood behind him. 'Master Hill,' began the King, 'you do not look refreshed by sleep. I trust this means that you've broken the cipher?'

'Your Majesty, I have not, but you will be pleased to learn that I have made much progress, and expect to break it very soon.' It was a lie, and Thomas suspected that the King knew it. He was playing for time.

'I would be a great deal more pleased if you were able to tell me that you had broken the cipher, as would Master Rush.'

'Indeed I would, Your Majesty.' agreed Rush, with a smirk that the King could not see. 'As you know, I was unconvinced by Master Hill's explanation of his previous effort and his lack of progress now reinforces my view. I wonder whether Your Majesty would be well-advised to entrust the message to another, more reliable, man. I have someone suitable in mind. Master Hill would not then be needed, and could be sent home, or, if Your Majesty wished, held at your pleasure.'

The King raised an eyebrow. 'What have you to say to that, Master Hill?'

Thomas knew he had to take care. This was dangerous ground. Rush would have him thrown back into that cell as quick as you like. 'I am at Your Majesty's service. I ask you to believe me when I say that I have made good progress, and am confident of success. We are dealing with a very complex cipher, with only one hundred and thirty four letters to work on, and anyone taking over from me would wish to start again using his own techniques. He would not wish, as I would not, to accept the workings of someone else. That would create more delay, which could be fatal to our cause.'

The King hesitated. 'I have always found Master Rush's judgement to be sound. Yet there is something in what you say. You have one more day. If you cannot bring me the decrypted message tomorrow morning, you will be released from your duties. In that case, Master Rush will advise me on what further courses of action to take. Good day, Master Hill.'

A stay of execution, thought Thomas, walking back to his room. Damocles's sword still held by a thread above his head. Twenty four hours to break the cipher. To work, Thomas, to work.

His room was just as he had left it, except for one thing. His working papers – all but the original message under his shirt – had gone. While he had been with the King, Thomas had had an unwelcome visitor. Another one. A tidy one, but nevertheless unwelcome. And there was only one person who could have arranged it, knowing for certain that Thomas would be otherwise engaged. Not that there was the slightest reason to inform the King, or anyone else. Rush would simply accuse Thomas of destroying the papers himself in order to provide an excuse for failing to decrypt the message. And, on reflection, perhaps it was not such a bad thing. An uncluttered table might help unclutter the mind. He still had the message itself, and could, without much difficulty, resume where he had left off. Rush might even assume that the copy that had been taken was the original, and that Thomas had no other. All the more reason to surprise the repulsive creature.

He started by reworking the distribution arising from a seven letter keyword. When the first letter threw up one each of C, E, J, O, Q, V, X, and Y and two each of A, I, L, and S, he knew he was wasting his time. Not enough letters, with or without tricks. Unclutter the mind, forget this approach, Thomas, and think of something else.

But what else? How could he break a Vigenère cipher without being able to attack it by frequency analysis? And a Vigenère cipher he was quite sure it was. Anything else would by now have revealed itself, and it was just what the devious Rush would have done. Find his enemy's strength and render it useless. A short message, the cipher, and tricks. Unbreakable.

Thomas was standing by the window deep in thought when Simon burst in carrying a sack. He was ashen. 'Thomas, Jane has been attacked. She was found this morning in the river, unconscious, and having lost much blood.'

'Is she alive?'

'She is. Just.'

'What happened?'

'We don't know. She was found by a student walking beside the river. It must have been shortly after the attack, or she'd have been dead. He dragged her out and carried her to Magdalen. An officer's wife there recognised her and sent word to Merton. She's there now.'

'In the name of God, why?'

Simon laid a hand on Thomas's sleeve. 'That, my friend, I cannot say. Thomas, there's something else. I fear Jane was raped, and cruelly so.'

Thomas slumped on to the chair and closed his eyes. One eye is brown yet the other is blue. Present tense. Is, not was. 'I must see her.'

'Thomas, if you're caught outside Christ Church, you'll be hanged. And if Rush is behind this, he'll be watching for you, even if he believes Jane is dead.'

'I must see her.'

Simon sighed. 'I thought you'd say that.' He tipped the contents of the sack on to the floor. 'I've brought you a habit, and I have an idea. It's dangerous, but I can think of nothing else. To try and leave by the main gate would be suicidal.'

While Thomas undressed and put on the habit, Simon explained his plan. 'When the Queen arrived in Oxford, the King had gates built in to the east wall of Christ Church, the walls of Corpus Christi, and the west wall of Merton. They enable him to visit the Queen discreetly. They are guarded only when the King is with the Queen, and, except when in use, the only keys are kept in the King's and Queen's private apartments. I have borrowed the Queen's keys.'

'Does the Queen know?'

'She does not. Nor, yet, does she know about Jane. I will tell her when the outcome is known.'

'I'm ready. Let us try.'

'Are you quite certain, Thomas? This is extremely dangerous for you, and probably for me.'

'I wish to see Jane.'

'Very well. Wait by the window. I will go down first, and signal to you when it's safe to follow. We'll walk together, as if in conversation. Don't hurry, and keep your head down. If there's anyone about, we'll walk past the gate and go round again. I'll lock it behind us, and we'll walk around the back of Corpus Christi to the Merton gate.' As soon as Simon had left, Thomas stood by the window, keeping himself from view. The encrypted message was inside his habit. He saw Simon walk towards the middle of the quadrangle, look up briefly, turn, and walk on. He made no signal. There must have been someone there. Thomas kept watching until Simon reappeared from the direction of the Great Hall. This time, he stopped under the window, and raised his hand. Within a minute, they were heading for the King's gate.

The gate was really a door. Cut into the wall, it was tall and thick, with oak timbers and iron fixings. No intruder was going to force his way through such a door, and, as Simon had predicted, it was unguarded. He produced a batch of heavy iron keys from under his habit, and inserted one in the lock. It would not turn. With a quick glance over his shoulder, he tried another. This one turned smoothly, and the door swung open. They were through it at once, and Simon immediately locked it from the other side. Seeing no-one about, they made for the path along the south wall of Corpus Christi, and turned left towards the gate in the Merton wall. As they approached it Simon again produced the keys, intending to open the gate and enter the college as quickly as possible. Once inside Merton, they would be safer. He had the key in the lock and was about to turn it, when four soldiers in the red uniforms of the King's Lifeguard of Foot appeared from the direction of Merton Street. Simon quickly removed the key from the lock, hid it under his habit, and walked briskly towards the soldiers. Thomas followed him. These Lifeguards had not spent their morning guarding the King's life. They were loud and drunk. Seeing Thomas and Simon approaching, one of them said, 'God's wounds, gentlemen, a pair of monks to keep us pure and holy. Just what we need. Good day, monks, what about a little prayer for our souls, or has the Queen used them all up?'

'God bless you, gentlemen.' replied Simon, as he tried to walk past.

A large Lifeguard blocked their path. 'He might, monk,' he said, a hint of menace in his voice, 'But we'd like you to. And your friend.' He looked at Thomas, who was trying not to show his face. 'A good friend, is he? We all know about monks and their unholy ways.'

'We are on the Queen's business,' said Simon sternly, 'and cannot be delayed further. Kindly let us pass.' The large Lifeguard did not move.

'What business might that be, I wonder?' asked the first one. 'Praying or poking? The Queen has lots of pretty ladies to tempt you.'

'That is a vile accusation, and I can see it comes from a vile man. We are men of God. Stand aside and let us be about our business.' snapped Thomas.

'And why would we do that, monk?' asked the large one. 'I don't care for men in skirts who keep out of trouble and leave us to do all the fighting. They might as well be women.'

'And we know what women are for, eh?' A third Lifeguard,

emboldened by his colleagues, entered the fray. 'What's under those skirts of yours, I wonder. Perhaps we should take a look.' He reached out and lifted the hem of Thomas's habit. Thomas grabbed his forearm and wrist with both hands, straightened the arm, pushed hard, and watched the soldier fall backwards and land on his backside in the dirt.

'No match for a monk, eh, Step?' The large Lifeguard bellowed with laughter. 'Let me show you how it's done.'

'I don't advise it,' said Simon calmly, 'Just because we're monks does not mean that we cannot defend ourselves. Furthermore, the Queen awaits us. If we're late, she will soon know why.'

Unimpressed, the Lifeguard took a wild swing at his head. Simon moved deftly to one side, avoided the blow, and hit the Lifeguard with a short, sharp, punch in the throat. With a strangled gurgle of pain, the man collapsed in a heap. Neither of the still upright soldiers made any effort to help him. Simon and Thomas turned and retraced their steps to the gate. Before the soldiers could stop them, they were through it and into Merton. Simon locked the gate, and put a hand on Thomas's shoulder. 'What a war. Even the King's men resent the faith of his Queen. What do they think they're fighting for?'

'Themselves, Simon.' replied Thomas, 'Themselves.'

Jane had been taken to her rooms near the Warden's Lodgings, where the Queen had set up her household. When Thomas and Simon entered, they found her on a large bed, cushions under her head, and covered by an embroidered blanket. An elderly lady sat by the bed, a pile of linen cloths beside her. She rose when they entered. 'Has there been any change?' asked Simon.

'None.' replied the lady. 'She's still losing blood, and has not yet spoken.' Thomas noticed a second pile of cloths on the floor, these ones stained with blood. He went to the bed and took Jane's hand in his. She did not stir.

'She's very pale. Can the bleeding not be stopped?'

'I am trying, Father, but the wounds are deep.'

'I am not a monk, madam,' Thomas said gently, 'though it's better you don't know my name.' The lady nodded, but said nothing. 'Would you leave us with Lady Romilly, please? We will call if she wakes.' With a glance at Jane, the lady quietly left the room.

Thomas sat on the bed, still holding Jane's hand. Simon stood at the and of the bed and said a prayer. When he had finished, Thomas spoke quietly, 'Abraham, now Jane. I wish to God that Abraham had never mentioned me to the King, or that we'd turned you away when you arrived at our door, Simon. Murder, torture, rape. All in the name of a stupid, vicious, war.' Before Simon could respond, Jane opened her eyes, saw Thomas, and smiled weakly. Thomas put his finger on her lips. 'Jane, don't try to talk. You've lost a lot of blood, but you're safe now.' Another tiny smile, and her eyes closed again.

To Thomas, it seemed like hours before Jane stirred again. He sat silently, holding her hand gently, and willing her to survive. She must come to Romsey to meet Margaret and the girls; they would walk together by the river; he would show her his books. Without warning, her eyes opened, he felt the slightest squeeze of his hand, and she whispered something. Unable to make it out, Thomas leant forward until his cheek was touching hers. He could just hear the words. 'They said Rush had sent them.'

Thomas lifted his head and nodded. 'He'll hang for it. Now rest.' But the effort had been too much. Jane's back arched, and she moaned in pain. Simon went to the door and summoned the nurse, who bustled in, and lifted the blanket. Jane's legs and stomach were covered in blood. Between her legs, the linen cloths were sodden. When the nurse removed them, blood gushed on to the bed. Her eyes had closed and there was no sign of her breathing. Simon bent to put his hand to her neck, and his ear to her mouth. When he rose, he shook his head, and made the sign of the cross. Jane was dead.

While Simon prayed for her, Thomas sat motionless, her hand still in his. Then, suddenly, without word or warning, he placed her hand on her stomach, got up from the bed, and left. While Simon prayed, he ran down the staircase, across the Merton courtyard, and through the gate. In Merton Street, he slowed to a fast walk. He passed soldiers, beggars, whores, merchants, and scholars, and saw none of them. He trod in mud and excrement, and was cursed when he collided with a fruit-seller, knocking the man's box of apples to the ground. He walked up Magpie Lane and Catte Street, along Broad Street, and towards the castle. He saw none of the staring faces, and heard none of the shouted insults. For an hour, and then another hour, he walked the streets, cursing Rush the murderer, cursing the King for his summons, cursing Simon for fetching him, even cursing Abraham. And, above all, cursing himself. For coming to Oxford, for Jane's death, for leaving Margaret and the girls, for his stupidity.

By the time Thomas found himself back at Christ Church, his fury had been replaced by cold, hard, anger. He strode through the college gates, and past two guards watching everyone leaving the college, but showing no interest in anyone arriving. He made his way around the cattle pen to his rooms. He met no challenge. If he had, he would have ignored it. He had work to do.

Chapter 12

XZFMGMAYTDSXPMFMMVNLAJCLTSDVWXLPTICVIPSUGZSRSAAKOAWVIOJ

WBVEMWBVRPFNUFGSVTEHZWLEAVEVAILMDPIXBFEMWKLTTHOCACAVS

RXKBYOAAINAXLQEIHLZLCIAWES

One hundred and thirty four letters. Thomas was sure they had not been encrypted by simple substitution, nor by a Caesar shift. That left Monsieur Vigenère, whom he had already defeated once. But this time, the message was short, there were no repetitions of more than two letters, his analysis of letter frequencies had yielded nothing, and the keyword was neither LEAVE, nor PARIS, nor LONDON, nor ROME.

Now what? Try every country and every city he could think of? Try random words that came to mind? Or think of something else, some new way of attacking Vigenère? For a long time, Thomas sat and stared at the text, occasionally scribbling words on a sheet of paper. Spain, England, France, Italy, Abraham,

Jane. ONE EYE IS BROWN YET THE OTHER IS BLUE. Jane Romilly. Rush, Parliament, Pym, Traitor. Romsey, Thomas Hill, Jane. He had no more than twelve hours to decrypt this message, and he had no idea what to do other than try possible keywords. Hardly scientific, nor even artistic. Where was Hill's magic when it was needed?

He wrote out a new square, and started with cities – MADRID, LISBON, ATHENS, VIENNA; then countries – SPAIN, AUSTRIA, ITALY, GREECE. Nothing. Not a thing. He tried a random assortment of words and names – FAIRFAX, MILTON, OXFORD, HONOUR, TRUTH, PIETY, PRAYER. Again, nothing. His head ached, and Michel Montaigne whispered in his ear. 'This is foolishness, Thomas. We need reason, not guesswork. Give this up. Rest. Relax your mind and the answer may come.' His eyes closed, and he dozed. From time to time during the night, he started awake, thought of some new word, took up his quill, and tried again. It was futile.

By dawn, he was beyond sleep, and had nothing left to give. He had failed. The message's secrets, whatever they were, remained secrets. His fate was out of his hands. Best to face it with as much courage and dignity as he could manage. He washed, shaved, put on a clean shirt, and waited to be summoned. He heard the guards tramping up the staircase, and rose to open the door. There were two of them, both ill-tempered, both complaining loudly. 'Backwards and forwards across the yard and up some damned staircase. That's all we do. We're soldiers, not servants.' grumbled one.

'I'd rather be killing roundheads.' said the other.

'Good morning, gentlemen,' said Thomas, as they reached the top of the staircase. 'Is the King ready to see me?'

'He is, sir,' replied one, 'and His Majesty is in no mood to wait.' With a final look around the room, and armed with the message and his copy of the square, Thomas followed the soldiers back down the staircase. They marched around the cattle pen in the middle of the quadrangle, and towards the Deanery. They were still complaining. 'Up and down, backwards and forwards, forwards and backwards. It's not proper work for the King's guards.'

'It is not. We might as well be messenger boys.'

Backwards and forwards, forwards and backwards. Why had he not thought of that? 'You silly shit.' said Montaigne. Before he could give the idea more thought, he was ushered into the receiving room where the King sat, guards stationed around the room, members of his household behind him, tapping his stick on the stone floor. There was still no sign of Rush. 'Master Hill. I trust you bring us good news.'

'Your Majesty, my efforts have failed. I have not been able to decrypt the message.'

The King's face darkened. 'In that case, I cannot see that we have any further use for your services, Master Hill. You will be taken to the castle and held there until I have decided what shall be done with you.'

'Your Majesty, although I have not yet broken the cipher, there is one idea that I have not yet had the chance to try. May I have your consent to make one final attempt?'

'Surely, Master Hill,' replied the King, 'you have had sufficient time by now. We have waited patiently for you to bring us the contents of this message, and we have been disappointed. The Queen should by now have left Oxford. What grounds are there now for believing that you will break the cipher?'

'I may not, Your Majesty. I may fail again. But is it not worth allowing a few minutes more – ten at the most – just in case I am right?'

'Tell me, pray, how this new idea has suddenly come into your head at the very last minute? Is that not a little strange?'

'It is, Your Majesty. I cannot account for it, except that providence can play unexpected games.'

The King hesitated, then beckoned to one of his servants. 'Fetch paper and ink. We will watch Master Hill at his final attempt.' The servant scurried off, and soon returned with quills, paper, and a pot of ink. Thomas took the message and his square from under his shirt, and sat at a small table in the corner. But for the scratching of his quill, the room was silent. Even the King had stopped tapping his stick on the floor. Thomas closed his mind to his audience, and concentrated on the message. Above the first ten letters of the text – XZFMGMAYTD – he wrote out the letters SIRAP twice. Then he referred to the square, and wrote a third line of letters above that. Within a few minutes, he had FROMRUSHTO. From Rush to. Surely this was it. The keyword PARIS one way, and SIRAP the other. Simple and clever. Very nearly too clever for Thomas Hill. Resisting the urge to shout Eureka and claim victory, he continued on across the first line. The stick started tapping again. Thomas tried to ignore it.

The eleventh letter of the text was decrypted as A. The recipient's name must begin with A. But the next three letters were PYM. A Pym? Why not John Pym or J Pym, or just Pym?

Thomas knew the answer as soon as he decrypted the twenty second letter. It was B. As he had suspected, there were nulls in this message, and it looked as though they occurred at every eleventh letter. That would be quite enough to eliminate any repetitions, and to render frequency analysis useless.

'I believe we have waited long enough.' said the King. There was a ripple of assent from the audience.

'Your Majesty,' replied Thomas, standing up and bowing low, 'I can inform you with confidence that my idea was correct. I have decrypted enough of the message to be sure that I have the keyword. It will take me ten more minutes to complete the decryption.'

The King stared at him. 'You are fortunate that I am a patient man, Master Hill. In the full knowledge of the consequences of failure, you may proceed.' Thomas worked as fast as he dared. Mistakes in decryption, especially using the square, were all to easy. After eight minutes he had:

FROMRUSHTOAPYMQUEENWIBLLEAVEWITHCI
NDAYSFORBRDISTOLENROUETEEXETERANFDF
RANCESHOUELDWEATTEMPTFTOEXECUTEPGL
ANINBRISTHOLIAWAITINISTRUCTIONS

And after nine:

FROM RUSH TO PYM. QUEEN WILL LEAVE
WITHIN DAYS FOR BRISTOL EN ROUTE EXETER
FOR FRANCE. SHOULD WE ATTEMPT TO
EXECUTE PLAN IN BRISTOL? I AWAIT
INSTRUCTIONS.

That was it. Rush the traitor, Rush the murderer. 'Your Majesty,' said Thomas, 'I ask that you and I are left alone. The contents of this message are so grave that no-one but you should know them.'

Another ripple from the courtiers, this time of dissent. The King waved it aside. 'The guards alone will stay.' The courtiers trooped out, and the King looked expectantly at Thomas. 'Well, Master Hill, and what is so grave that I alone should hear it?'

'This message reveals that the Queen will travel to Bristol and Exeter, and then to France.'

The King was on his feet. 'That cannot be. The Queen's route has been kept a close secret. Almost no-one knows it.'

'I fear, sir, that the sender of this message knows it.'

The King held out his hand for the text. He read it twice, and sat down. 'I cannot accept this without further evidence. Tobias Rush is a loyal and trusted servant. To be told now that he is a traitor is beyond comprehension. And you, Master Hill, after your theatrical display, what am I to make of you?'

'I can understand Your Majesty's dilemma. I wish that the keyword had occurred to me before. That it came to mind only on my way here this morning is indeed strange. I blame myself for not thinking of it sooner.'

'And what is this keyword which eluded you for so long, Master Hill?'

'Your Majesty will recall that the keyword to the first intercepted message was PARIS. This one turned out to be the same letters, but backwards. SIRAP. Messages go back and forth. So did the keywords.'

'Could you be mistaken as to the sender's name?'

'No, sir. The sender's name is Rush.'

The King closed his eyes. 'It is beyond belief.'

'If I may, Your Majesty,' went on Thomas, 'there are other things of which you should be aware. I am quite sure that Erasmus Pole was not murdered in Brasenose Lane, but his body dumped there after he had been killed somewhere else. Why would the murderer do that other than to conceal his motive? The murderer of Abraham Fletcher was looking for something, and tortured him when he could not find it. He could not find it because I had it. It was the first message. My room was also searched, but, fortunately, the message was not found. Master Rush arranged for me to be imprisoned in an effort to get rid of me, and to retrieve the message. Again, we were fortunate. It was hidden, and, in your absence, the Queen graciously commanded my release. Without her intervention, I would certainly be dead. Your Majesty will also know that Lady Jane Romilly, lady-in-waiting to the Queen, was cruelly raped and murdered. However, she lived long enough to reveal the identity of the man behind this bestial crime. It was Tobias Rush.'

'Merciful God. Tobias Rush, to whom I have entrusted many secrets, and whom I trusted with the Queen's life. Is there more?' asked the King.

'Rush knew how I had decrypted the first message. He's a clever man. He used the Vigenère square again, but in a very short message with no repetitions or numbers, and with nulls – that is, extra letters inserted in the text to confuse a decrypter. Without the keyword, the message was impregnable. It was only by chance that I guessed it.'

'Master Rush knew of our plan for the Queen to travel to Exeter from Bristol. He is away now making arrangements.'

'When does he return, sir?'

'Tomorrow.'

'Your Majesty, Tobias Rush is ruthless. He must be apprehended before he gets wind of what we know. The Queen herself might otherwise be in danger. He would almost certainly have sent a copy of such an important message by more than one carrier.'

'He will be met by my Lifeguards when he arrives at the city wall. They will escort him here to face his King. Only when I have interrogated him myself, will I know for certain whether or not he is a traitor. Meanwhile, Master Hill, you will remain in your rooms. A guard will be posted outside the door. Master Rush's rooms will be searched. I will send for you if I wish to speak to you further.'

After little sleep and no breakfast, Thomas was tired and hungry. There was no elation at breaking the cipher and proving Rush's guilt, nor relief at his own reprieve. Food and rest must come first. Having scavenged bread and cheese from the college kitchen, he returned to his room, lay on his bed, and slept while the King's guard stood outside the door.

He was still asleep when the guard threw open the door. 'Master Rush, the King wishes to see you at once.' In the bedchamber, Thomas heard nothing. The guard went in and shook him. 'Master Rush, you must arise, sir. The King has summoned you.' Thomas struggled awake. Four hours sleep felt like four minutes. The guard helped him up. 'Get dressed, sir. I will take you to the King.' Please God, thought Thomas, no more ciphers. I haven't the strength.

On a table beside the King stood a small iron box. It had been forced open. 'This box was found concealed behind a wall in Master Rush's rooms.' said the King in his quiet voice, 'It contained these two documents.' He handed them to Thomas, who unrolled one. On it had been written a column of letter sequences. The sequences were five or six letters in length. He put it down and unrolled the other one. On this was a column of numbers, which did not correspond to the number codes used in the first message. In both cases, Thomas recognised the hand of Tobias Rush. 'What do you make of them, Master Hill?' asked the King.

'The alphabetical list is probably an encrypted list of keywords, sir, and the numerical list a list of code words. They are both written in Tobias Rush's hand.'

'Of that I am aware. Can you decrypt them?'

'As we already know some of the number codes being used, and we know PARIS is one keyword, it should not be difficult, Your Majesty.'

'In that case, start work at once, and bring me the results the moment you have them.' Taking the two documents, Thomas bowed and left. Ciphers for sleep. A poor trade.

He started with the letters. If he was right about the numbers, they were less important. He looked at the list.

MQQHTT
WKHRSG
NCGVNJ

QCUMX
BUKISY
MKYFTT
OCSPJY
NKOES

If they were keywords, one of them would be PARIS. Only two of the sequences had five letters – QCUMX and NKOES – one of which would be it. It did not take Thomas long to find out which. He very quickly found that each letter of the plain word was encrypted by a letter of the alphabet the same number of places after it as its position in the word. So in PARIS, P became Q, A became C, R became U, I became M, and S became X. He soon had the list in plaintext.

LONDON
VIENNA
MADRID
PARIS
ATHENS
LISBON
NAPLES
MILAN

Keywords to Vigenère squares or alphabetic shifts, which would be used in turn, replies using the same words backwards. After MILAN, the sender would go back to LONDON.

The numbers also submitted without a fight. The man who

had devised these ciphers was not the most imaginative encrypter that Thomas had ever faced. He had disguised the numbers in a similar way to the letters, only backwards. He had used the numbers one to nine, and returned to one after nine. Thus, the numbers appearing in the first message – 769, 371, 574, 852, 182, 264, 421, 775, and 637, had been encrypted as 646, 257, 451, 738, 968, 141, 397, 652, and 514. There were ten further numbers which Thomas decrypted, but could not, without a context, put names to. And there, for all to see, was 775, now revealed to be Tobias Rush. The senders of messages would have committed to memory the names represented by each number.

On receiving the decrypted lists, the King said only that Thomas would no longer be under guard, that he may leave Christ Church as he wished, and that arrangements would be made to escort him back to Romsey. He now knew with certainty that one of his most trusted advisors had been sending and receiving encrypted messages on behalf of his enemies, and that he would have had access to all incoming and outgoing messages from the man who had replaced Thomas. Thomas went immediately to Pembroke, where he found Silas Merkin and apologised for not contacting him earlier. Then he went to Merton, where the Queen's household was preparing to travel. In Merton Street, horses were being groomed and carriages polished. Inside the college, under the watchful eyes of the Queen's ladies, servants bustled about with bags and boxes. Thomas doubted if any of them knew when they were leaving or where they were going, but whenever and wherever it turned out to be, they would be ready.

Simon was in his room, reading his Bible, when Thomas arrived. 'Not preparing for the journey, Simon?' he inquired.

Simon looked up and smiled. 'Thankfully, a Franciscan monk has little to prepare other than his soul. He has everything invested in that.'

'Judging by the number of horses and carriages, and the heaps of baggage, you won't be dining on shaggy inkcaps this time.'

'Probably not. I wouldn't mind, but Her Majesty's household expects something rather more substantial.'

'Does anyone know when you're leaving?'

'I don't think so. Even the Queen is vague on the matter. Do you know why?'

'I do.' replied Thomas, taking a seat beside Simon. He told Simon about backwards and forwards, his last minute decryption, about the contents of the message, and about the lists found in Rush's rooms.

'Is the King now persuaded?' asked Simon.

'Almost. He has sent a troop of Lifeguards to intercept Rush on his way into Oxford. He intends to interrogate Rush himself. I have warned him, however, that such a message would certainly have been sent by more than one route and that Pym will know of the plan for you to travel to Bristol before Exeter.'

'Then no doubt the plan will change. And when will you go home, Thomas?'

'The King is arranging an escort for me. If you're going to Exeter, perhaps it will be you. With Rush in gaol, I hope to leave soon.'

They talked of the Queen, Margaret, Polly and Lucy, Oxford,

and the war. And, finally, they talked of Jane. 'The Queen insisted that her body be taken to York.' said Simon, 'She would have wanted to be buried near her family.'

'If Rush should hang for nothing else, he should hang for Jane. Rape and murder of a woman guilty only of having been my friend. And why? To get me out of Christ Church, so I could be arrested, or just out of spite?'

'That I cannot say, my friend. Rush is beyond my understanding. Thank God he's on the way to the gallows at last. Without you, he might never have been caught.'

Thomas knew all was not well the moment he set foot back in Christ Church. A group of guards stood inside the college gate, shuffling their feet and looking sullen. A second group had congregated at the other end of the cattle pen, near the Great Hall. Both groups seemed to be waiting for something. He asked one of the first group what news they brought. 'News that our captain is giving the King at this very moment,' replied the soldier, 'and I thank God it's him not me.'

'I am Thomas Hill, advisor to the King. May I know what the news is?'

The soldier exchanged a glance with the man next to him. 'The King will know by now, Master Hill, so I may as well tell you. We were sent to intercept Tobias Rush on his way into Oxford from the west. The King wanted him brought straight here.'

'Is he dead?'

'No, sir, far from it. While we were engaged with his guards, he slipped away. Just turned his horse and galloped off. We hadn't time to stop him.'

'Did you give chase?'

'We did, sir, but he was gone. His Majesty will not be happy. The captain told us it was a task we had better not fail in.'

'Thank you,' said Thomas, 'better to know.' and left the guards to their waiting. Damn them, and damn Rush. Damn the man to hell, where he should be rotting. He'd be among friends by now, and out of reach. So now what? Would the Queen still leave, or would she stay in Oxford? And how much longer would he have to stay here? And how could they catch Rush?

For two days, there was no news. No word from the King, nor from Simon at Merton. The King's mood had descended on Christ Church like the blackest of clouds. Voices were hushed, the college was quiet, there was little activity. Men and women spoke and moved as if wary of incurring the King's anger. Only the cattle in their pen were oblivious. Thomas sat in his room, reading a little, but mostly thinking about Margaret and his nieces. He wondered if the King would remember his promise to provide an escort home, and, if so, how long he would have to wait. Thomas Hill, cryptographer and bookseller, for all the service he had given, would not be high on the royal list of priorities. New codes would have to be devised and distributed for all messages to and from the King's commanders, an assessment of the damage done by Rush would have to be made, and new plans put in place.

And, all the while, news of the war was not good. Oliver Cromwell's cavalry, supported by the Earl of Manchester and Sir Thomas Fairfax, had sent a Royalist army running for their lives through the Lincolnshire countryside, and, in Scotland, the Earl of Leven was gathering his forces for an advance towards Newcastle. Nottingham and Manchester were in Parliament's hands, and Chester was under threat. In the south and the west, bands of clubmen had become serious obstacles to the occupation of towns and villages, with the result that the King's soldiers were going hungry. It would not be long before they started deserting – just what the clubmen wanted.

Thomas heard no news of Romsey, still in Royalist-held territory, but the forces of Parliament now held both Southampton and Portsmouth. If the town's merchants were unable to send their cloth to the ports, trade would dry up, and everyone in the town would suffer. Simon had brought plenty of money for Margaret, and they had a decent amount under the stairs, so Thomas had no fears on that score; even in times of scarcity, food could always be bought. For her safety, however, and that of the girls, he feared greatly. He had experienced soldiers from both sides in the town, and he knew what they could do. They could drink, fight, steal, rape, and kill. He wondered, too, if there had been any more threatening letters. The chances were that they were nothing, albeit a frightening nothing. And if they were something, God alone knew what might have happened.

On the third day, Thomas awoke desperate to escape the confinement of his room and the oppression of the King's mood. He walked round Christ Church meadow, now crammed with artillery pieces, mortars, and stores of small arms, up St Aldate's and Cornmarket, and back towards Merton by Broad Street and Catte Street. Everywhere, there were even more beggars and whores, and more filth and decay, than when he had first arrived in Oxford. Evacuees from villages burnt down to prevent their falling into enemy hands had poured into the town, as had the maimed and wounded from each new engagement, and the reinforcements demanded by the King were arriving in their hundreds. Barely a house or a college room remained unoccupied by soldiers, or by members of the royal households. Thomas saw neither scholars nor teachers. Instead, he saw disease, poverty, and degradation. Oxford was no longer a university town; it was a military encampment.

A military encampment with a difference. In Catte Street, a line of revellers, the men in the blue and red uniforms of the King's Guards, their masked ladies in flowing gowns, danced down the street to the sounds of flutes and pipes. They were led by a young man whom Thomas recognised as Prince Rupert, a lady on either arm, singing lustily, and trying vainly to keep in time with the music. Thomas stepped aside to let them pass. The dancers took no notice of the limbless beggars lining either side of the street, nor of the abuse shouted at them by watching townspeople. A woman in an old straw bonnet and a torn dress, who tried to join the dance, was shoved roughly aside. It was a spectacle that Thomas had not before encountered. Starving beggars and dancing soldiers. What a war.

Before Merton, he went to the Physic Garden. It was there that Jane had shown him Daisy Fleabane, and they had walked together between stands of lavender and beds of violets. The violets were over, but the lavender still flowered. He twisted a head from its stem and rolled it between his fingers. Its scent was the scent of Jane. He had never had the chance to impress her with his knowledge of flowers, to invite her to Romsey, to woo her properly. Now there never would be a chance. Jane was dead. Rush had murdered her.

At Merton, he found Simon sitting on a bench in the little quadrangle behind the Chapel, a quiet spot, away from the comings and goings in the front quadrangle. Thomas sat down beside him. 'Has there been any news?' he asked.

'None that I know of.' replied the monk, 'The Queen awaits instructions from the King as to her day of departure, and her destination. Her mood, as ever, reflects his. Black, sullen, ominous. She has even cancelled the farewell masque she had planned for the King.'

'Then matters must be serious.'

'Indeed. Have you heard nothing from the King?'

'Nothing. I still hope for an escort home, but His Majesty will have other and more pressing affairs to attend to.'

'Among them, the capture of Tobias Rush, I hope.'

'I doubt he'll be caught now. He could be in Manchester or London or Cambridge. Somewhere where he can't be reached.'

For an hour they sat together, sometimes talking, sometimes sitting in silence. By the time Thomas rose to go, he had made up his mind to seek an audience with the King and to ask for permission to go home. Surely His Majesty would not refuse such a request. He would ask him at once.

That evening, however, Thomas's request for an audience was refused. The King was too busy to see him. Frustrated and furious, he stormed out of Christ Church, hoping to cool his temper by the river. He had come here under sufferance, he had done what was asked of him, and he wanted to go home. Well, if the King would not honour his promise to provide an escort, he would take his chances and go anyway. Tomorrow morning, he would just walk out of Oxford, find a horse, and make his way to Romsey. If he had to, he would hide in woods and live on toadstools. He had lost a lady he loved. He had been away far too long. It was time to go home. Much cheered by his decision, Thomas returned to Christ Church, going over in his mind the practicalities of the journey. He had money, he could buy a horse, he knew the route. Three days on the road and he would be home. At last.

The blow that knocked him cold came from behind the door as he entered his rooms. He saw and heard nothing. It was a blow from a heavy object, delivered by someone who knew what he was about. A blow to render his victim unconscious, not to kill him. An expert blow to the back of the head. When Thomas came to, he was on his back, ankles bound together, and wrists tied to the frame of the bed. His movement was restricted to raising his throbbing head, and wriggling his backside. Through eyes that refused to focus, he thought he saw the door to the bedchamber open, and a black-clad, crow-like, figure, enter and approach the bed. The figure stooped over the bed to examine its prey. In its hand it held a cane with a silver top. It spoke. 'Master Hill, we meet again.'

Chapter 13

Rush pulled up a chair and sat by the bed. He pushed one strip of shirt into Thomas's mouth, and secured it with a second, tied around his head. Then he held up the silver-topped cane where Thomas could see it, and drew out of it a very thin blade. 'The finest Spanish steel, Thomas, made especially for me by the best swordsmith in Toledo. Its point is as sharp as one of your sister's sewing needles. As you can see.' Holding the sword by its silver handle, his eyes never leaving Thomas's, he touched Thomas's arm with the point. A trickle of blood appeared. 'The secret is in the mix of metals. That and the exact heat of the forge and the length of time the sword is in it. The smiths measure the time by reciting prayers. Then the blade is cooled with oil. A fine Toledo sword is every bit as much a masterpiece as a Michelangelo sculpture.'

A slow smile crept across the narrow face. 'I can see that you're surprised to find me here, Thomas. I quite understand. I could be in London by now, yet somehow the idea of our meeting again proved irresistible. I am unaccustomed to defeat – a poor loser, you might say – and unwilling to concede victory, especially to so unworthy an adversary. Tobias Rush bested by a Romsey bookseller? I think not. With a little help from some friends, it was not difficult to return unnoticed to Oxford, nor to enter Christ Church and wait for your return. You'd be surprised just how many of us there are in the town, and we are more each week. Disenchantment with the King grows with his every extravagance, and those of the Queen, and it does not take a military eye to see which way the war is going. I believe I may claim, in all modesty, to have been instrumental in recruiting a good many to our cause. And I had expected to go on doing so. Until, Thomas, you stumbled upon a means of decrypting our messages. You look surprised. Of course I know about the second message. Not only did it arrive by only one of its two routes, but certain friends here alerted me to its interception. So you discovered our plan. An excellent plan, too, if I may say so, devised by myself. Imagine it. The Queen and her unborn infant in our hands, her devoted husband unable to do anything to recover her but to accede to our demands. The war would have been over within days.' Rush bent his head to Thomas's ear and whispered, 'Now, Thomas, I am going to allow you to speak. But if you so much as raise your voice, you will immediately lose your right eye. Do I make myself clear?' Thomas nodded, and Rush removed the shirt from his mouth.

'There, now we can talk man-to-man. How is your head?' Thomas said nothing. 'Very well. I recall from my visit to the prison that you are prone to spells of sullen silence. I shall continue. Assuming that my rooms have been searched, we will no longer be using the codes and keywords that may have been found there. Monsieur Vigenère has served us well for over a year, but he too will now have to go. How clever you were, Thomas, and how fortunate, to discover his secrets, and ours.'

'Why did you kill Erasmus Pole?'

'Ah. He speaks. A question, though not a very interesting one. Pole had become a liability. After the affair at Alton, we had to decide whether to keep him. We decided not to. He was an old man and had outlived his usefulness.'

'Why did you take a blind man's eyes?'

'Now that is more interesting. They were no use to Master Fletcher, of course, but that is not quite all. I find a certain satisfaction in the neat removal of an eye. I imagine a surgeon feels the same way when he cleanly removes a musket ball. A neat incision and out it pops. A good job, performed by an expert. Does that answer your question?'

'Did you rape Jane Romilly?'

'I thought we would come to that. I myself did not. Rape is not one of my pleasures. The men who did rape her, however, did so on my instructions. I understand they were a little rough.'

'She bled to death.'

'Such a pity. A lovely lady. And so available.'

'You'll burn in hell, Rush.'

'Very probably. And you'll be able to tell them to expect me.'

'You're a vicious murderer, a traitor, and a coward.'

A shadow passed over Rush's face. 'A coward? No, Master Hill. I have no time for soldiers or soldiering, but a coward I am not.' He shoved the shirt back into Thomas's mouth and secured it. 'Now we shall see who's a coward.' He ripped Thomas's shirt down the front, and dragged the point of the blade diagonally across his chest. Thomas's back arched against the pain, and blood from the wound dripped down his stomach. Again the blade sliced his flesh, its line forming a cross with the first cut. Rush rose and fetched a pail of water from the washstand. He threw it over Thomas's chest. 'There. We don't want you bleeding to death quite yet, do we? The water will help to keep you going.' Thomas closed his eyes and bit down on the shirt in his mouth. The cuts had been finely judged. Deep enough to cause pain, not so deep as to kill.

Rush sat back on the chair, and admired his work. 'Not a bad start, although the smaller cuts are more difficult to make precisely. How fortunate that we have all night. A man's pleasures should always be taken slowly. Speaking of which, I found an excellent bottle in your cupboard. Are you thirsty? No? Well, I am.' The bottle produced, Rush poured himself a glass and sipped it appeciatively. 'The college cellars are one of the few good things about this city. I daresay that's why the King chose to come here. This is a splendid claret. Are you sure you wouldn't care for a glass?' Unable to speak, Thomas forced himself to keep his eyes open, willing Rush to see the contempt in them. At the same time, he wished he could close his nostrils. The stench of the man was overpowering. It was a foul stench, a stench of evil. If witches carried the smell of evil, Rush reeked of the devil himself. Thomas gagged on the shirt in his mouth, and swallowed the bile in his throat.

'Your sister, I'm told, is a handsome woman,' went on Rush, 'and your nieces very pretty young things. I have not yet had the pleasure of meeting them myself, although I hope that will not be long delayed. Ah, you're wondering how I know. I have friends in Hampshire. One of them has been keeping a close eye on your sister and her daughters. He even wrote to advise them to take particular care in these uncertain times. Such a kindly man.' The threatening letters. Rush's doing. 'We did think you might hurry home when you heard about them. Alas, you chose to stay in Oxford. Most unwise.'

Rush poured himself more wine and took his glass to the window. 'A lovely city, Oxford, as is Cambridge, which I know better. I was there myself, you know. I studied law at Peterhouse. Nothing like as grand as Christ Church, of course, but a charming college. Do you know the most unusual thing about both places? People listen. They learn by listening. Everywhere else, I find people do not listen, they merely wait for their turn to speak. Sometimes, they don't even do that. They interrupt. I learnt to listen at Peterhouse, and the habit has never left me. In gathering information, I find it an invaluable skill.' Taking up the sword, Rush pressed the point under Thomas's ear and drew it down his neck and across his throat. Thomas felt a trickle of blood. 'I do hope you're listening, Thomas. You would be foolish not to. I'm going to give you another chance to speak, but do remember what I said. A shout or a scream will cost you an eye.' The shirt was removed, and Thomas swallowed hard, the taste of bile still in his mouth. Rush continued his monologue. 'The best thing about this war is that it has brought with it opportunities for a man clever and daring enough to take them. Opportunities to become rich, opportunities to become powerful. Military men are so splendidly stupid. They hack each other to death while others are quietly taking these opportunities. When they realise what has happened, it will be too late.'

'Hell will be too good for you, Rush.' Thomas's voice rasped in his throat.

'So you have made clear.' laughed Rush, 'Fortunately, I don't believe in hell. Or heaven, for that matter. Believing in either makes life so much more difficult. Nor do I care much whether the country is ruled by King or commoner, Catholic or Puritan. Charles Stuart, John Pym, Oliver Cromwell, the Vicar of Rome, it's all the same to me. There will be rich and poor, clever and stupid. Happily, there will always be more poor and stupid.' He took another sip of wine. 'Which are you, Thomas, I wonder? Clever or stupid?' Thomas turned his head and spat out a mouthful of bile. 'If that is an answer, I fear I do not understand it.' continued Rush, 'Let me put the question another way. There is a place on my staff for a man as skilled as you. In view of recent developments, I shall be returning to London, where John Pym, as you will know, is dying. There I shall take up a new position under his successor, working to spread fear and discontent among the soldiers of the King. I shall need clever men around me, and I shall need one who can ensure that our communications go undetected by the enemy. A chief cryptographer. For the right man, the rewards will be great.' Deceipt, treachery, subversion – Rush's weapons, and every bit as lethal as his blade. 'Have you nothing to say to my generous offer?' Thomas remained silent. 'In that case, I will try a little persuasion.' Holding Thomas's head still, Rush drew a neat circle of blood around his right eye with the point of the blade. 'There, just right if I should happen to need a target. And if you persist in this stubborn silence, I shall indeed need one.'

With his chest, neck, and face, cut and bloody, and unable to see much out of his right eye, Thomas considered risking a scream. But Rush would not hesitate to plunge that blade into his eye, and, in any case, a scream might not be heard. Rush sat on the left side of the bed, so he concentrated on wriggling his right hand. There was a slight give in the rope that held him to the bed frame. With a lot of work, he might be able to loosen it enough to slip his hand through. The question was, would he have enough time to do it? The blade appeared again. This time, it sliced through his breeches and down his leg to the knee. Then it travelled up the other leg, stopping just short of his groin. Blood dripped on to the bed. Rush threw another pail of water over him. 'So important in discussions of this sort to know when to pause.' he whispered in Thomas's ear. 'One wants one's listener to be able to give one his full attention and to encourage him to make a sensible decision. I have made my offer, Thomas. The matter is now in your hands.'

'I would require a guarantee of absolute safety for my family.' whispered Thomas, trying to ignore the pain.

'And naturally, you shall have it. They will join you in London, where you will be found an excellent house, with appointments and servants appropriate to your position.'

'How will this be arranged?'

'That need not concern you, Thomas. I shall personally supervise the arrangements for their safe passage from Romsey. And I shall escort you to London myself.'

'How do I know I can trust you?'

'Trust? What has trust to do with it? Be pragmatic, Thomas. Why would I lie? You have something of value to me. I'm offering you the chance of saving your own life, and their lives, or a painful death, ignorant of what lies in store for them. Which shall it be?'

'I need time to consider.'

'Don't be absurd. Time to consider what? Which eye I shall take first? Whether you will bleed to death? The issue is clear. Decide.'

'I need time. You said I have something of value to you. Allow me an hour to consider your offer.'

'Very well. An hour. Not a minute longer, or be sure that you have seen your last dawn.'

Thomas closed his eyes. Perversely, Homer, of all people, came to mind. When his beloved 'rosy-fingered dawn, child of the morn' arrived, would Thomas be able to see it or not? Rush was expert with his Spanish blade. A twist of the hand, and his eye would be gone. At least the bleeding from his neck and chest had stopped. He tried to think clearly. The rope around his wrist had moved very little, despite his efforts to work it loose, his ankles were tied together, and Rush was sitting no more than a few feet away. Go with him or die here. Scylla and Charybdis – more Homer. With no idea of what to do if he did manage to free his hand, he clenched his teeth and kept working on the rope, which had already rubbed his wrist raw. Rush had twisted it twice around his wrist, then looped it around the wooden frame of the bed, and knotted it tightly. To release his hand he would have to loosen the knot enough to pull it through. The indestructible Odysseus might do it; Thomas Hill probably would not.

After no more than a few minutes, Rush, who had been sitting very still, stirred. 'Did I say an hour, Thomas? How foolish of me. I find that my patience has already run out. What is your decision?' Thomas needed more time. The rope was definitely looser, and, by squeezing his fingers together, he could pull his hand through the loop as far as the ball of his thumb. Ten minutes might be enough.

'How will we get out of the college undetected?'

Rush smiled and pulled from his pocket an iron key. 'The King's private gate should serve us. I took the precaution of having a key made for myself when it was built.'

Thomas feigned ignorance. 'The King's private gate? Is there such a thing?'

'There is. Now tell me your decision.'

But Thomas did not have to answer. There was a loud hammering on the door, and an urgent voice outside. 'Thomas. Wake up. We're leaving within the hour, and you're to come with us.' It was Simon.

Rush was on his feet at once, his sword at Thomas's throat. 'Not a sound, Hill, or it will be your last.'

Simon hammered on the door and called out again, this time louder. 'Thomas. Wake up. We must hurry.' Thomas felt the point of Rush's sword prick his throat. Rush would have locked the door after knocking him out, and Simon would not have a key, although Rush would not know that. He had to alert Simon without being immediately skewered. He made his hand as small as he could and wrenched it hard. It very nearly slipped through the rope. One more try and it would come. He had to make Rush look away. Risking the point of the sword, he turned his head towards Rush, looked past him, widened his eyes, and raised his eyebrows as if in astonishment. Rush caught the look and turned. Thomas jerked his hand free and grabbed Rush's wrist, twisting it as hard as he could. The sword dropped from his hand and rattled on to the floor. He shouted as loudly as his dry throat would permit. 'Simon, kick the door down.'

Rush snarled, pulled his wrist free, and bent to retrieve the sword. As he did so, the door, with a crack like a musket, broke free of its lock and opened into the room. Rush picked up the sword and moved towards the door, where Simon stood watching him. 'Well, monk, not a good time to call.' The words were hissed. He took two quick steps and thrust the sword at Simon's groin. For a big man, Simon could move very quickly, as Thomas had seen before. He stepped to his left, and chopped down on Rush's arm with the edge of his hand. Rush cursed, but did not drop the sword. Now he knew what his opponent could do, he would take more care. Simon still stood at the door, not giving Rush the chance to get past him. Even unarmed, he would be a difficult obstacle to move. Rush circled cautiously around him, the sword pointing at his face. A false move and this man might disarm him. To test his speed, he jabbed at his eyes and stomach, his own eyes never leaving Simon's. Simon deftly avoided the jabs, until Rush subtly changed his angle of attack, and drew blood from his cheek. Simon barely flinched. Again, Rush drew blood and again Simon ignored it. Given a chance, he would break Rush's arm, and Rush knew it.

While they watched each other, Thomas struggled with the knot that tied his left hand to the bed frame. He got it free and reached down to tackle the rope around his legs. Rush must have seen the movement from the corner of his eye. He backed away from Simon towards the bed. A quick thrust into Thomas's unprotected throat, and he would turn back to Simon. Thomas could not free his legs in time. He sat up and waited for the strike, hoping somehow to parry it. It never came. The moment Rush turned his head towards Thomas for the thrust, Simon launched himself at his back. Both men crashed on to the bed, pinning Thomas underneath them. Simon grabbed Rush's arm in both hands and bent it backwards. Rush screamed and the sword fell from his hand. Winded, and unable to move his body, Thomas managed to free a hand and jab his fingers into Rush's throat. At the same time, Simon grabbed him by his hair and jerked his head back. Rush screamed again and flailed wildly with his arms. It did no good. Simon de Pointz was a strong man. He held Rush easily, pulled him off the bed, and dumped him on his face on the floor. 'The ropes, Thomas, if you can.' he said. 'We'd better tie this thing up before it can slither away.' Thomas freed his legs and used the ropes to tie Rush's arms and legs securely, while Simon sat on his back and held him down by the neck. Unarmed, Rush was no match for the tall monk.

'You are an unusual monk. I thought Franciscans were peaceful souls.' said Thomas, standing up to examine his handiwork.

'In the backstreets and alleyways of Norwich, a boy learnt to defend himself. St Francis would not disapprove of self-defence.' Holding him by his hair, Simon hoisted Rush to his feet. 'And if he had known this creature, he might even have advocated striking first.'

For the first time since Simon broke down the door, Rush spoke. 'Curse your eyes, monk.'

Simon shook him by the hair. 'Save your breath, Rush. You'll need it for the King.'

Rush spat on the floor. 'Pathetic little man.'

'You can tell him that yourself. Clean yourself up, Thomas, and then let us escort Master Rush to His Majesty.'

In the early hours of an October morning, His Majesty was not best pleased to be roused from sleep to be told that Master Hill and Father De Pointz were outside and must see him at once. His first thought was that something untoward had happened to prevent the Queen leaving the city quietly. They had said their farewells the previous evening, swearing undying love and reassuring each other that they would meet again soon. Arrangements for her journey had been hastily revised and she would now travel to Salisbury on the way to Exeter. Both Hill and De Pointz were supposed to be going with her. What were they doing here?

He soon found out. A long fur robe over his nightgown, he stormed into the receiving room, where Thomas and Simon held Rush between them. Six Lifeguards stood around the walls. It took the King a moment to take it in. Tobias Rush, the traitor who had escaped capture, back in Oxford, and held by these men. How? 'I once observed that my birds had flown.' he said, regaining his wits, 'Now I observe that one has returned. Guards, take this man in charge.' Two guards jumped to it, taking Rush from Thomas and Simon. 'Now, gentlemen, perhaps you would explain yourselves.'

When they had done so, the King turned to Rush. 'I once

trusted you. Now I know you to be a traitor and a murderer, and of the foulest kind. Before you are executed, you will reveal everything you know about our enemies. Take him to the castle.'

'Your Majesty, If I may explain…'

'Take him.' With a protesting Rush between them, the two guards marched out of the Hall. 'Betrayed by his own vanity and greed. How foolish.' Indeed, thought Thomas, but he isn't the first and he won't be the last. The King spoke to Simon. 'Is the Queen safe?'

'She is, sir.'

'Then we shall delay her departure until Master Rush has told us what he knows. I will send word to her. Master Hill, you will be summoned when there is news.'

Outside the Deanery, Thomas asked, 'A word of thanks would not have been out of place, Simon, don't you think?'

Simon shrugged. 'His Majesty takes the loyalty and suffering of his subjects for granted. He expects no less.'

'Royal vanity. Doubtless an altogether finer quality than the common variety. For his sake, I do hope so. Now, Simon, as the door to my room has been kicked in by an intruder, I would rather lay my head elsewhere. Have you any suggestions?'

'Merton always welcomes you, Thomas. My bed is your bed. I must attend the Queen.'

Thomas returned that afternoon to his room at Christ Church, to find that royal vanity had allowed a gesture of royal kindness, and the lock on his door had been repaired. The only thing I know is that I know nothing, he thought. Socrates, or possibly Plato. They're easily confused. Very few men survived more than a day of the type of rigorous examination conducted at the castle, and he guessed that the royal summons would come that day or the next. There was little to do but sit and wait.

It came that evening. Thomas was escorted to the Deanery and shown straight into the King's receiving room. 'Master Hill,' said the King without preamble, 'I have just received word that Tobias Rush is dead. He died an hour ago under examination, having told us nothing. I have ordered his body quartered and burnt. I shall pray for his soul, evil and treacherous though it was.'

'His death was quick, Your Majesty.'

'It is often the way when a man is not going to talk. He allows himself to go quickly. So it was with Rush.'

'I cannot say that I'm sorry. He was a traitor, a torturer, and a murderer.'

'He was, and a clever and devious man. How he hid his treachery from me for so long, I do not know. He has done our cause much harm, and only time will tell if it can be repaired. Thank God he is dead and can do no more. Now, the Queen and her party will be leaving Oxford tonight. You may travel with them to Salisbury. From there, you must make your own way home.'

'Thank you, Your Majesty.'

'Good. Then it's settled. Farewell, Master Hill. God be with you.'

Chapter 14

Three days later, the Queen's considerable party of courtiers, guards, and servants, with ten carriages and twelve baggage carts, arrived in Salisbury, where Thomas was to take the road to Romsey. Simon saw him off. 'Farewell, Thomas Hill. I shall pray for you and your family. May you find them well.'

'Farewell, Simon. I have enjoyed your company, but little else since first meeting you. I shall hope never to see you again.'

Simon laughed. 'Come now, Thomas. It's Rush whom we shall never see again. I may call upon you at any time.'

'Please don't. It would be rude to send you away empty-handed.'

Carrying the bag he had brought from home, his leather water flask, and a silver-topped cane left in his room at Christ Church, Thomas covered the fifteen miles to Romsey in less than two hours. On the outskirts of the town, he dismounted and led his horse through Market Square and up Love Lane. Having tethered it, he knocked as hard as he could on the door of the bookshop. It was a new door, made of very stout oak, and fixed with three large iron hinges. It was not a door that a thieving soldier would be able easily to kick in. The windows were also new, with thick shutters, and sturdy frames. There was no answer. He knocked again, and heard footsteps inside. 'Who is it?' inquired a muffled voice.

'Margaret? It's the owner of this bookshop, and he would like to come in.' The door was immediately unlocked and pulled open. Without a word, Margaret threw herself at him and held on as if her life depended upon it. She started crying. 'Good Lord, my dear, I wasn't expecting quite such a welcome.' said Thomas, gently patting her back. 'Are you quite well?'

Margaret let go and stood back, wiping her eyes on her sleeve. 'I'm sorry, Thomas. It's such a relief to see you.' She sniffed loudly. 'I'm quite well, thank you, and so are the girls. And they will be even better for seeing you. She studied him. 'You look well. A little thinner, perhaps, and the beard will have to go, but otherwise well.'

'Where are they?'

'They're staying with Andrew's sister in Winchester.'

'Oh? Have they been there long?'

'Come in. We'll eat first. Then we'll talk.'

After they had eaten, Margaret fetched a handful of letters from upstairs and put them on the table in front of Thomas. 'There are six of them. The last one arrived two weeks ago. They were all pushed under the door at night, for me to find in the morning. Read them, please.'

It did not take Thomas long. They were short letters, and very much to the point, each one more threatening than the one before. Their message was the same. At a time of war, a young widow and her daughters were not safe alone, and should take particular care. Who knew what awful things might otherwise happen to them? Who knew what vile ideas might enter the heads of drunken soldiers? They were all in the same hand, and unsigned. Thomas looked up. 'Are these why you sent the girls away?'

'Yes. I thought they'd be safer.'

'You were probably wise. However, I know why these letters were written, and I know who was behind them. The writer himself is actually of no account. It was the man who composed them who was dangerous.'

'Was?'

'Happily, yes.' It took Thomas over an hour to relate the story. He missed out the worst of the gaol, and left a certain amount unsaid about Jane Romilly. Otherwise, he gave Margaret a full account. 'So,' he ended, 'there is nothing now to be frightened of. The girls can come home, and we can reopen the shop. Tobias Rush is dead. I have the King's word on it.'

The next morning, Margaret set off for Winchester to collect the girls. After a busy time putting books on shelves, and arranging his writing materials on the table, Thomas wandered down to the Romsey Arms to see what news there was, and for a little refreshment. At the junction of Love Lane and Market

Street, he stopped to admire the view. The autumn leaves were red and orange, the fields a deep green. He could hear voices coming from Market Square, and guessed that the inn was busy.

There were no drinkers outside, but, inside, it was noisy and crowded. A troop of the King's dragoons, in their multi-coloured coats and feathered hats, were keeping the serving girls busy. When she saw Thomas, Sarah shrieked a greeting. 'Master 'ill, haven't see you for ages. Where 'ave you been?'

'Nowhere much, Sarah. How's Rose?'

'Much too big to work, silly cow. Baby'll drop any day.'

'You're busy today.'

'Soldiers on their way to Oxford. Same lot as was 'ere a few weeks ago.' Thomas looked around. Sure enough, there was the fat dragoon who had sat on him, and there was Captain Brooke. He took his ale, and found a seat in the corner, from where he could watch and listen. He was not in the mood for argument or banter. Or for being sat upon. He heard the dragoons recounting their experiences of being in Lord Goring's army, which consisted mostly of monumental bouts of drinking and whoring, his lordship setting an excellent example to his men in both pursuits, and he watched them spending a good many shillings on ale, shillings they had doubtless removed without consent from their owners. He was about to leave when the captain noticed him in the corner.

'Well, well. If it isn't our friend the bookseller. Hill, isn't it? We met when we last visited Romsey.'

Thomas rose. 'Thomas Hill, sir. Your memory does you credit. I gather you and your men have been serving with Lord Goring.'

'That we have, the drunken old goat. Now we're on our way to Oxford. The King has demanded reinforcements. Do you know Oxford?'

'I was a student there many years ago. It's a beautiful town.'

'Then let's hope we don't have to defend it from rampaging puritans. And what have you been doing since last we met, Master Hill?'

'Oh, business as usual, captain.'

'The quiet life, eh? I envy you. And what about that French fellow of yours? Mountain.'

'Montaigne, captain. Michel Montaigne.'

'What was it he said? I couldn't make head nor tail of it.'

'To learn that we have said or done a stupid thing is nothing; we must learn a more ample and important lesson: that we are all blockheads.'

'That was it. Damned odd.'

Thomas grinned. 'Not so odd, captain, when you think about it. Now I must be away before one of your men knocks me down and sits on me. Good bye, captain.'

'Good bye, Master Hill.'

AUTHOR'S NOTE

The Vigenère square, which gave Thomas so much trouble, was perfected by Blaise de Vigenère, a French cryptographer, in the middle of the sixteenth century. Other than Thomas, no-one found a way of breaking the cipher until the nineteenth century, when the remarkable Charles Babbage, using much the same technique, did so.

Thomas was fortunate in two respects. The first message contained as many as eight repeated letter sequences, and, except in the fifth file, the key letters e,a, and t were easily found. Having identified these, he was able to find the displacement, and thus the keyword, PARIS. It might not have been so. The second, much shorter, message, he could not decrypt by analysis, and only managed it with an inspired guess.

In writing *The King's Codebreaker,* I referred, in particular, to the following:

Christopher Hibbert: *Cavaliers and Roundheads*
Michael Braddick: *God's Fury, England's Fire*
David Clark: *The English Civil War*
Diane Purkiss: *The English Civil War: A People's History*
Simon Singh: *The Code Book*

I thank my friend Florence Benoit d'Entrevaux, my son Tom, and, above all, my wife Susan, to whom this book is dedicated, for their help and support.

Thomas Hill will be back for his next adventure in

Blessed Rain

On a frosty March morning, the soldiers came at dawn. Thomas Hill, asleep above his bookshop in Love Lane, was woken by the crack of their boots on the frozen cobblestones. Their captain hammered on the bookshop door and demanded it be opened in the name of Parliament. Thomas was wide awake instantly and pulling on his clothes; it would not do to answer the door in his nightshirt. The hammering continued while he dressed. They were not going to go away until they had got whatever it was they wanted. He went downstairs, through the shop, and opened the door. There were four of them, each wearing the round helmet and breastplate of a parliamentary infantryman, and each armed with a pistol and a sword.

'Are you Thomas Hill?' demanded the captain.

'I am.'

'Are you the Thomas Hill who served the King at Oxford?'

'I am. What of it?'

The captain pulled a single sheet of paper from inside his tunic. 'Thomas Hill, are you the author of this?'

Thomas took the paper from the captain and glanced at it. There was any number of political pamphlets circulating, but he could guess which one this was. It was the only one to which he had ever put his name. Several pamphlets on mathematics and philosophy, but only one on politics. 'I am. What of it?'

'Thomas Hill, in the name of the people, I arrest you for inciting actions against Parliament.'

'Can you read, captain?'

'I am obeying orders.'

'I thought not. If you could, you would be aware that this pamphlet, written by me, argues for a strong Parliament to represent the people, and for that Parliament to work in conjunction with the King for the common good. Am I to be arrested for that?'

The three soldiers, who had been standing to attention behind their captain and staring straight ahead, shuffled their feet and looked sheepish. 'My orders are to arrest you and take you to Winchester gaol to await trial.'

There was to be no argument, and resistance would be foolish. 'My sister and nieces are upstairs. Am I not permitted to say goodbye?'

The captain hesitated. 'Very well. Two minutes, no more.'

Thomas ran back upstairs. The girls were crying. Margaret was ashen. They had heard everything. He hugged each of them.

'Now don't fret. This is nothing. Just a mistake. I'll be home again in no time. I'll send word. Pass me that shirt, my dear. I may need a spare.' He put it on over the other. 'There. Should keep me warm. Now kiss your uncle, girls, and look after your mother while I'm gone. I'll see you again very soon.' He turned to Margaret. She too was weeping. 'It's really a harmless pamphlet, my dear. They can't keep me locked up for long.'

'I wish you hadn't written it, Thomas. I knew it would be trouble.'

'Indeed. But it's really nothing. I'll be home tomorrow, just see if I'm not.' He kissed her cheek and left. A moment longer and he might be weeping himself. The soldiers were waiting outside.

'Right. Bind his hands, Jethro – tightly mind, we don't want him escaping – and we'll be on our way.' The captain was impatient to be gone. He had three more to collect today.

The rope was bad enough, the indignity worse. More embarrassed than frightened, he was marched down Love Lane and across Market Square, with only the clothes and shoes he was wearing. Although it was early, the soldiers had been heard, and, as they clattered over the cobbles, he was aware of curtains moving and faces peeking out. He squared his shoulders and fixed his eyes on the back of the head of the soldier in front of him. Even in these uncertain times, no magistrate would pay much heed to an innocuous pamphlet written by a humble bookseller. He would be home again soon, the whole thing forgotten; although if a tear did come to his eye, he did not want it seen by a watching friend.

That evening, hungry and exhausted after marching from village to village, they arrived at Winchester gaol. On their way, three more men had been arrested on charges of speaking against Parliament, but, other than the charges, Thomas knew nothing about them. They had not been allowed to talk on the journey but there had been brief halts to rest and they had been allowed to drink brown water from wells in the villages.

The prison was crowded, and the four men were put into the same cell as two others. Six men in one small cell was bad enough; filthy straw on the floor and a bucket in the corner made it worse. Compared to Oxford Castle, however, from which Thomas had been lucky to escape alive, it was almost comfortable. He backed into a corner from where he listened and answered questions, but volunteered nothing and took no part in the general banter, which was more bravado than bravery. Happily, one of the prisoners, an innkeeper from Hursley, was a natural jester. Robert Rich was a large man, red of face and loud of voice, who stood accused of saying that he would rather serve Oliver Cromwell for dinner than serve him with it. Unfortunately for him, he had been overheard by one of Cromwell's spies and reported. He claimed that he was looking forward to his trial, when he would offer the defence that he had said no such thing, and, if he had, he must have been speaking in jest, because he made a point of serving only the very best meat, and no customer of his would want anything as mean as Cromwell. Listening to him, Thomas thought that Rich was just the kind of man he'd want beside him in times of trouble but that his chances of avoiding a spell in prison were remote.

Through a long night Thomas kept his spirits up by examining the crime of which he stood accused. It really was so trivial, if indeed it was a crime at all, that he should have no difficulty in persuading the magistrate to release him. He would be home in a day or two. By the following afternoon, however, doubts were creeping in. There had been no information and no contact from outside. He might need someone to speak for him. The magistrate would almost certainly be in someone's pay. One of Cromwell's men probably. A more serious charge might be concocted. He had not been able to send word to Margaret and, by evening, he was frightened. Separation was punishment enough, never mind the noisome cell and gruesome scraps of food. He wondered what on earth had induced him to put his name to the offending paper, balanced and reasonable though it was, and prayed that justice would be done, and done without delay.

On the second morning, they were roused by a commotion somewhere outside the cells. They heard orders being given, doors being unlocked, and men being taken out. Soon their own cell was opened, and the head gaoler, accompanied by two guards carrying pistols and muskets, stood at the door. 'These men come with me.' he ordered, and called out three names, of which Thomas's was the third. Robert Rich was not among them. The three men were assembled and led away by the soldiers to a small courtyard where a larger group of prisoners was waiting. It was easy to tell that they were not new prisoners because they were gaunt and filthy and trying to shield their eyes from the light. A short, fat, man, in the drab uniform of the army of Parliament, stood before them. 'I am Captain Fortescue.' he announced, 'I have been granted permission to remove you from this place and transport you to the island of Barbados, in the Caribbean, where you will be sold as indentured men. We will travel to Southampton where my ship is anchored, and proceed from there to the Irish port of Cork where we will take on board more men to be indentured.'

Thomas could not believe his ears. Arrested for nothing, thrown into gaol, and deported without trial? It could not be. 'Captain,' he said, with as much authority as he could muster, 'My name is Thomas Hill. I stand accused of who knows what and I demand to be heard.'

'Hill?' replied Fortescue, consulting his list, 'Ah yes, Thomas Hill. Hold your tongue Hill, or it'll be the worse for you. Your indenture has been arranged and I shall make sure it happens.' Indenture arranged? How and by whom and for what? It was impossible. 'And I demand a fair trial.'

'Enough, Hill. One more word and you'll pay. Bind his hands. This one could be trouble.'

His hands bound behind his back, Thomas was led away with the others. They were loaded like sheep on to two large carts, each drawn by two shire horses, and guarded by four soldiers. Captain Fortescue rode behind them.

When they arrived that evening in Southampton, Captain Fortescue's ship, The Dolphin, was anchored in the harbour. It was a stout cargo ship, quite new by the look of it, and designed to carry goods from England to the new colonies in the Caribbean, returning with cotton, tobacco, and sugar. Still unable to believe what was happening to him, Thomas looked desperately around as they were marched to the quayside, as if hoping to see a friendly face. Labourers were unloading barrels and crates from carts and carrying them on board, sailors were hauling on ropes and shouting instructions, and a small group of well-dressed men, merchants probably, had gathered at one end of the quay to see that their goods were safely loaded. Not one of them took any notice of the prisoners being herded on to the ship.

They were led to a section of the hold towards the bow, partitioned off from the cargo, and fitted with narrow hammocks no more than a foot apart. It was a dire place, reeking of human waste, cold, dark, and threatening. Thomas's sensitive nose betrayed him and he started retching. The door of the hold was shut behind them and twenty miserable, frightened, men had no choice but to find a hammock and await events. At that moment, Thomas knew that he was trapped. Someone, God alone knew who, had used the pamphlet, innocuous though it was, to have him arrested and deported. He longed to shout, to demand a fair trial, to rail against the injustice, to force someone to listen. But no-one was going to listen to one insignificant prisoner. Too shattered to speak, he closed his eyes, and concentrated on survival.